When We Kiss

By Tia Louise

This book is a work of fiction. Names, characters, places, and incidents are products of the author's imagination or are used fictitiously. Any resemblance to actual events or locales or persons, living or dead, is entirely coincidental.

For good girls, bad girls, hot cops,
and everyone in between...
For the Mermaids,
And for Katy Regnery.

Kissing makes everything better.

Contents

Chapter 1

Tabby

August, last year…

The air is electric when you're being bad.

Little currents zip through your veins like lightning bugs grazing the tips of tall grass, and your stomach is tight. You're right on the edge, holding your breath…

Or maybe it's just me.

"Climb through." Blade squints up at me, the devil in his blue eyes.

He's holding the corner of a chain-length fence, and it makes a metallic screech as he lifts it higher.

Eleven thirty, and the night air is hot and humid — a warm washcloth on my bare skin. I duck through the opening, putting my hands up to protect my hair, my ears.

The space is just big enough for me to fit, hidden behind the tool shed. A rustling and a *BANG!* lets me know we're both through the breach. My naughty escort stands grinning in the moonlight. His hair is dark, his skin pale, and shadows deepen his eyes, nose, and mouth. He's like one of those scary-sexy vampires.

Or maybe I'm a little high.

"Let's do this!" He lets out a whoop and jerks off his black leather jacket.

His white tee is next, revealing a coiled serpent tattooed on his upper back. Jeans off, I catch a glimpse of his tight ass as he runs straight to the pool and breaks the glassy surface with a loud splash.

I shimmy out of my calf-length jeans and unbutton my short-sleeved shirt. I'm buzzing from the pot we just smoked at my small house, the old parsonage in town near the church, before we got the idea to break into the Plucky Duck Motel pool.

The Plucky Duck is off the Interstate, too far from the beach to be a tourist attraction. It's a million years old and completely deserted.

"Nobody ever stays here." I walk slowly down the steps into the shallow end.

The water is warm as it rises up my calves, to my knees, to my panties, to my waist. Blade is under the diving board watching me, his mouth submerged like a shark or a crocodile. His eyebrows rise as the water reaches my waist.

Through a blue haze of pot smoke, he demanded we do something I've never done before. I said there isn't much in Oceanside I haven't done. Until I thought of this old place.

Skinny dipping with Mayor Rhodes's tattooed bad-boy nephew is the perfectly spontaneous, irresponsible way to kick the last memories of Travis Walker from my heart.

Acid burns in my stomach. Tattooed Travis blew into town three months ago on a Harley, kissed me, and said I was the prettiest girl he'd ever seen. We screwed around for six weeks, until I caught him sneaking out of Daisy Sales's bedroom window.

He didn't even deny sleeping with her. He said Oceanside was getting "too restrictive," then he hopped on that Harley, lit up a cigarette, and drove away.

Asshole.

Serves me right for letting my guard down.

Pushing off the bottom, I keep my head above water as I glide to where Blade waits at the deep end. It's darker under the diving board.

"How long you planning to stay in Oceanside?" I don't really care. Blade's a fling I'm going into with my eyes wide open.

"Not sure." He reaches for my waist, his palms hot against my bare skin. "Ma said Uncle John needs to straighten me out."

He grins, and a dimple pierces his cheek. That bit of information makes me laugh, and I rest my elbows on his shoulders.

"I've been told something like that before." I give the field where we came in a longing glance. I wish we had more pot or at least a six-pack.

"Who's trying to straighten you out?" he asks, running his fingers up and down my sides.

My eyes return to his, and I do a little shrug. "My uncle's Pastor Green."

"No shit!"

The way he says it with a laugh makes him seem young, like a kid. I don't like the way it makes me feel, especially with the iron rod of his erection pressing against my stomach.

Twisting my lips, I reach up to hold the sides of the diving board, moving out of his arms. "I lived under his roof, his rules, until I was old enough to get out."

"I hear that." Blade reaches up to hold the diving board, mirroring my behavior.

We're facing each other, and I admire the lines of his lean muscles. Another snake is tattooed around his upper arm, but it looks amateurish, almost like he did it himself.

"So you're staying?" My red velvet lips purse, and he winks.

"That's what they tell me."

His muscles flex as he walks his hands forward, bringing our bodies closer together.

"Future's a lot brighter now that you're here."

I don't know if I'm sobering up or if his enthusiasm is killing the mood.

Blade had waltzed into the bakery where I work earlier this afternoon looking for trouble. The memory of Cheater Travis was looming large, and I decided I needed to do something reckless to blow off steam.

"You're new in town," I had said, cocking my hip to the side.

"My uncle's the mayor," he'd replied with a swaggering shrug.

"Good enough for me." I'd trotted out the door behind him, down the steps, and into the beat-up old Buick he'd parked out front.

We started on the strip at Oceanside Beach, where the high-rise condos line the shore like a wall and the tourists block up the sand. Then we had a few beers at the Tuna Tiki, the local beach bar-hangout, before he pulled out a dime bag of weed and we went back to my place to smoke it.

All in all, it was a fun, reckless day, but my buzz is definitely wearing off.

He gives me a boyish grin, and I decide I'm not looking for some *Grease*-inspired Danny and Sandy summer romance.

He walks his hands closer until my boobs smash against his chest. His legs pull my lower half flush against his, and I feel him hard against my panties. It's been a while since I've had a non-solo orgasm, and I'm not opposed to a fling with the town's newest bad boy.

He flashes a cocky grin before tilting his head to the side and kissing my cheek. His lips are soft, and I turn my face, ready to kiss him.

Still, before I do, I issue a warning. "Don't get attached."

His laugh reminds me of a young James Dean, and I'm ready. Our mouths inch closer. Another second, and they'll meet, tongues entwining. The space between my legs grows hotter, and I briefly consider I don't have a condom.

There's no way in hell I'm doing this without protection, when…

FLICK! It's a loud switch, like the throwing of a main breaker.

The entire pool floods with light, and I let go of the diving board, lowering my body into the water.

"What the fuck?" Blade does the same, joining me at the side of the pool.

The water offers little protection, as the lights fully illuminate our half-naked bodies under water. Looking up, I see we're surrounded.

"There she is! I knew I heard her voice." Betty Pepper is on the side of the pool, leaning down. Her lavender bouffant glows around her aged head, and she's wrapped in a peach terry-cloth robe pointing a bony finger in my direction.

"What are you doing in my pool, Tabitha Green?" Her voice is stern as always, the quintessential school marm.

"What does it look like I'm doing?" I snark. "Having a prayer meeting?"

"The pool closes at dark, *Tabitha*. And it's for registered guests only." She says it like I don't know very well we're out here breaking the law. "Who is that with you? Is that Jimmy Rhodes? Jimmy, is that you?"

My eyes flick to Blade. His face is downcast, and if it weren't so dark, I'd be sure his cheeks were red.

"It's me, Mrs. Pepper."

"I told your mamma I'd be looking out for you today. Did you check in with Wyatt at the hardware store? What are you doing running around with Tabitha Green?"

She says my name like it's a bad word.

Like I'm the bad influence.

I hiss at him. "You know Betty Pepper?"

He shrugs, and a male voice cuts through my irritation. "Tabby, did you take Jimmy to the bar at the Tuna Tiki?"

My brows tighten, and I squint up at Sheriff Cole. He towers over us from where he stands at the side of the pool, and his cowboy hat blocks the security light from blinding me. Otherwise, it's pretty much a police interrogation.

I answer truthfully. "I rode down to the strip in his car."

"We need you to get on out of the pool now," Sheriff Cole says, tipping his hat.

I look down at my transparent bra and panties, and there's no way in hell I'm climbing out in front of Sheriff Robbie Cole, Betty Pepper, and what I now see is a tall, quiet guy who's also wearing a khaki uniform.

He's quite a bit younger than Robbie, although he's older than me, and he stretches that polyester in a way I've never seen before.

Muscled arms hang from broad shoulders, leading down to narrow hips. His dark hair is short, and from under his lowered brow, I can see he's observing everything.

"Who's that?" I jerk my chin in his direction. "A storm trooper?"

The big guy's square jaw tightens as a muscle moves in his cheek. He gritted his teeth at me, and the heat in my panties reignites.

"Now's as good a time as any." Sheriff Cole, steps back gesturing to Mr. Tall, Dark, and Sexy. "Chad Tucker's my new deputy sheriff. He'll be working with me until I retire next year."

My lips press together. *No, thank you.* No Sheriffs. I don't care how square his jaw is or how well he fills out that uniform.

"Chad," Robbie continues. "This here is Tabitha Green, Reverend Green's niece, and this young man is Jimmy Rhodes, Mayor Rhodes's seventeen-year-old nephew."

"Seventeen!" The words are like a splash of water in my face, and I jerk off the wall, dog-paddling as fast as I can away from Jail Bait to the shallow end, humiliation burning in my chest.

"You hear that, Tabitha?" Betty shrills after me. "Not only are you breaking and entering, you're contributing to the delinquency of a minor."

Robbie continues introducing the baby wanna-be bad boy. "Jimmy is staying with his uncle until he finishes high school next year."

Every word is a cringing flash of shame, and I stomp up the pool steps, scooping my shirt off the tattered lounge chair and over my shoulders. My tight jeans are next, but it's a challenge getting them up my damp legs.

13

"What would your uncle say if he saw you?" Betty continues regaling me.

I stomp back to where Sheriff Cole and his new storm trooper stand, not even casting a glance at the kid in the pool. "Are you planning to arrest me?"

Lines form around the sheriff's eyes as he suppresses a grin. "Well, Mrs. Pepper here has listed your potential crimes."

"You're turning into a Jezebel," BP continues nagging. "If you're not careful, you're going to end up just like—"

My eyes flash at her, and her voice dies. She'd better not say my mother. If she knows what's good for her, she'd better not say it.

Instead she tightens her robe. "It's a slippery slope."

"What do you think, Chad?" Robbie exhales, straightening his posture and tugging on his waistband.

Mr. Silent But Deadly's eyes skim the front of my transparent bra before meeting mine. When they do, I realize they're light brown. I also realize they're hot, and chills break out over my skin in the warm night air. It strikes me this sexy future sheriff might be the real bad boy in the group.

His voice is a nice, low vibration. "I think you're playing a dangerous game… Miss?"

"She's single," Betty interrupts, as if not being married is another of my offenses.

Chad's eyebrows twitch ever so slightly. I'm pretty sure he doesn't think my being single is a crime.

My stomach is tight, and I swallow the knot in my throat. *Get a clue, Tabby.* The last thing on God's green earth I have any intention of doing is getting mixed up with a lawman.

"I don't play games, Mr. Tucker." My voice is higher than his, but just as determined. "And I don't check IDs on people I've just met."

"Maybe you should start." I can't tell if Chad Tucker is being a smartass or if he's just naturally cocky.

Seeing as he's a deputy, I'm willing to bet it's the latter.

Robbie's chuckle breaks the tension. "I think we can let you off with a warning this time. Do you need a ride home?"

I've managed to get my feet into my slides, and I see Jimmy standing on the side of the pool, pulling on his jeans and tee. He looks so skinny and young now. I wonder why I ever fell for his counterfeit tattooed bad-boy routine.

My phone is in my hand, and I tap the icons quickly. "No thanks. I just ordered an Uber. Looks like it'll be here in two minutes."

Gripping my shirt closed, I stomp up the sidewalk that leads to the front of the hotel.

Betty Pepper calls after me, getting her final jab in. "Consider your ways, Tabitha!"

I grind my teeth and fight the urge to flip her off as I round the corner. I'm saved by the headlights of a Dodge Dart with a white U in the windshield. It's too late to call my best friend Emberly, but when I get to the bakery tomorrow...

A billboard on the Interstate catches my eye, and I get an idea. Not Robbie Cole, Betty Pepper, or even Mr. Tall, Dark, and Sexy will see this one coming.

Chapter 2

Chad

One year later…

The highway leading from the beach into sleepy Oceanside Village is tranquil tonight—as usual.

I've made my rounds, driving past closed businesses, along the strip where the tourists have all gone home, past deserted beachfront mansions closed up for the season. I've driven through neighborhoods, where residents have turned in for the night. I've checked on the single moms, the shut-ins, the bars that will be shuttered in another hour.

I've spent a year in this place, and I know its rhythm.

I know what will and what won't happen as the shadows lengthen, as the noise of the cicadas rises louder than the crashing of the waves on the shore less than a mile away.

When I told my dad I'd taken a job as a sheriff's deputy in a tiny county of less than twenty thousand, he said I wouldn't last a month.

I said he was wrong.

He was wrong.

Taking this job was a 180-degree turn from the life I grew up in, from the forces that led to my sister's death, a death the detectives still haven't ruled out as a suicide.

I came to this hamlet along the coast to get away from the city, from my family, and from the memory of Charity lurking around every corner.

She died, and a month later I started basic training.

I'd already enlisted before it all went down. We buried her, and I buried myself in learning to protect and serve. I couldn't save my sister. Maybe I could save somebody else.

It seemed like the best way to kill the pain, to silence the questions, the never-ending *whys*.

Why did she do it?

Why would a 23-year-old woman climb out the window of a car and stand facing a semi-truck racing head-on in a demented game of chicken?

Her body exploded on impact, the police said. Her friends were too traumatized to speak. I can still hear their hysterical screams.

Was she just a daredevil? An adrenaline junkie? A "bad girl" gone too far?

These were answers we would never get.

No note. No explanation.

We were left to pick up the pieces, carry on as survivors of her reckless existence. My parents chose to stay in their gilded bubble, to walk around town like nothing had changed.

I walked away.

Actually, I sailed away with the U.S. Navy to the coast of Africa onboard a destroyer. It was a risky mission after the bombing of the Cole.

I didn't really care.

Nothing made sense anymore, and if life was so fragile, it seemed pointless to care about the expectations of my pedigreed past. It grew harder and harder to worry about the things my friends would get so hung up on.

Yeah, I probably should have gone to therapy or seen a counselor or something. Looking back now, it's water under the bridge, a rough patch I had to walk through. Not too many visible scars.

I know the scars. I wanted answers I would never find.

Four years and several letters of commendation later, I retired from service with my degree in psychology and criminal behavior.

Looking at my options, I wanted to get as far as possible from the place I once called home. I never wanted to hear the sound of eighteen wheelers barreling down the highway or the buzz of a Jake brake splitting the night.

I wanted to find a place where life existed like it did in those old TV shows — the ones from the 1950s, where people lived and worked and grew old in quiet towns smiling and happy, surrounded by familiar faces.

Where the worst thing that could happen was a kid stealing a baseball card from the drugstore or sneaking a cigarette under the bleachers.

Oceanside is that place.

Here, I've found that life.

It's Saturday night, and I'm sitting in my cruiser off the county road leading into town. The hum of the cicadas is the only noise, and with my windows down, the air hangs thick and damp, pushed occasionally by a stray ocean breeze.

It smells like salt and fresh fish.

I really like it here.

I like the busybody old ladies like Betty Pepper, who owns the grocery store. I like the laid back old men like Wyatt Jones, who runs the hardware store, and my boss Robbie Cole, soon to retire and hand me the reins.

Emberly Warren and Daisy Sales are the two single moms in town. They have preschool daughters, and I check on them every evening. It's just a simple drive-by, a glance around the perimeter, before I call it a night.

This place is peaceful, idyllic. It's an America I wanted to believe still existed when I joined the service. Saving strangers because I couldn't save the person I knew best. *Why didn't I know she needed help?*

My thoughts are slipping back to the darkness when a car blasts past me, clearly speeding, windows down, radio blaring. It snatches me back to the present, and I look up in time to see a streak of yellow before red taillights illuminate the night.

The car pauses at the stop sign and turns with a screech down Oak Alley.

"That was not a complete stop," I mutter, flipping the switch for my lights, but not turning on the siren.

Whoever it is will see the flashers, and I won't have to disturb the whole town. It's an unusual occurrence, but I'm not concerned.

Concern melts to a different feeling altogether as I slowly get closer and recognize the yellow Volkswagen Bug. My stomach tightens. It's a feeling I've grown used to ignoring. Especially in the presence of this person.

Still, I hit the button to give the siren a little bark. Red lights illuminate the night as she slams on breaks and pulls to the side of the road. I ease onto the shoulder behind her and type in the number of her license plate, even though I know how this will go.

Switching off the ignition, I leave my lights flashing as I exit my cruiser and walk slowly to where

Tabby Green is sitting in her car in front of me.

The window is down, and I lean forward. "Where's the fire, Miss Green?"

Red velvet lips purse briefly before she flashes emerald eyes at me. "Is something wrong, officer?"

Fake innocence is in her voice, and I hold off a smile. Tabby and I have been circling each other for almost a year now, ever since the night I was on hand to bust her skinny dipping in Elmer Pepper's Motel pool. The Plucky Duck… an artifact from another time.

Elmer's cousin Betty had been keeping an eye on the place, and the minute she heard a suspicious noise, she was on the phone with Robbie.

Robbie told me to get used to it. Betty Pepper calls the station at least five times a week.

"Would you please step out of the vehicle?" My voice is level, full of authority.

"Step out?" Her brows lower, and I see her prickle against the rule of law in my tone. It's crazy how much I like her response. "Why do I need to do that?"

"Because I asked you to." Straightening, I put my hands on my hips.

Her hands tighten on the steering wheel, and she wiggles around in her seat.

"Is something wrong, Miss Green?"

Frustration flickers across her face and she jerks the door handle before pushing it open roughly. She steps out, and I see she's wearing one of her usual skin-tight dresses. This one is red, and it hugs her curves.

She reaches down to tug the hem, and I tear my eyes away from the moonlight glistening on the soft rise of her breasts.

Heat rises below my belt as a memory flashes to the front of my mind. I'll never un-see Tabitha Green standing wet, in only a transparent lace bra and panties. Her dark hair was piled on top of her head, and her dark nipples were straining through her bra. Damn, she was sex on wheels.

Clearing my throat, I focus on my job. "Looked like you were going about forty-five just now."

"That's not really very fast." She lifts her chin, our eyes meet, and it's the same as it always is between us.

Sparks.

Truthfully, I haven't been avoiding her, but I know she does her best not to be in the same room as me at all times. It's confusing, because I know girls like Tabby. I grew up with one, and being fearless is her most valued character trait.

She's not afraid of me.

"It's too fast at night driving through Oceanside. You could hit someone walking or riding a bike."

"Nobody is out at night in Oceanside." Her tone is defiant, challenging. "You know that as well as I do, Deputy Tucker."

"You can call me Chad."

"Not while you're on duty."

I want to laugh, but no way. I have to keep the upper hand on this lady. "May I see your driver's license?"

Her bottom jaw drops, causing her lips to form a little *O*. I clear my throat against the pornographic image it conjures.

"You're going to give me a ticket?"

"Maybe. I need to see your license."

"But…"

"License, please."

She turns to the car and hesitates a moment before turning back. "I don't have it with me."

Now it's my turn to frown. "You're driving without a license? Weren't you just at the Tuna Tiki?

Did they even card you?"

"I couldn't find it. Anyway, everybody knows everybody around here. You know me."

Straightening to my full, six-foot two height, I cross my arms, thinking about this interesting situation.

"So speeding, driving without a license, blowing a stop sign..." My eyes travel down to her bare feet. Her toenails are painted red. "Can you walk a straight line?"

"Of course I can." She turns quickly, walking on her tiptoes away from me.

My eyes are drawn to the sway of her perky ass. *Jesus, get a grip, Tucker.*

She stops and walks back slowly. "Are you planning to arrest me?"

Her voice is a sultry challenge. A hint of a grin is on her lips, and yep. It's a total turn-on.

I'm pretty sure she's trying to flirt her way out of this, and while I like it, I'm not that easy. My hands go to my hips, and her eyes go to my biceps. They widen slightly before quickly returning to meet my gaze. If it weren't so dark, I'd almost think she was blushing.

"I could take you to jail... Or I could give you a hell of a ticket... However, I'm willing to let you off with a warning."

That gets me an immediate smile. "Thanks." She starts to get in the car again, but I stop her.

"I wasn't finished."

She pauses and looks up at me. "You weren't?"

Tabby is the niece of Bob Green, pastor of the small church in town. I attend somewhat regularly to keep the townsfolk happy. She is rarely there. It gives me an idea.

"I'll let you off with a warning and…" Stepping back, I turn as if I'm ready to walk to my cruiser. "You'll be in church tomorrow to make up for it."

"Church!" Her voice is just short of a shriek, and I bite back a grin. "Why do I have to go to church?"

Pausing, I allow a cocky grin. "Because I have a feeling it's the one thing you'd hate more than a hefty fine."

Her hands are on her hips, and I can almost see her doing an angry little stomp. "That's blackmail."

"I could give you the ticket instead. I expect it'd be around… Five hundred dollars."

"Five hundred!"

"You're breaking at least three laws."

"Bastard," she whispers.

"What was that, Miss Green?"

The cicadas grow louder, filling the empty air like a pitcher of water.

"I said I guess I'll see you in the morning."

"I'll follow you home. No more driving without a license. I won't be as lenient next time."

"That was lenient?" She's grumbling, and I grin at the cute sass in her walk away from me.

I'm in my car, shutting off the flashers and starting the engine. It only takes her a moment to do the same, and we slowly follow the highway into town, through the oak-filled neighborhoods and out past the four ancient storefronts belonging to Betty, Wyatt, Emberly, and Daisy.

She takes a turn and drives to a little strip of land down the road from the church, a small cottage I know she calls home.

I wait until she shuts off her car and gets out. A pair of red heels dangle from her fingers, and she doesn't even look back as she jogs up the short flight of steps to her front door. A jiggle of keys, and she disappears into the house with a slam.

Her lights flicker on, and I'm sure she's in for the night. I can't help thinking about how I'll see her tomorrow in the tiny sanctuary. I'm headed home myself now, looking forward to what the next day will bring.

Chapter 3

Tabby

Chad Tucker is the most annoying man on the planet.

Dropping my heels on the floor of my bedroom, I slip out of my skirt and go to my small bathroom. I step into my footed tub and turn on the hot water, sitting on the side as I wash the sand off my feet with the sprayer.

Making me walk a straight line...

I know he did it just to piss me off. As if I'd drive drunk. I do some crazy shit, but nothing that would endanger the lives of others. He should know better with his damn biceps and that damn tight waist. My panties got hot when he put his hands on his hips.

He just grinned with that ridiculous square jaw and those dimples. For a man of the law, he doesn't have to be so damn sexy busting me for speeding and driving without a license.

Go to church.

My eyes go to the clock. I need to call Emberly and tell her what happened. I also need to be sure she's going to be there tomorrow. There's no way in hell I'm walking into that building by myself.

Betty Pepper will corral me in beside her and her stinky son Bucky wanting to know if I've recommitted my life to Christ.

As if.

The water is getting a little too hot, and I crank up the cold to cool it down. I consider sinking into my oversized copper tub. Last year, I took a semester's worth of night classes in web design. Then in January, I launched my own website design business. I'm slowly building my client list, but it's netted me enough money to afford some luxuries. This tub is one of my favorite things.

I actually saw it in the photos for Daisy's antiques shop when she sent me the updates to her page on the Oceanside Village website, which I designed and maintain *pro bono*. That's a fancy word for *free*, and it's the only time I've ever done something like that.

It's mainly for Emberly because she's such an amazing baker and she's so broke. I wanted to figure out a way to make her famous locally and maybe even worldwide without costing a ton of cash. If anybody deserves it, she does. She works so hard as a single mom to build a life for her and her daughter, my adorable god-daughter Coco.

Daisy is also a single mom, and she has a real eye for antiques. But after the way she slept with Travis Walker the five minutes he and I were together, no way in hell would I go in her store and buy anything from her. We're not speaking.

So I bought it online and had it delivered—one of the special features I added to the site.

Of course, Jimmy Rhodes is her delivery boy. Emphasis on the word *boy*.

Daisy shares him with Wyatt at the hardware store. He's "staying out of trouble" while he finishes high school, and he's been making eyes at me ever since I had my bout of Travis-induced temporary insanity and spent a long afternoon with him last year.

God, I shudder at that memory.

Sometimes this town feels so small.

It was when everything started with Chad Tucker. It was the first time I ever saw him.

Shrugging off the rest of my clothes, I slide down into the warm water filling the tub, using my red painted toes to adjust the temperature. I showered before I went out tonight, but after that flashback, I need a little relaxation. I wish I'd poured a glass of wine.

Chad Tucker looked at me that night like I was a filet mignon and he'd been on rations for a month. He stood there all strong and silent, that muscle in his sexy jaw flexing back and forth.

Moving the sprayer between my legs, I slide it gently up and down over my clit as I close my eyes and remember his dark ones on me. I walked past him without a word, but he radiated heat.

The lines in his forearms, the way he fills out that uniform… He looked at me the same way tonight, like he wouldn't just kiss me. He'd devour me. Those eyes, burning with lust. That body, so hard and powerful…

Oh! Oh my goodness…

"Shit!" I hiss as currents of pleasure shudder through my thighs.

I move the sprayer to my stomach and curl closer in the warm water, giggling at the idea of me jilling off to the image of a hot cop.

A cop.

Get your head straight, Tabitha. I'm not interested in a square officer of the law any more than he would be interested in me.

Oil and vinegar.

We do not mix.

But damn, that fantasy felt like heaven…

The door to the sanctuary makes a loud squeak as I pull it open, and the entire congregation turns to look at us.

My best friend stands next to me, and while she's a regular church attender, the weight of their stares makes me feel like I owe some sort of explanation.

Ridiculous.

This is exactly why I don't go to church.

Organ music blasts through the one-room building, and everyone turns to the front, pulling red-bound hymnals from the pews in front of them.

I grab Emberly's arm and drag her into the closest open seats. Just my luck, we're two pews behind Chad Tucker. Although, I suppose it is lucky, considering he's the reason I'm here in the first place. *Blackmailer.*

"Crown him with many crowns..." Everyone sings in unison, and the person behind me is hitting all the wrong notes.

"I don't think he saw you." Emberly sings the words in tune to the descending notes of the hymn.

I look over my shoulder to see who all is staring at me. Of course, Betty Pepper gives me a smug look. It makes my stomach turn.

"Who are you looking at?" Emberly says right in my ear, making me jump.

"Nobody!" I say too loud.

The people in front of us give us a glance, and my eyes lock with Chad's. His lips curl in that cocky grin, and it's like a lightning strike straight between my legs.

Damn, he looks even hotter in a gray suit. The one-room sanctuary isn't well-air conditioned, and it's stuffy. I pull one of those little accordion fans out of the pew in front of me and wave at my face.

The song changes to surveying the wondrous cross, and I survey Chad's wondrous backside. I decide God is okay with this since he made Chad's wondrous backside.

"You can say hello after the service," Emberly sings.

She's been pushing me to date Chad since he appeared at Robbie Cole's side last year. I keep telling her it won't work. It's a match made in screaming, coming to blows, nearly killing each other hell. Chad Tucker and I are like night and day.

The song ends, and we take our seats. My uncle rises to the podium above us, and I swear, a light flickers in his eye when he sees me. I'm ready to stand up in the pew in front of everybody and announce, *Chad Tucker made me be here!*

They'd all think I was possessed by the devil, but at least they'd stop looking at me like I've finally seen the "error of my ways."

Silence falls over the room, and I brace myself for the start of the sermon. I've hated this since I was a little girl.

"*Idolatry!*" My uncle's voice is so loud the windows rattle.

An old man in front of us snorts and wakes up, and I drop my chin, pinching my nose so I don't laugh. "Sex and idolatry are the workings of the flesh, and in the last days they will grow stronger and stronger amongst the children of men..."

Uncle Bob continues blasting about how lustful and depraved we all are then he moves on to the Ten Commandments and putting God first in all things.

My eyes drift across the room to Emberly's mom. Marjorie Warren is the richest lady in town and possibly the most powerful. Her father was one of the founders of Oceanside Village and the first city councilman.

Emberly rejected all of that, choosing to restore the empty space above her bakery shop on Main Street and live there instead of in her family's mansion in the garden district. She had Coco out of wedlock—everyone's words but mine—and she's been working hard to be financially independent ever since.

We are a match made in best-friends heaven, and we've been tight since pre-kindergarten. I catch half the blame when Emberly steps off the straight and narrow. *If she weren't hanging around with that bad influence Tabitha Green…*

As if Emberly has no mind of her own. It's the kind of thinking that drives me crazy.

My own mother ran away from this town when I was just a baby. She left me with Uncle Bob and never looked back. While I don't blame her for wanting to get out of here, it kind of stings she never at least sent for me or called or anything.

Emberly wouldn't ditch Coco like that. Hell, I wouldn't ditch Coco like that. I guess that's why Emberly made me her godmother.

I try to trust people in spite of my "troubled childhood," but at times I still feel like everybody's just in this for themselves.

"…and you shall be saved," my uncle ends ominously. "Let us pray and beg the Father to expose our hidden sins and save us from ourselves."

My eyes roll involuntarily. Scanning the room, everyone is either pale or slightly green, and I can't resist.

"That's what I call church," I mutter, leaning forward.

Emberly snorts and elbows me in the ribs. I swear I see the muscle move in Chad Tucker's jaw, and I bet he's grinning. It almost makes me second-guess my straight-laced thoughts about him...

My uncle drones on reciting a noticeably specific, guilt-inducing prayer I'm sure he hopes causes all the wayward sheep who've stumbled into this place to repent — specifically me.

Dream on, Uncle Bob.

I think about Chad and how I've done my best to avoid him ever since the night he stood by watching as I climbed, humiliated, out of Elmer Pepper's ancient motel pool.

It was the same night I saw the billboard that changed everything. *Start a new career in web design and change your life!*

Turns out you actually need money up front to change your life, but I like web design. Ever since I was a kid, I've always dreamed of traveling, seeing the world — getting out of this dumb town — and after a year, it's all coming together.

"Ah-Men."

It's finally over, and we all make a beeline for the back door. "Thank the lord for fresh air," I say inhaling deeply.

Betty Pepper intercepts us on the front lawn. We're waiting for Coco to get out of Sunday school, and I guess I should check in with my blackmailer.

Betty is going on about how Emberly should consider dating her stinky son Bucky, the creepy taxidermist, when I see Chad appear at the top of the steps. An old lady is on his arm as if he's an Eagle Scout.

All the old ladies want to hold his arm. They act like they're so feeble they can't walk to their cars without his help. The truth is they're just pervy and want to stroke his muscles.

He catches my eye and hands Gwendolyn Smith off to a noodle-armed old man before slowly walking down the steps to where I'm standing. Today, I'm dressed in a demure yellow sundress, sandals, and I've traded my signature red-velvet lipstick for a nude matte. My eyes are still done, though. *Duh.*

That smug grin on his face shouldn't be so sexy at church. "Good morning, Miss Green, I trust you had a restful night."

"I'm a little tired, actually." I pretend to yawn, looking over my shoulder at the gardenia bushes.

"Trouble sleeping?"

"Not really. I drove down to Fireside and played poker with the truckers off the Interstate for a while after you left. I guess it was about four when I got to bed. If I hadn't promised to be here today, I'd probably have slept until noon."

His eyes narrow, and I know he's trying to decide if I'm lying.

Of course, I'm lying, but I'm not about to say I slipped into a warm bath and rubbed one out to the memory of his sexy bod until I was so relaxed, I slept like a baby.

Standing in front of him in my sandals, my head only reaches the top of his broad shoulders, and up close, in broad daylight, it's hard to look him straight in the face. He has a rugged manner like a soldier, but his features are elegant, refined—a straight nose, square jaw, and light brown eyes.

When he smiles, those dimples just push it all over the top. Not to mention he smells like heaven, all fresh and clean and manly.

He really is too sexy to be our future sheriff. I foresee a rise in petty crime among the blue-haired Sunday school ladies. *Oh, Sheriff Tucker! Did I do that?*

He lets my story about playing poker with the truckers pass. "How did you like the service?" he asks instead.

"It was okay, I guess." I'm acting bored. I should get an Oscar—or at least a Daytime Emmy. "Uncle Bob used to have more fire when I was a kid. He seems to be cooling down now. How can anyone be expected to have anxiety and indigestion all week on that milquetoast? I'll be lucky if I even need a Tums after lunch."

Chad grins at that. A little glint hits his pretty, pretty eyes, and I notice he has one crooked tooth on the side. It's right in line with that cheek dimple, and when my gaze meets his, my panties melt right off.

"Have lunch with me." He says it so fast, I'm pretty sure the invitation surprises him as much as it does me.

My breath leaves my lungs, and it takes a second for me to remember why this is a bad idea. "I'm having lunch with Emberly."

His dark brow furrows. "Don't you have lunch with Emberly every day?"

He's right. I work at the bakery, so I spend every day of the week with my best friend.

"Yes... well... today's special." I glance over to where she's still talking to Betty Pepper. "We're supposed to be planning out a way to attract more of the tourists up this way."

Not only do I sound nervous, I'm talking too fast. All of it makes me want to hit stop and start all over again. Being flustered in front of Chad is not how I want to come across.

He nods, semi-accepting my answer. "I have to work tonight."

He looks down at his shoes. He's so tall, and his shoulders are so broad. I picture myself climbing him like a tree.

"Robbie's getting ready to retire." My voice is quiet, thoughtful.

A young, male voice interrupts us. "Hey, Tabitha. How's it hanging?"

It's Jimmy Rhodes, and I want to crawl inside the gardenia bushes. Everything is replaced with my humiliation from last year. I was caught. Skinny dipping. In the nine hundred year old Plucky Duck motel pool. In my underwear. With this child pretending to be a man.

Oh. My. God.

I'm never smoking pot again.

"Keep walking, Kid." Chad laughs as he says it, but there's a hint of something more in his tone.

Something like jealousy?

Jimmy's shoulders slump, but he does as he's told. As much as I'm burning with humiliation, and as much as I do *not* want to encourage Jimmy's teenage crush, I can't help feeling a little ruffled feathers. Chad is acting awfully possessive.

"Go out with me on Friday." He turns to me again, and his expression is serious, a little fierce.

It does strange things to my insides.

"No," I say too fast, and he exhales a laugh.

"So it's still like that?"

Between humiliation, lust, and church, my emotions are as mixed up as a bowl of spaghetti.

I don't know what it's like. I just know bad girls don't date cops. It's a recipe for disaster. One of us will end up wanting more than the other is willing or even capable of giving, and it will be painful and awful.

"I don't think it's a good idea." My voice is quiet, and I'm being as honest with him as I've ever been with anybody.

His grin melts, and a little line forms between his brow as he processes what I've just said, like he understands. "Then I guess… I'll see you around."

"Not if I see you first."

I swear my mouth has a mind of its own. It doesn't matter. That irresistible dimple appears, and I know I haven't scared him off.

The knowledge of that fact scares me even more.

"Either way, I've got my eye on you," he teases.

"I don't need a guard dog."

"Everybody needs somebody watching their back."

"I've got Emberly."

We take a pause while our eyes travel across the bright green lawn to where my best friend is still talking to Betty Pepper. Only now, Coco is hopping all around her. My goddaughter is an adorable bundle of energy, brunette ringlets, and sunshine, and she's been on a kangaroo kick for a month. It makes me smile, and when I glance up, I notice Deputy Tucker has a grin on his lips as well.

"She might have her hands full." He turns those sexy eyes on me, and I almost cave.

Can't do that. "We look out for each other."

He slides a large hand in his front pocket. "Have a nice day, Tabitha."

He's letting me go for now, but it's getting harder to resist the temptation.

Chapter 4

Chad

Red velvet lips and soft brown curls are in my mind as I roll over to stop my blasting alarm. For a minute I blink at the white wall, regaining my bearings and thinking how it's the third time in a week I've opened my eyes on the tail end of a dream.

A nice, round tail end.

One that leads up to a narrow waist, full tits, sassy green eyes and a broad, white smile. The dream is gone, and I'm left with a tent in my sheets. *Shit.*

I groan, tossing them aside and getting up. I came here to find peace. Getting mixed up with a girl like Tabitha Green is a recipe for disaster. I need coffee and a wake-up call. A mental smack in the face and a stern *Snap out of it.*

My bare feet pad on the warm hardwoods of my warehouse apartment over the sheriff's office, and I stumble to the bathroom to take care of business and get to work.

After surprising both Tabby and me with that spontaneous lunch invitation, I'd spent the afternoon with Sheriff Cole, listening to his old war stories from the days when Oceanside Village was the center of tourism, before the strip of land now known as Oceanside Beach was developed.

That billion-dollar development resulted in a lot of bad blood between the business community and the man who developed it, but it also cut way down on the petty crime here.

In the past, I enjoyed spending an afternoon that way. I'd spent the better part of last year getting back to normal, learning how to believe in something again.

Clearly I'm cured. I can't get fucking Tabby Green out of my mind.

I'm in my car in less than thirty minutes, ready for café au lait and beignets when I take my foot off the gas. "What the—?"

Tabby is walking on the side of the road about a half-mile from town. Her long legs are bare leading up to tight, navy short-shorts and a red and white checked short sleeved shirt. It's knotted in the front, and her dark hair hangs over one shoulder in a thick, curled ponytail. I growl, shaking a vision of me wrapping that dark rope around my fist from my mind. She's a sexy little pinup with white sunglasses perched on her nose.

My dick perks up at the sight of her, and I have to shift in my seat. It's a bad idea, but I pull to the shoulder, slowing down as I approach.

"Oh!" She skips back, reaching up to lower her sunglasses so she can peer at me over the frames.

I come to a stop when I reach her. "Good morning, Miss Green." Her cheeks turn pink, and fuck me. It's sexy as hell.

Still, she's defiant, which only encourages the heat in my groin. "Good morning, Deputy Tucker. Do you mind?"

"Mind… what?" My brow furrows, and I look side to side.

"You're blocking my way to work."

"I was going to offer you a ride." Glancing down at her shoes, I cut my eyes up to hers. "Those aren't made for walking, especially not on this highway."

She inhales deeply, and I divert my eyes from the swell of her breasts. She really is the real deal. She's also knows I'm right—even if she's pretending like she doesn't.

"Come on, Tabby, I don't bite." I give her a grin. "Until I know you better."

Her eyes widen, and I love that I throw her off balance. Surprise melts quickly into a frown, however, and she starts walking again. "I like the exercise."

Lifting my foot off the brake, I turn the wheel so the cruiser rolls slowly, keeping pace with her journey on the shoulder of the road. Her chin is lifted, and we continue a bit further, her giving me the silent treatment.

Teasing her seems to come naturally to me. "You should wear tennis shoes if you need exercise."

She gives her feet a passing glance. "I wasn't planning to walk when I got dressed this morning."

"What happened?"

"I still can't find my driver's license." Her tone is impatient, but at least she's talking now.

"I'm impressed, Miss Green. You do obey the law."

She takes a deep breath, causing those perfect breasts to rise. I look away, to the road ahead.

Her reply is pure sass. "If I didn't obey the law, Deputy Tucker, I wouldn't have made it this far."

"Call me Chad."

She stops abruptly, putting a hand on her hip. "Isn't there some law against stalking private citizens?"

"Stalking is a pattern of behavior. I'm trying to be a Good Samaritan. This road isn't designed for pedestrians. You'll turn an ankle."

"Is that any of your business?"

"Actually, it is. I've sworn to keep the people of Oceanside safe."

"So you're just going to drive along the shoulder at one mile per hour while I walk?"

"It'd be easier if you'd let me give you a lift."

Her green eyes narrow, and she studies me a moment. She looks down at her feet then ahead at the town. Finally, with an exasperated exhale, she stomps around the front of the car, jerking the passenger door open. I bite back a grin as she climbs inside and fastens her seatbelt.

She keeps her face turned to her open window, and the cool breeze pushes her dark hair behind her shoulder, exposing the fair skin of her neck. We don't speak for a minute, and I consider making a turn around the block to give us a little more time. Her presence fills the space, and my awareness of her is electric.

She breaks the silence, looking up and around the car. "I've never been inside one of these before."

"Really?" I don't hide the surprise in my voice.

That gets me another annoyed glare. "How bad do you think I am, *Chad*?"

Even with that tone, my name sounds good on her lips. "Hopefully, just bad enough."

Her cheeks flush pink again, but the ride is over. I stop at the corner of Main and Elm, and she doesn't give me a chance to open the door for her before she's out and heading down the row to Emberly's bakeshop.

Betty's pack-n-save is first in line followed by Wyatt's hardware store. Emberly's bakery is next, and down a bit is Daisy's antiques store. A smile lifts the corner of my mouth as I watch her go, that ass from my dreams swaying side to side.

The bell over Betty's door rings as I pull it open, and the aroma of café au lait and beignets hits me.

"Right on time," a rumbling male voice calls from behind the counter.

André Fontenot is Oceanside's best-kept secret. He's got a pop-up sandwich store in Betty's place, and he makes coffee and poboys to rival anything you'd find in the French Quarter in New Orleans. He and Emberly recently combined forces to add her pastries and launch a breakfast menu. They're determined to draw tourists up from the beach and back into town, and so far it's working. Once the word starts to spread, people are going to be lining up.

"Morning, Dre." I hand him the cash and take the paper cup, giving it a quick puff before taking a sip. Rich, dark coffee surges through my veins, and all is right in the world.

"Saw Tabby getting out of your cruiser just now." Dark eyes are worried beneath the brim of his Saints ball cap. "Everything okay?"

I lean back against the bar lining the window and nod as I take another sip. "Lost her driver's license."

"Shit." A bright smile splits his dark lips. "I was worried for a second."

Tabby's website development has been a big part of their plan, and her penchant for getting into trouble would keep me on edge as well.

"I think I've found her Achilles heel."

He cocks an eyebrow, and I lower my voice. "Making her go to church."

That earns me a loud laugh. "Is that legal?"

"She hasn't questioned it yet."

André nods, seeming impressed. "Not bad, Tucker."

"They don't give those badges out to just anybody."

He's still chuckling as he passes me a small paper bag. "Emberly made beignets. Take a few for the road."

"Thanks." I put the plastic lid on my cup. "I'll be around. Holler if you need anything."

He shakes his head. "If you'd told me this time last year I'd ever be glad to see a cop, I'd have called you crazy."

It's a compliment I'll take, and I tip my coffee at him before heading out the door. I'll stop in and check on each of the stores along Main Street before I head out to the beachfront strip to finish my rounds. It's the off-season, so our days are gradually slowing down.

From now until spring break, my job is pretty quiet. Wyatt is busy helping a guy with toilets and plumbing supplies when I stick my head in to say good morning. He's tied up, so I move along, down the row to Emberly's shop.

Again, a little bell rings as I enter the store. Emberly is at the large table in the back, her chestnut hair gathered on top of her head as she rolls out what looks like white paste. Tabby is at the counter, pecking on a calculator with a pen in her hand.

"Morning, ladies." Her head snaps up at the sound of my voice, and she frowns again.

"How long does the pattern of behavior have to occur before it's considered stalking?"

"Just doing my job, Tabitha." I take a few steps inside when Emberly, looks over her shoulder and gives me a friendly smile.

"Good morning, Chad! Did you try the beignets today?"

I hold up the small brown bag. "André hooked me up. Just finishing my coffee."

"They go with the coffee!" She waves her hand over to where a carafe stands in the window. "We're combining forces. He gave me some of his coffee."

She takes my cup and crosses the large, open space to get me a refill, and I stop at the counter where Tabby is suddenly very focused on number crunching.

"Web design and accounting?" I lean over, looking down at the notebook in front of her.

Straightening, she slaps it shut. "You might be surprised to learn girls can do math and computer science. Even if they don't wear glasses."

"I'm not surprised." My eyes flicker to her red lips before returning to those fiery green eyes. "I bet you can do whatever you want."

That melts her. I don't know why I have a one-track mind toward this girl all of a sudden, but I just go with it. What the hell? "I've got Friday night off. I'd like to cash in that rain check if you're free."

"What rain check?" Her voice is quieter, defiance gone.

"From lunch yesterday. Go out with me on Friday."

"I told you no."

I confess, her immediate rejection stings a little, but I see the fear in her eyes. It eases the blow somewhat. "Really?" I can't wait to hear her excuse this time.

"I... I promised Emberly I'd keep Coco."

"Tabby!" Emberly is with us again, handing me the fresh coffee. "Coco can stay at Mom's Friday night."

Tabby cuts her eyes at her friend. "But I promised—"

Emberly shrugs. "It'll be a good reason for me to call it an early night. Besides, you haven't done anything fun in—"

"I do what I want to do." Tabby cuts her off, glancing at me before turning on her heel and going to the coffee carafe.

"I don't want to cause any problems…" I start.

"It's not a problem at all." Emberly gives me an encouraging smile coupled with a little wink. Then she tilts her head toward where her friend is standing.

I look from her to where Tabby is pouring coffee. I don't like causing conflict, but I'm encouraged by the unexpected support. "What do you say?"

Tabby turns to face me. "You're barking up the wrong tree, Deputy Tucker. I'm not looking for anything right now."

"Then we should do just fine. I'll pick you up at seven." Crossing the space, I'm headed for the door when her voice stops me.

"But… What are we doing?"

I go to where she's standing by the small table. She straightens as I approach, as if preparing to defend herself.

"May I have your number?" I catch her eye and smile in what I hope is a friendly manner.

It only seems to fluster her. "I guess so."

"Here." I reach for her phone, which she hesitates before putting in my hand. Quickly, I type in my number and send myself a text. "Now we're connected."

"You're going to keep me in suspense?"

"Seems you like surprises." I start for the door again, but pause before leaving. "You'll need to wear something you can move around in…Something you don't mind getting dirty. I'll text you more later."

Her brow furrows, and I grin as I head out the door.

I do love knocking her off balance.

Chapter 5

Tabby

My phone buzzes at eight a.m. with a text from Chad, *Do you have full use of your arms and stomach muscles?*

Sitting up in the bed, I rub one eye as I text back, *What the hell kind of question is that?*

A pretty easy one. Do you?

My nose wrinkles. *As far as I know.*

Any issues that would limit the use of one arm and both legs?

Is this about tonight?

Maybe.

I have no special needs.

Time change. Okay if I pick you up at five?

Pressing my lips together, I contemplate replying about him just assuming I'm sitting around waiting to go out with him. I don't. *What the hell are we doing?*

Wear something you don't mind getting dirty.

You already told me that.

He doesn't respond, leaving me antsy all morning.

Since Monday, Chad hasn't stopped in the bakery at all. At his usual, morning check-in time, he only peeks in the window and gives us a wave. He grins, and that damn dimple pierces his cheek, causing my insides to clench. If our eyes meet, it's like a bolt of lightning.

I remind myself I'm not doing relationships now. I'm working on my business, and once I've saved enough money, I'm taking a trip around the world. I've got my American Airlines credit card to buy all my gas. I'm racking up the points every time I go to the station, and I'm well on my way to 120,000 points — the magic number to book a RTW flight.

I got the idea from my newest client, Travel Time. They're a travel agency, and I'm setting up a streamlined, elegant site for them, directing travelers to packages based on where they want to go, categorized by location, duration, price, and star rating.

In the evenings I search for blog posts, photographs, and travel diaries to accompany the different packages they offer. Many nights, I have my dinner reading them and dreaming of seeing the sites up close in personal. Maybe I can add to the photographs and travel logs...

So while Chad Tucker is an interesting diversion, he is not distracting me from my goals. Cheater Travis Walker was the last man ever to do that to me. I plan to be financially independent and to see the world.

My best friend used to say she'd go with me, but having my gorgeous goddaughter and launching this bakery have put her travel plans on hold for now. I watch as she carefully guides the frosting bag around the edge of a three-layer chocolate cake, creating perfectly shaped purple flowers.

"He's not giving you the chance to change your mind." Emberly straightens, putting one hand on her lower back and giving it a stretch before returning to her work.

"He's wasting his time is what he's doing." I pick up a fruit tart and carefully lower it into a cardboard box.

"Spending time with people isn't a waste." She gives me a wink.

"You know what I mean."

"Give me five more minutes, and you can take this one, too."

Checking the clock, I see it's almost eleven. "The tart is for the Ladies' Auxiliary First Friday luncheon, and the cake is for..."

"Betty Pepper's Sunday school class is having a birthday party for her."

"You made it awful early." Emberly usually makes her cakes closer to the time they'll be eaten to keep them fresh.

"She said they might have the party tomorrow if Roxanne is going out of town."

Shaking my head, I assemble another box. "I can't keep track of all these old biddies. I thought you slowed down as you got older."

Emberly shrugs, finishing the final purple rose. "Roxanne Philpot isn't slowing anything. Since her husband died, I heard she has a profile on Hookup4Luv dot com. Donna said her mystery trip is to Hedonism."

"No way!" My jaw is on the floor. "If that old lady has a better sex life than me—"

"Whatever." Emberly cocks an eyebrow at me from where she's finishing Betty's cake. "Your sex life is as good as you allow it to be."

"I don't know what that means." It's bullshit. I know exactly what it means.

The bell over the door rings, and in waltzes Jimmy Rhodes like some kind of living visual aide. He's dressed in his usual—dark skinny jeans and a tight black tee. What I now recognize as a homemade tattoo peeks down his lined bicep. I cringe. *Good lord.*

"Afternoon, ladies." He leans on the counter, giving me a wink.

"What do you want, jail bait?" Turning my back, I carry the box to the table where Emberly is finishing up.

"Aw, come on, Tab. That was a whole year ago." A cocky grin curls his lips, and he hooks a thumb at his chest. "I've aged a lot since then."

"To what? Seventeen?"

"No." He acts offended. "Eighteen."

"Did Wyatt have that bulb?" Emberly pushes past me, wiping her hands on her apron and inspecting the box Jimmy is holding.

"Yes, ma'am." He pulls out a small, oddly shaped bulb. "He said it should fit that old refrigerator, but he's not sure how much longer he'll be able to stock them. Says they're getting harder to find."

My friend's face pales. "What does that mean?"

Jimmy shrugs as if it's an easy math quiz. "Time for a new fridge?"

Emberly rubs her stomach, and I know full well she can't afford an expense like that. Daisy helped her find this old commercial-grade heap through one of her antiques dealers.

"That it, kiddo?" I'm ready for this bad flashback to be on his way.

"Almost… Go out with me again. I've got Uncle Milt's Lincoln all weekend long."

"No, thank you." I do a full-body shudder. "I've got a car."

I finally found my driver's license in the clothes dryer at Uncle Bob's house. It's probably been there a month. He doesn't check these things very well. He raised me without a strong female role model, and I've been improvising ever since.

"Come on, Tabby. Things were just getting good when—"

"Thanks for the delivery. You and I are never happening."

His shoulders droop, and he starts for the door.

"I've heard everything changes once you start college." My best friend is too kind hearted for her own good.

Jimmy only shrugs. "I'm not going to college."

"Well, either way, there are lots of fish in the sea!"

I've heard enough. "See you Monday."

A quick air kiss, I stack the fruit tart on top of the cake box. Walking past my car parked out front, I mentally note Deputy Tucker hasn't even pulled me over to be sure I'm not breaking the law since I started driving again on Tuesday. It makes me feel a bit uncomfortably predictable, but I don't have time for that. I've got to get these pastries delivered.

* * *

André grins at me like he knows something when I push through the door of Betty Pepper's pack-n-save.

My eyes narrow. "What?"

He shrugs. "Nothing."

André is in the middle of bagging up poboys for a customer, and I decide to let it go. He and Chad are always joking around, and I'm sure it has something to do with tonight. Those mysterious texts are on my mind as I approach the door at the back of the store. It leads to a storage room that doubles as the office where Donna does her bookkeeping for Betty.

"Hey, Tabby!" Donna White is a mousey girl, timid but sweet. "I was planning to walk down and pick this up. You didn't have to bring it all the way over here."

"It's not that far." I put the large box on the end of her desk. "We should probably put it in the cooler so it doesn't melt."

"Is it ice cream?" Her brows furrow as she lifts the lid.

"No, the frosting will melt in the heat."

Donna's frown instantly transforms into delight. "It's beautiful! Oh my goodness. Emberly is so talented."

I lean over to check out the deep chocolate cake topped with beautiful purple roses and little white dots of baby's breath. The happy birthday message is inscribed in perfect calligraphy.

"She's got the talent. It's the customers she needs. There aren't enough birthdays, anniversaries, weddings, and... well, reasons to have cake in this little town."

Donna nods as if she knows exactly what I'm talking about. She's probably never thought about it in her life.

"I hope I can help bring in a little extra business."

"You're great. Thanks, Donna." She closes the lid, and that's when I see it sparkling like a drop of water on the third finger of her left hand. "What's this?"

I snatch it up and turn her hand side to side as the light hits a small emerald-cut diamond. The girl starts to giggle, covering her nose with her right hand.

"Liam finally proposed last Friday. He drove me all the way up to the Dairy Queen in Fireside and right in the middle of dinner, he pulled out a black box."

My lip goes between my teeth, and I start to laugh, too. "I'm not sure many people would consider a proposal at the DQ the height of romance."

"Oh he knows how much I love those dip cones. I dream about them some nights."

"You're not pregnant, are you?"

Her eyes flash wide. "No! We haven't even... you know." She clears her throat and hurries on. "We could have gone to the Blue Crab or one of those fancy restaurants out on the strip. But that's never been our thing."

I consider the tall plumber with the floppy brown hair who hangs back quietly at most events in town.

Donna's voice is quiet as she adds. "I'm sure you think it's stupid, since you're so sophisticated and all."

"Not a bit!" Reaching out, I pull her to me in a hug. "I was actually thinking how sweet that is. If Liam pays that much attention to the little things you like... well, he sounds like good husband material to me."

She returns to the box and carries it along the line of refrigerator cases. "Help me with the door, will you?"

I'm turning it all over in my mind as I open the large glass door. "He sounds a lot better than the assholes I seem to pick..."

"Still no word from Travis?"

"Of course not. That player is never coming back."

Donna makes a sad face. "I can't believe he did that to you. Daisy is so sweet, and she has that little Melody... Well, it's just a shame, that's all."

"Maybe he's dead."

"Tabitha!" The door slams shut with a muffled thud, and Donna laughs louder. "You say the craziest things."

"I'm just saying. The way he drove that bike." *I wish he were.*

"He was a bit careless." Her voice is quiet shock as we walk slowly back to the desk where she works.

"Careless doesn't come close to what he was. Heartless. Worthless…" Something else flickers in my mind. "So you and Liam have never… done it?"

Clearing her throat, she quickly takes her seat. "It's never been a good time." She's acting way too suspicious, but she charges on before I can question it. "God doesn't want us to, right?"

My lips curl. "I don't know. A lot of that stuff was said when people got married at fourteen. God might understand adult needs."

She takes her seat, picking up her pencil. "You sound like the old ladies in my Sunday school class. You know, I think Ms. Roxanne is going to a sex club for her vacation?"

"Don't even say it!" My hands fly up, and I turn on my heel. "I've got a fruit tart to deliver."

I beat a hasty retreat to the door, calling goodbye and best wishes over my shoulder as I push through the door. The last thing I want in my mind is images of wrinkly old farts frolicking on a nudie beach.

I've got bigger fish to fry… and a mystery date to prepare for tonight.

Chapter 6

Tabby

Standing in front of the mirror, I go back and forth between my kitten heels and my black Vans. Chad has been so freakin mysterious and absent all week. I have no idea what's going on—other than I'm supposed to wear something I don't mind getting dirty.

Not much in my closet fits that description. I don't dress to get dirty ever, and as much as I've been trying to fight it, I do want to look cute for my date tonight.

I'm standing in my denim capris and a black, sleeveless sweater going back and forth on my shoes when the doorbell rings. A kaleidoscope of butterflies takes off in my stomach, and I growl at them to settle down.

I don't know why I'm doing this.

I don't need distractions right now.

Especially not hot ones with big muscles and tight ends.

Pulling the door open, my breath catches when I see Chad standing in front of me in loose, faded jeans and a camo tee that stretches across his pecs in such a way he might as well be shirtless.

I kind of like his sexy G.I. Joe look. *Unexpected.*

His dark brow lowers, and those full lips press into a frown. "Nope." He shakes his head and walks past me into my small house.

"Rude!" I manage to pick my jaw off the floor and call after him. "Did I invite you in?"

"You can't wear that." He ignores me, looking around the room. "You need layers. Do you have a sweatshirt you don't love?"

"I don't have a sweatshirt at all. You've seen how I dress."

His eyes flash the way they sometimes do when I see him around town, and I'm pretty sure Chad Tucker just had an impure thought. The way my panties catch fire, I'm pretty sure my body is right there with him.

My brain is the only holdout.

Chad Tucker is nothing but trouble as far as my plans are concerned. Tall, dark, and sexy trouble, but trouble nonetheless.

"Never mind. I've got something in the truck. Wear the tennis shoes."

"Give me a second."

He waits as I go to my bedroom and grab the other shoe. When I return, he seems to completely fill my living room. His eyes rake over my body, and my breath catches.

"You look great. Ready?"

"Ready as I'll ever be." I exhale, doing my best to halt my involuntary response to him. "Where are we going?"

He catches my hand in his, and I swear to God my heart jumps to my throat. *He's only holding your hand, Tabby.* Jeez, I've been holding boys' hands since fifth grade. It's just never sent a humming vibration up my arm before.

When we get to his silver Chevy, he releases me, opening the passenger door and actually taking my arm to help me climb the step side.

"Aren't you the gentleman?" I tease.

He looks confused, and I totally fall for him right then.

What a lie. I fell for him the first day I saw that ass in those polyester uniform pants.

I have *never* seen polyester look that good on anybody.

"I got to thinking about it." He turns the wheel and heads up the road away from town. "I figured you're probably bored with the usual Oceanside stuff."

"So you've been thinking about me all week?"

"I did ask you out. I'd like you to have fun."

Okay. I look out the window at the passing scenery. He's driving on roads I only take if I'm going on a trip somewhere, leaving town.

After a few more minutes, he turns down a narrow dirt road I've never even seen. "It's a good thing you're a cop. Otherwise, I'd be nervous."

"I don't believe it. You're not afraid of anything." He winks at me, and my stomach flips.

"I wouldn't be too sure of that." The way my body responds to him scares me to death.

The road opens on a large field and what looks like an obstacle course or some place where military guys do drills. Massive, gray tree stumps are stacked on top of each other, with big canvass bags dotted among them. A few small thickets with trees are in the four corners, and two old sheds are at the very back. The closer we get, I see guys are running around inside carrying guns, and a big sign over it all reads Fireside Paintball Battleground.

"What the..." I don't finish as Chad parks the truck.

My lips are parted, and I'm staring at the scene in front of me. Chad's at the door again, holding it open and waiting. "Come on."

"Chad... I..." I don't move, but he takes my arm, giving it a gentle pull. "I don't know anything about this. I didn't even know this was here."

"Me either. One of the guys who works here stopped in for poboys last week." Pride is in his voice as he leads me to the back of his pickup. "Put this on."

He hands me a black sweatshirt, and I pull it over my head. I'm practically swimming in it, but it smells yummy, clean and fresh with a warm manly undertone. I think it's just soap mixed with Chad, but if it were bottled in a store, I'd buy it.

"I have these masks." He holds up what looks like a black ski mask. "They don't fog up, but they also don't cover your whole head. I can rent one for you if you'd rather—"

"These are good." *I have no idea.*

I take the mask and follow him to the ticket booth, tying my hair back in a long braid as he pays for us. Then I follow him around to the supply shed, where we're handed guns with big barrel things on the tops of them, and a canvass vest.

"I rented the vest for you." He slips it over my shoulders, fastening it in the front like I'm a little kid. "It'll add extra padding so it doesn't hurt."

My eyebrows shoot up. "Hurt?"

Chad chuckles. "Don't be such a wuss. It just stings a little. Watch your step out there or you'll slip."

He picks up the gun like he's been doing this all his life. When I think about it, he probably has been handling weapons for years.

I study the strange gun. "I think you've got the advantage on me."

"We're on the same team. Don't worry. I'll cover you. Just stay close to me."

"I plan to stick to you like glue."

He gives me that panty-melting grin again, and my breath skips. "Sounds like a good strategy. Remember, the pellets are heavy, so aim a little higher than you normally would to hit a target."

I follow him to the field, and Chad stops to talk to a few guys. I'm surprised how many people are out here. It looks like ten men, the two of us, and one other woman a little older than me. She gives me the stink-eye, and I know who's going to be aiming at me.

As we fall back to the starting line, he explains. "They play last man standing. No rounds, so it could go a while."

I have no idea what that means. "I'll probably be the first to go. Katniss Everdeen has me in her sites."

Confusion lines his face, and I nod in the direction of the blonde. He gives me a wink and flicks my dark braid over my shoulder. "You're Katniss. She's more like... Glimmer."

My jaw drops and I pull back. "You've read *The Hunger Games*?"

"Hasn't everybody?"

"I guess. I didn't expect you to—"

"Just leave her to me."

"Not a chance." I pull the mask down over my face. "I fight my own battles."

"You don't even know how to use the gun yet."

"I'll figure it out."

"Remember what I said. Stay to the sides and keep yourself covered."

The air horn sounds, and we all run up the sides. Chad is faster than me, and I have to dig in to stay at his side. Noises like whizzing rocks fly past me, but I manage to get to the first canvass bag without getting hit. Chad is pressed in front of me, and I'm right beside him, breathing hard and looking all around.

"That was intense," I whisper.

Chad doesn't respond. Sure enough, Glimmer is behind a stack of stumps scowling at me. I bet every one of those near misses was her trying to hit me as I ran.

Chad turns to the side, pressing his back into the bag. "If you get hit, you're out."

"Anywhere? Or somewhere where it would be a real kill?"

"Anywhere. I'm going to run to the next bunker. Stay here and shoot anyone who tries to hit me. I turned your safety off."

"No!" I whisper-shriek, my heart flying in my chest.

I'm really panicked.

It's ridiculous!

He's takes off, running low to the closest stack of stumps. I see Glimmer lifting her gun to shoot at him, and I scream as I pull the trigger, holding the tip of my gun slightly higher than her head and unleashing a flurry of little round pellets.

To my surprise, it leaves a line of yellow paint in an arc on the stump where she's hiding. She pulls back fast, and Chad is safely at the next bunker. I'm guessing *bunkers* are these barriers placed around the field for us to hide behind.

I have no idea why, but I'm breathing so hard, you'd think we were in a real war with real bullets. My entire body is vibrating, and I peek out to see Chad give me a thumbs up and a grin.

I'm so proud, I want to do a dance. *I did it – I covered him!* Instead, I lower my brow, very serious, and give him a sharp nod in response. Like I do this all the time.

I have no idea what to do now, and there's no way in hell I'm leaving this spot. Looking around the edge, my eye is on Glimmer. I want to take her out more than anything, and I can hear myself panting.

A guy from the other team darts out from behind a tree, and Chad pelts him at least fifteen times with blue paint. The guy drops to one knee and puts his hands above his head. I figure it's the signal he's out because everyone ignores him as he leaves the field.

Blue paint is concentrated in a palm-sized circle in the center of his chest, and I realize Chad is a great shot. I only have a second to think it because Glimmer is on the move—headed straight at me with a determined look on her face. She raises her gun, and I'm looking right down the barrel.

With a scream, I drop to my knees, lifting my gun and holding the trigger. My eyes are closed, but I can feel the multiple shots as the pellets fire from my gun. It smells like smoke and chemicals and oil, and slippery goo on my hands.

Then hear her growl, "Dammit! You can stop now."

I lower my rifle, and when I look again, I see red paint all around me, but only splashes on my arms and legs. No direct hits. Glimmer, by contrast is covered in a line of yellow from her crotch up her chest almost to her face.

Biting my lip, I fight back my laughter. It doesn't stop my snort, though. She looks like a wild person got after her with a paint gun, which I suppose is what happens when you shoot with your eyes closed.

She stomps past me, hitting me with her shoulder, leaving a smear of yellow on my arm. I shake my head as I watch her go. These people are nuts, and very serious about this game.

"Cover!" Chad's low shout snaps me out of my wonder, and I look up in time to see another big guy running toward where I'm standing. I do a quick dive, sliding around the bag with my back still pressed against it.

Another flurry of paint, and the guy is coated in blue. Chad got him, but I hear him mutter, "Shit."

Looking down, I see my leg has a purple dot on the thigh. *Damn*. I didn't even feel it, but I'm out. He got me. I do the motion with my hands over my head and walk slowly off the field, squishing in paint and feeling like a failure.

It takes almost an hour for Chad to ultimately win the game. I'm not surprised since he's a cop and all, but the last guy he's trying to get looks like Rambo. It's quiet for long stretches, then they duck and dash from bunker to bunker almost hitting each other.

I let out a little yip when Chad is nearly hit with orange paint, but he manages to dodge it. He's really amazing to watch. He's so big and muscular, yet sleek and stealthy as he moves around the field. I'm surprised by how much I love watching him work.

When I returned my gear, the guy gave me a plastic bag for Chad's enormous sweatshirt, which was covered in paint. I'm in my purple-stained capris and sleeveless black top, and paint is spattered all over me. I wish I had my red lipstick, especially when I see Glimmer a few cars down watching the guys with as much interest as me.

Finally, Rambo takes a turn and his foot goes out from under him. He slipped on paint, and Chad shoots him in the shoulder. He goes over and helps the guy up, and they're laughing and talking like old friends as they leave the field.

"Good game." Chad claps his shoulder, stopping at the booth to return the paint gun.

"You have to come back for a rematch," the guy says, and Chad shrugs.

"I'll have to see what the schedule looks like."

He walks to where I wait on the front of his truck. I'm ridiculously proud of him, especially when I see Glimmer go up to Rambo and slip her hand in his. It's silly, but I give her a superior look as Chad helps me down. Then I shake my head and wave. Who am I kidding? I like badass bitches, and this was fun.

I glance up at Chad holding the door for me. "You don't want to stay and have a beer with them?"

His eyes are bright. We're both pretty adrenalized. "I can't drink beer on an empty stomach and drive you to dinner."

"Oh, right," I nod slowly. "Breaking the law. You can't do that."

"I don't have to break the law to have fun."

He's such a square. I roll my eyes and start to climb in, but he stops me with a hand on my shoulder. "You had fun."

A smile splits my face, and I laugh. "I really did."

"Let's get some food."

"Like this?" I look down at the paint on my clothes and hands, not to mention the paint splattered on his neck and shoulders and feet. "Our shoes are ruined."

"André's got us covered. Put this over your seat." He grabs a towel from the back and hands it to me. I arrange it before climbing inside.

He walks around the front of the truck, speaking again to the other group and doing a little wave. The sun is setting, and it smells like night air, fresh grass, and stinky paint. We're driving back into town, and I haven't felt this relaxed and happy in a long time.

What is this hot cop doing to me?

Chapter 7

Chad

"Muffuletta for you and chicken salad. Her favorite." André gives me a nod as I head in to collect our dinner. "You planning to get cleaned up first?"

I glance down at my paint-spattered body. "Maybe. If I'm lucky."

I give him a wink as I slide the cash across the counter, and André's chuckle follows me out the door. Tabby's waiting in the cab of my truck, and my stomach tightens when our eyes connect. I've seen her as sexy pinup girl, but she's even prettier like this, natural with her hair in a braid and little pieces falling around her cheeks. Our differences are on my mind, but after tonight, I'm willing to explore more, see how deep those divisions go.

"No wonder André's been so sly all day today." She teases as I drop the bag on the bench seat between us. "He was in on the plan."

The windows are down, and the breeze whips away the funky paint smell. At least we both smell like paint. "I thought you might be hungry after."

"You are something else, Chad Tucker." She slants an eye at me, and my body responds.

I swear, this woman. She's got me hungry for more than food. Our eyes meet, and hers flutter away. Her cheeks flush pink, and I clear my throat, returning to her statement.

"Something good?"

"Surprising. You found something in Oceanside I've never done."

"It was technically outside the city limits."

"Still…" She gives me another side-glance. "You were kind of a badass out there."

That makes me smile for real. "You were kind of a badass yourself. That's quite an aim for somebody who's never played before."

"I've used a gun."

I'm surprised. "You have?"

"Uncle Bob's taken me deer hunting. I never shot anything, but he taught me how to aim."

It's an interesting story, and one I don't expect based on my limited experience with her. "I didn't think you got along with your uncle."

She exhales a laugh and looks out the window. "We get along okay. He just wants me to be a straight-laced Sunday school teacher. It doesn't interest me."

We're at my place, and I park the truck. Her eyes return to mine, but now a brow is arched. "I figured since we're covered in paint, we might as well go to my place." Her hesitation makes me pause. "We can go somewhere else if you're uncomfortable—"

"No, it's okay. You are a cop. And where else would we go?"

"Carry the food?" I take the paint-covered towels off the seat. "I should have mentioned bringing a change of clothes."

While I unlock the door, we both slip off our shoes at the bottom of the staircase leading up to my warehouse apartment. "You can leave them there."

She follows me up the narrow flight of stairs. "This is nice."

It's a big, open space with exposed brick lining the exterior walls. It's industrial and very male, with a brushed metal bar dividing the kitchen from the living room, where an enormous flatscreen TV hangs over a gas fireplace.

"Thanks." I cross to the washroom located behind the refrigerator. "The rent's unbelievably cheap. Robbie restored it, but he couldn't get any renters."

"Why not?" Turning to look at the whole space, her confused gaze lands on mine.

"Who wants to live over the sheriff's office?"

"The sheriff's deputy?" She drops the bag on the bar, and I walk back, giving her a nod.

"Right. And nobody else."

That makes her laugh. It's a bright, melodic sound I haven't heard much up to tonight. She's always scowling when I'm around.

Taking down the plates, I level my eyes on her. "So what's the deal, Tabby? Why have you spent the last year treating me like the enemy?"

Her jaw drops. "I haven't been doing that."

I pull out the foot-long, paper wrapped sandwiches. They smell like heaven. "You've been doing exactly that."

She clears her throat and shifts from one foot to the other. "I've been really busy that's all."

She turns and walks across the living room to the built-in bookcase beside the television. I'm not looking to kill the mood. As much as I want an answer to my question, I'm mostly teasing.

"Want that beer now?" It's offered as a truce.

She looks over her shoulder. "Got anything stronger?"

The braid is out of her hair, and in the small spotlights, I see she has caramel highlights in the front.

Even with paint spattered on her cheek, she's really beautiful. Maybe the paint adds to it. All I know is for a second, my brain decides not to work.

"Chad?" Her voice snaps me out of it.

"Right. Um… I've got whiskey and tequila."

"Tequila it is." She turns to the bookcase again, and I give her cute backside a once-over before going to the refrigerator and taking down the gold bottle.

"Want to mix it with something?"

"Look at you!" She crosses the space between us carrying a picture frame.

Stepping toward her, I stop when she's beside me, small in her bare feet. She's holding my graduation photo from military college.

I give it a glance, and exhale a short laugh. "That was a while ago."

"Did you serve?"

"Four years."

Her slim brows pull together, and she glances up at me again. "Why?"

Placing the bottle on the bar, I take out a can of sprite and some orange juice. "Pretty early in the night for that conversation."

"So it wasn't just for love of our country?"

"There might have been other reasons."

"Okay, we can table that." She climbs onto one of the wooden stools across the counter from me and puts the picture aside. "What are you making?"

"Modified tequila sunrise." I have ice in tumblers, which I fill half way with soda before adding a few fingers of tequila and topping off with orange juice. "See what you think."

Green eyes meet mine, and her smile is genuine. "It's good!"

"Don't sound so surprised. Hungry?" I slide her plate toward her and lean against the bar where my plate remains.

"I can't eat all of this." She lifts half a poboy and inspects the side. "Chicken salad. My favorite. How did you know?"

For a second I consider taking credit. *Nah.* "André made them for us. I told him we'd need something quick and easy."

"He knows me so well."

I'd like to know her so well. "So you grew up here?"

She nods, chewing a minute before answering. "Born and raised. What about you? Where were you before all of this?" She twirls a finger in a circle over the bar.

"My family is in Charleston."

"Is that where you graduated high school?" She's rocking on the stool, and I take another sip of my drink.

"Yep."

"Football player?"

"Yep."

She puts her sandwich down and picks up her glass. "Let me guess... Star quarterback, captain of the football team. Straight-A student, graduated college with honors."

Straightening, I cross my arms over my chest. "Guilty as charged."

Her eyes flicker to my biceps then to my eyes again. Yeah, I did it on purpose.

"Such a good boy." Her tone is softer, and she takes another sip. "What brought you to Oceanside Village?"

I walk around the bar and pull out the stool beside her. It's close enough that our knees touch, but not so close to be crowded. "I like the beach. I finished my tour of duty, and I wanted peace and quiet, something small."

"If by peace, quiet, and small you mean boring, backward, and closed-minded, you've come to the right place."

I only laugh. The tequila is warm in my blood, and I like being close to her. "I haven't found it to be that way."

"Give it a little more time." She trades the glass for her sandwich and takes a small bite. My eyes travel from her slim shoulders up her neck to her full lips.

"My turn. Let me guess... Preacher's kid, wild child, drove all the boys crazy —"

"Hold it right there." She drops the sandwich and holds up a finger, laughing. "Preacher's *niece*, and just because I don't like Uncle Bob's shouty sermons, I'm not as wild as you think."

"You're not a wild child?" Disbelief is in my voice, and I reach out and trace my finger down the line of the tattoo on the inside of her wrist. It's an infinity symbol with the word *Believe* in one curve.

"Get with the times, Tucker. Tattoos don't mean anything anymore."

I slide my finger across the symbol again, and her lips tighten. I want to kiss her. "Why believe?"

Her shoulders lift slightly. "To remind myself to do it? I might not like shouty sermons, but I do believe."

"So you stayed here because it's safe." Somehow I've edged a bit closer to her.

Shaking her head, she wrinkles her cute little nose. "Safe makes me restless."

"So I've noticed. You like surprises, being caught off guard." Rising to my feet, I push the plates back, lift her off the stool, and sit her butt on brushed metal top of the bar.

Her arms go to my shoulders, eyes wide. "What are you doing?"

"Kiss me." I'm between her legs now, and I lean down so our mouths are a breath apart.

Her fingers flex against my muscles, and her green eyes sparkle. She bites her lip, and we're both breathing a little faster.

"You're too law-abiding for me." Her words are a warm whisper of a promise on my lips.

"How so?"

"That uniform? Those handcuffs?"

"Maybe I should put you in handcuffs."

"Maybe I'd like to see you try."

Heat floods my pelvis, and my cock perks up. I can imagine her in handcuffs. Her hands over her head, round breasts heaving, legs twisting. *Fuck, that's hot.*

"Kiss me, Tabitha."

Her green eyes flicker to mine, and they smolder like emeralds. "You're too bossy."

"You like being bossed."

Another nose wrinkle, a little curl of the mouth into a smile, and she leans forward. The moment our lips touch, fire ignites between us. Her arms tighten around my neck, and my fingers on her waist curl. I pull her soft body flush against mine as my mouth parts hers. Our tongues touch and slide together, and it's a match to kindling.

It's sweet orange with the bite of tequila. It's electricity humming in my veins. She exhales a sigh, and I can't hide the erection in my pants. I pull back, tugging her lips with mine, taking a gentle bite of her jaw. Another soft moan, and her fingers are in my hair.

I lift my head and our eyes meet.

Damn she's just what I want...

Chapter 8

Tabby

My lips throb from the best kiss I've had… *Ever.*

Beard scuffing my skin, I scratch my fingernails through his hair and chase his lips as he bites my jaw. *Shit,* that feels good. His cock is hard against my thigh, and I'm so wet.

He lifted me off my stool like I weighed no more than a doll. It's sexy as hell, rough and demanding, and when he pulls back, when our eyes meet…

A current shoots from my chest to my core, tingling between my thighs before making its way to the arches of my feet.

We're both breathing fast, blinking into each other's eyes. I see the hunger there, but he hesitates. We both do. Our chemistry is crazy, and as much as I want more, I need to hit the brakes, think about who he is, who I am…

Dropping my chin, I loosen my arms, sliding my hands to his forearms. I'm not sure what to say. *Holy shit!* is on repeat in my head.

"Sorry." His voice is gruff, and he steps back, helping me off the bar and onto the stool again.

His eyes are diverted, and he walks around into the kitchen area.

"No need to apologize." My voice is a little shaky, so I clear my throat. "I think we both participated in that."

He turns to the refrigerator. "I think I'll switch to beer. Want one?"

"Sure." I reach for my sandwich, but I'm not really hungry anymore. Not for food anyway.

He places two bottles of amber in front of me. "Frosty mug?"

"Nah." I take mine before he can pour it into the glass. "I'm easy."

He does that sexy wink before taking a sip. "Is that so?"

"Not the way you said it."

Setting the beer on the counter, he leans on his forearms. "Tell me, Tabitha Green, something I've been wondering about for a while."

His forceful tone makes me shift in my seat. "Okay."

"If Betty Pepper hadn't called us, would you have gone through with it?"

I frown. "With what?"

"Jimmy, that night at the Plucky Duck."

"Oh…" Blinking rapidly, I try to remember how I felt that night. "It's hard to think of it now, knowing what I know about him."

"You didn't see right through that act?"

My cheeks are hot, and I press my lips together. "I wasn't using the best judgment at the time. I was pissed off at everybody."

When our eyes meet, his are still warm, searching for something. He reaches out a large hand across the bar and slides his finger down the inside of my forearm, starting at my tattoo and going to the bend of my elbow. "Why?"

It's such a simple question, I feel silly answering it, especially in view of that kiss just now. *Who was Travis again?*

"I was dating this guy." I pick at the label on the bottle. "He turned out to be a real jerk. Then he skipped town." When I glance up, I notice Chad's brow has lowered, and I can't tell if it's about Travis the Jerk or Jimmy. "I was having second thoughts, anyway. I wasn't sure about the condom situation, and I wasn't sure I was even into it anymore…"

He nods slowly. "You look out for yourself."

"I'm not stupid." Sitting up straighter, I feel defensive. "Sometimes it's nice to be with someone, a warm body when you're feeling lonely. I guess that sounds wrong… Sinful."

I can't believe I said that out loud. *Am I drunk?* I'm pretty sure I sound like a total slut right now.

"It sounds human to me." Chad clears his throat and straightens. "I just wanted to know."

Squinting up at him, I try to decide what to make of Chad Tucker. "You're doing it again."

"What's that?"

"Being something else."

"Something good?"

"Let's play a game."

He walks around the bar again to sit beside me. "Sure. Get the mood back on track."

I slap my hands on my thighs, then I lift my palm. "Ew…" Purple paint covers it.

"Here." Chad stands in his chair, reaching for the roll of paper towels. "Let me get you something to change into."

He crosses the living room to what I now see is a bedroom off to the side. Scrubbing the paint off my hand, I inspect my jeans, wondering if this crap will ever come out. It smells like gasoline.

My lip curls, and I call after him. "If you're bringing me clothes, I can't imagine you own anything that would fit me."

He's back pretty fast, changed into sweat pants and a white undershirt. My eyebrows shoot up, and I tear my eyes away from his crotch before he catches me staring. It looks like a snake swinging heavy and low in those pants. An Anaconda. I want to touch it.

Again, *Holy shit* is on repeat in my head.

"How's this?" He holds out a large, navy tee and a pair of dark blue boxer shorts.

I take them, loving the way they smell. "I'll be swimming in these."

"I've got this." He jogs around into the kitchen again, pulling a narrow drawer open and digging in it. "What do you think?"

He's holding an enormous safety pin. "What the hell... Are you MacGyver? Where did you get that?"

He frowns as if trying to remember. "I think it was on some dry cleaning. I figured it might come in handy one day, so I threw it in the sauce drawer."

"The sauce drawer?"

"You know, where you throw all the sauce packets. Don't you watch SNL?"

"Not enough." I hold out my hand, palm up. "Hand it over."

I'm changed and pinned in his boxers in no time, the shirt knotted in the front. He has two more beers on the bar waiting when I return, and when he notices I'm not wearing a bra, I see the same struggle on his face as when I saw his trouser snake.

Glad to know I'm not the only one enjoying the view.

Pretending like I don't notice, I slide my palm over the bright red circle on my thigh faintly shaded from the paint that seeped through the denim.

78

"Looks like I got punched in the leg."

Concern replaces lust, and he crosses to me quickly. "Does it hurt? I have an ice pack…"

"I think it'll be okay. It might leave a bruise, though."

"Sorry."

"What's this?" I point to the bar where the beers are waiting.

He gestures to them. "You wanted to play a game… Quarters?"

I snort and frown. "No."

"Truth or dare?"

"Never." I've been burned too many times by that game.

"I'm all out. What you got?"

Climbing on the stool, I run through the least offensive drinking games I know. "Never Have I Ever?"

He tilts his head to the side, and the way the light hits his square jaw is like some classical painting. "I don't know that one."

"How can you not know that one?"

Broad shoulders rise in a shrug, stretching that tank, and I inwardly sigh. "I guess Oceanside is more sophisticated than you give it credit for." His reply is a total tease.

"Not a chance." I take two more beers and twist off the caps. "It's easy. I'll start by making a statement of something a person might do. If you've done it, you drink. For example, never have I ever gone skinny dipping." Lifting my beer, I take a short pull. "Get it?"

His frown softens, and he starts to nod. "I think so. You drink when it's something you've done."

"Right. First one drunk… Wins?"

"Then loses tomorrow."

"Or later tonight, depending on how your stomach works."

His full lips part, and I'm treated to that white smile again, coupled with that deep dimple in his left cheek. *Holy shit.*

"Was that your first statement?" He points the neck of his bottle at me. "You've gone skinny dipping?"

"Yep. Drink up, Tucker."

Lips press into a grin, and he shakes his head.

My eyes go wide. "You are shitting me right now. You've never been skinny dipping?"

"Never had a reason."

"Who needs a reason?" He shrugs, but that grin is still there. I narrow my eyes. "I don't believe you."

That makes him laugh. "I'm a man of the law. Would I lie to you?"

"Yes." I answer so fast, he laughs louder. It makes my stomach all tight and tingly. "It's a game of honor. There are no rules for lying."

"I'm not lying." A laugh, soft and low rolls from his throat, and my insides are all warm and fizzy.

"It's your turn."

His eyes travel around the room. "Let me see..."

"The object is to get to know the other person better."

"I understand." He gives me a glance like he wants to get to know me better naked. It's hot. "Never have I ever... Hmm... watched a porno on a date."

He takes a drink, and my eyebrows shoot up. I sit motionless, like a dummy, not drinking. "You've watched porn on a date? Isn't that illegal or something?"

"It's not going to work if you doubt everything I say."

Taking a deep breath, I shake my head. *Just when you think you have somebody figured out...* Chad Tucker is not such a square after all. I slide my fingers down the cool bottle.

"You haven't?" The disbelief in his voice makes me self-conscious. I shrug, and he murmurs. "I'd like to get that cherry."

I have to clear the lust from my throat. "Never have I ever..." My eyes circle the room. "Had phone sex."

I sit back and take a drink. Chad only looks at me, but this time the smirk on his face is hot. "Maybe you can get that cherry."

"You are not serious right now. You've watched porn on a date, but you've never had phone sex?"

"I didn't have access to cell phones for a while."

"Where was that? Tibet?"

"On a destroyer in the Indian Ocean."

Leaning my head on my hand, I feel buzzy thinking of him in uniform out there defending our country. "Were you lonely?"

He crosses both arms in front of him, leaning forward. His biceps are so round and bulgey. A vein runs down the center of one...

"A little. I was pretty messed up for a while myself."

"Why?" It's the same simple question he put to me earlier. In my defense, all his sexy has pretty much depleted my brain's store of clever comebacks.

"My sister had just died... Or committed suicide." He looks down then takes another long drink. "They never knew for sure."

Sadness fills my heart, and I slip off the stool, going around to hug him. "I'm so sorry."

He leans down, engulfing me in a warm, strong

embrace. I'm surrounded by that clean, manly scent I'm starting to crave. My cheek is against his chest, and I can hear his heart beating solid and strong.

"I thought she was the coolest person in the world." His voice is quiet, tender. "Her nickname was Cherry… She was a wild child." A sad smile curls his lips, but this time there's no dimple. "Five years older than me. She knew everything I didn't."

I step back so I can meet his eyes. "I can't even imagine."

"I went straight into the academy after it happened, then I left for active duty. When I got out, Robbie Cole offered me this job. He'd been friends with my dad since way back." He exhales deeply. "I figured it was time to stop running away. Time to be still and make peace with it."

"It sounds like you had to live your life."

He nods. "Life keeps going. No doubt about it."

"Her name was Cherry?"

"Short for Charity."

"Charity." I say it softly, imagining a girl who looked like Chad. A bad girl who might or might not have committed suicide.

Without thinking, I step forward again, wrapping my arms around his waist and pulling him close. His face dips lower, beard brushing my temple, and I lift my chin.

Our mouths touch, open. It's a small kiss at first, a brush of lips, a nip, a pull. All at once, it's too much to resist, and with a groan, he lifts me off my feet.

My arms go around his neck and my legs around his waist. He pushes my mouth open, and our tongues curl and stroke. Heat blazes between us as I devour his luscious mouth. He keeps time with me, large hands sliding up my thighs, gripping my ass.

I grind against him, feeling the hardness of him at my core, only thin scraps of cotton separate us.

My mouth breaks away with a moan, and I look up at the wood ceiling. "Oh, God," I gasp as his lips trace a line down my neck, his beard scratching my skin. My heart's beating wildly, and I want this so bad.

He sits my ass on the bar again then reaches up to my breast. My nipples are tight, tingling, and he slides his palm over them, squeezing and kneading. I can't stop making little noises. My whole body is hot, wet, and when he goes in for another kiss, I hold his cheek, ready to rip off his clothes, my clothes...

What am I doing? The thought rises unwelcome in my head. Pulling back, I know I have to grab the reins on this. We're going too far, too fast.

Chad doesn't hesitate. He leans forward, kissing me again, and I whimper as I kiss him back. I'm still in his arms, and this moment of clarity won't last long.

"Wait..." My palms flatten against his chest, and I move away this time. "I can't do this."

His brow furrows, and ahh, *holy shit*, he's so handsome. "I have condoms."

"I bet you do." *Magnums, from the feel of it.*

"So what's the problem?"

"We've had too much to drink. I can't... I—" *I can't do this with you...*

Chad is a good guy. He's the type of guy who wants a family and a home right here in this small town. He wants peace and quiet. I *hate* peace and quiet. I'm not a good girl—just ask any of the old biddies in town. I'm a Jezebel. Maybe I'll have a family one day, but it'll be later, after I see the world...

Oh, God, all my excuses sound so lame with this gorgeous man standing here, burning with lust for me, that massive snake straining in his sweatpants.

"Right. You're right. We should… slow it down." Chad steps back, scrubbing a hand behind his neck. It drops quickly, covering the anaconda in his pants, shoving it down. Poor anaconda. "I need a few minutes before I can drive you home. What is it? One hour per drink?"

Both our eyes go to the tequila and empty beer bottles on the bar.

"It's okay." I pull out my phone and slide down to my feet. "I'll call an Uber."

"No, I should drive you. Or at least let me pay…"

I turn my phone face to him. "Already done."

I know myself. I have to act fast, rip off the Band-Aid, or I won't leave at all. Now my only question is why the hell did my brain pick tonight to do the right thing?

"I still can't believe they have Uber in this town," Chad mutters.

"It's because of the strip." Looking down at my phone, I feel guilty. "Listen, I didn't mean to—" The device dings. "Shit, it's already here."

I pick up the plastic bag holding my clothes and start for the door. My shoes are down on the landing.

"Wait…" Chad puts a hand on my forearm. It's warm and inviting, and I hesitate, looking up into his whiskey eyes. "I had a great time tonight."

I step forward and give him the quickest peck on the cheek. "Me too."

Then I run down the stairs, snatching my ruined shoes off the step as I dash into the night before I can second-guess myself.

Chapter 9

Tabby

The universe hates me.

The second I jump into the Uber, I nearly jump right back out again.

"Tabby?" None other than Jimmy Rhodes is behind the wheel. "You're World Sites, LLC?"

"What are you doing here?"

"Earning money. What are you doing at Deputy Tucker's place? Drunk?"

"I am not drunk." Seeing him is a total buzz-kill, and I slump back against the seat crossing my arms. "Are you even old enough to drive for Uber?"

"I told you I'm eighteen now." He's driving too slow down the short road through town. He doesn't turn at the stop sign like he should, and I sit up quick.

"You're taking the long way."

"I'm following my Uber directions. It's how I get paid." He's silent, but it doesn't last long. "Really, Tab? Chad Tucker? He is not the guy for you. You're too different."

Tell me about it. "I expect you think you're the guy for me?"

"Maybe."

"Snap out of it, Jimmy. I'm never going out with you."

His shoulders slump and all the cockiness is gone. Now I feel doubly bad.

A quiet growl ripples through my throat. "Look, I'm sorry, Jimmy. You're just too young for me."

"One of these days you're going to see what you let slip away. I hope it's not too late."

Leaning forward, I look out the window. We're finally approaching my house, and my hand is on the door handle. "We'll see." I'm out before the car even comes to a complete stop. "Thanks for the lift."

Ditching my shoes and the plastic bag at the door, I head straight for the shower. I carefully place Chad's tee and boxers on my bed. As soon as I finish getting the paint off me, I'm back in his clothes, surrounded by luscious Chad-scent. *Why, brain? Why tonight?*

I know the answer. Chad is sexy and strong and good. Very, very good. Straight As, captain of the football team, military, future sheriff, future dad… *porn on dates?* Talk about a wild card. He'll make some lucky girl a great husband one day. In the meantime, I've got to keep my eyes on my dream.

For now, I snuggle down in the sheets, burying my nose in the neck of Chad's tee.

* * *

"Hellooo?" Emberly's voice rings through my cottage, pulling me from a deep sleep. "Anybody alive in here?"

"Aunt Tabby!" Coco's little voice joins my bestie's, and I sit up fast.

Then I clutch my head and sink into my pillows again. "Oh, shit."

"Hey!" Two bodies bound onto my bed, climbing to the top to lay beside me. Emberly pulls the blanket off my face. "How'd the date go? Uh, oh."

"What's wrong?" Coco's little body struggles to sit up beside me.

"Aunt Tabby looks a little green around the gills."

"I am not." I grumble—softly so as not to shatter my skull.

"You need to wake up now, Aunt Tabby. Mama says if you sleep all day it messes up your arcadian rhythms."

My eyes squint through the blasting sunlight. "My what?"

"Circadian!" Emberly laughs and reaches across me to muss her daughter's hair. "Your circadian rhythms."

"What's Circadian, Mama?"

"It's your body clock."

Coco starts to laugh, bouncing on the bed. "I'm not a clock!"

Pulling the blanket over my head, I struggle to crawl lower. "Five more minutes!"

Emberly catches me. "What do you need? Ibuprofen? Emergen-C? Hair of the dog?"

"Mama!" Coco cries again, rooting around beside me like a little piglet. "Aunt Tabby doesn't want dog hair!"

I poke my head out of the blanket considering it. "We drank tequila. I don't have any tequila."

"Ooo…" Emberly nudges me in the side with her elbow. "A tequila night. Sounds naughty."

Coco stops worming around and gets still. Emberly and I are lying head to head on my pillow facing the ceiling. I think we're going to have a moment of calm when my goddaughter's thoughtful voice breaks the silence.

"Mama says tequila makes you pregnant," she announces.

Our heads snap to facing each other, eyes bugging out. Then we both explode with laughter, and I roll over, catching Coco around the waist and moving her between us. She squeals with delight and wiggles all around as Emberly tickles her.

"That's right," my friend says. "You never, *ever* drink tequila unless you're with the man you're going to marry."

Dark brown eyes widen at me. "Were you with the man you're going to marry, Aunt Tabby?"

"No!" I answer fast, cutting off Emberly's snorts of laughter. "I was with Mr. Chad, and he made this... modified tequila sunrise. We weren't doing shots or anything"

Coco's brown eyes go wider. "Like with his gun?"

"Yes, Tabby," Emberly joins her being bad. "Did Chad shoot his gun?"

"Okay, that's enough." Scooting to the side of the bed, I leave them both rolling around laughing as I stomp into the kitchen and pull out a packet of ginger tea.

"What the heck happened here?" Emberly's with me as I fill the kettle, leaning down to study what's slowly turning into a bruise on my thigh.

"Oh, that." I switch on the gas and wait for it to ignite. "I guess Chad did shoot a gun last night." She straightens, studying my face. "A paintball gun."

"Did he take you to that place Jimmy's always going on about? The way he talks, you'd think it was some kind of magical kingdom."

"Like Disney World?" Coco is up on a stool at the bar, and I reach in the cabinet to get her an Oreo Pop Tart.

"It was pretty elaborate. I'd never seen any of those people before in my life. How is that possible?"

"They were probably all from Fireside and elsewhere. I can't imagine too many of the senior citizens in Oceanside playing paint ball."

Shrugging, I put the Pop Tarts up and take down a box of ginger snaps for me. "It was actually a lot of fun."

"So you had a fun date with Chad?" Emberly crosses her arms, nodding like she won a bet or something.

"Saying *I told you so* is so unattractive." I crunch into a ginger snap then grab a washcloth to wipe the dark brown crumbs off Coco's face.

She hops off the stool and runs across to my small living room, where a flat screen is hung above a real wood fireplace.

"I've been telling you so for a year."

Coco puts the TV on some kid show about a cat and a fish in school, and Emberly leans close over the bar so we can talk in private. "Did you sleep with him?"

"No."

She frowns, pulling back. "You didn't?"

My nose wrinkles, and I bite into another ginger snap. "I don't like how that makes me sound slutty."

"I've never called you that a day in your life." She drops back onto the bar stool like she knows something. "So you didn't sleep with him… Interesting."

"What's so interesting about that?"

"You'll run out the door to hop on the back of Travis's bike—"

"That was different. Did you see Travis? He was like… Jax Teller with black hair."

Her lips twist, eyes cast to the side. "It's true. He did have that Sons of Anarchy sex appeal."

"He was a lying, cheating, sack of shit is what he was." Inwardly, I cringe. "I can't believe I trusted him for so long. I can't believe I thought he was the one."

"You never told me that." My friend's voice goes soft, gentle. It makes me uncomfortable.

"He was *not* the one." I snap a gingersnap hard between my fingers. "I blame all the old ladies in this town constantly going on about missing your chance and shit. Bullshit."

Maybe I do need some hair of the dog.

"If it's meant to be, it'll be." Emberly nods, then her eyes narrow. "I bet if we saw Travis Walker now, he wouldn't look like Charlie Hunnam at all."

"He'd look like the south end of a northbound mule. One that can keep heading north."

Emberly starts to laugh. Then we both laugh, holding each other's hands until we're out of that dark place.

"Oh..." Emberly wipes her eyes, exhaling a sigh. "I think you're onto something with the hot cop. Chad's like... some kind of sexy, muscle-bound, all-American action hero. He's like Thor with brown hair... Why are all of my favorite actors blond?"

I arch an eyebrow at her. "Sounds like you should be dating him."

Her chin drops, and she reaches for a ginger snap. "You know that's not my type."

"Yeah." I feel bad for saying it. I know Emberly's type. Jackson Cane, the one guy she's always loved, who left for college and never came back. I heard he's some hotshot lawyer in the city now. *Asshole*. "Sorry, Em."

"Forget about that." She blinks a few times, then smiles up at me. "You, on the other hand... You're different somehow. I think this good guy might be good for you."

"That's too many *goods* for my taste."

She pats the watch on her wrist. "Gotta go. Are you sure you're okay with keeping her tonight? If you're not feeling up to it—"

We're crossing the living room, headed for the door. "Of course I'm up to it. We're going to have fun tonight, aren't we Coo-coo?"

"Oh..." The little girl nods her head knowingly. "That's how I'm a clock. Because you call me Coo-coo."

Emberly stops to kiss the top of her daughter's head. "I won't be late in the morning. You be sweet and mind Aunt Tabby." She comes to me next and gives me a hug. "Not too much sugar."

Coco starts to whine, but I'm right there with the save. "Would I do that?" My voice goes high, and when I hug my friend, I give Coco a wink over her shoulder.

The little girl laughs, and her mother only shakes her head. "I felt that. Y'all have fun. Thanks for letting me borrow the car."

"No problem. You left me your bike?"

"I parked it right around the corner. Remember to put the chain on."

"You drive safe. You don't have much practice."

My best friend prefers riding her bicycle all over the county. I don't blame her, except I don't wear the right shoes for biking.

"I'm an excellent driver!" Emberly cries.

"That's what Rain Man says."

She's out the door, and I prance over to give my goddaughter a kiss. "Okay, sugar puss. Let me check my emails and we can decide what we want to do this afternoon."

Last night was a little crazy, with me not getting home until after midnight. In the past, I wouldn't have gotten home until three, but I've turned a new leaf this year. I'm being more responsible.

Take last night for instance, not sleeping with Chad. That's what I should have told Emberly. Why didn't I think of that?

Not sleeping with Chad is part of my professional makeover. I'm not falling for some good guy. I'm being a responsible businesswoman, keeping my eye on the goal.

The tightness in my chest when his dimpled smile flashes through my mind is just residual hangover feelings, nothing more.

I do not want to pet the snake in his pants.

I want to get this website finished, cash that big check, and hop a flight to Tahiti.

Okay, I might want to pet the snake one time.

Stop it, Tabby!

Chapter 10

Chad

The alarm on my phone is like a freight train barreling through my room.

"Shut up," I growl, slapping it off.

I went to bed with the worst case of blue balls I've had since ninth grade, and now my head aches. I start to roll over, when fuck me again. Apparently my dick is still ready to party. It's awake like I'm fourteen and just seeing Pornhub for the first time.

"Tabby…" My voice is thick from sleep and too much alcohol, and I'm pretty sure I dreamt about her all night.

She was right to put on the brakes. It was a first date, for chrissake. Although it feels like we've been dancing around each other for a year. Closing my eyes again, I see her walking out in my boxers and tee. She tied the shirt up so I could see a peek of her waist, her cute little navel with a tiny gold loop.

My dick aches harder, and I get up, ripping the covers back and stalking down the hall to my walk-in shower. It only takes a minute to switch on the water and get it warm enough for me to step inside and take care of business.

A squirt of conditioner, and I grasp my aching cock, propping my other hand against the wall and letting my mind travel back to the feel of those tits through my tee. Her nipples were so tight, I wanted one in my mouth. I can taste it.

Her little moans ring in my ears, and the way her soft ass felt in my hands, the way her hips moved as she rocked against me. My hand moves faster, and it won't take long today. The orgasm races up my legs, tightening my ass and…

"Yes," I hiss, as it streams out in pulses.

My knees go weak for a moment, and I brace myself as it rolls over me—longing, desire, release. I carefully hold my hand over my now-sensitive dick. Damn, that girl is so sexy. I pull off the shower head and wash the evidence down the drain.

I have to see her again.

It's probably a bad idea.

Still, we had a great time last night. My initial worry that she might be put off by paint ball melted the minute I saw her sizing up our opponents, competition sparkling in her green eyes. She was adorable, closing her eyes and screaming as she shot. She did pretty damn good. Then, when we we came back here…

Scrubbing shampoo through my hair, I soap up and wash off. I have a short shift this afternoon, then I plan to drop by and see if she's free tonight. I've been guarded, staying out of the mix, keeping my head down. It's almost as if I've been figuratively out to sea.

Now it's time to come home.

* * *

Robbie's feet are propped on his desk, studying what looks like a legal dossier.

"Nah, I'm just not ready to do it." Dropping his feet, he grabs a mug of coffee and gives me a nod.

"Morning, Chad. How'd it go last night? Tabby like that paint ball idea? I tell you, sometimes these kids just need a hobby."

"We had fun. What are you looking at there?" As much as I like Robbie Cole, I'm not about to delve into the details of last night with him. He's as gossipy as Betty Pepper.

"Chad…" he rises out of his seat, crossing his arms over his chest, hands under his armpits. "I've decided. I'm not going to retire."

"Okay." He's been saying this every month the closer his retirement date draws. We're six weeks out, and it's getting worse.

"I was just looking over the numbers for the county. We've got more than enough to give you that raise you were expecting."

"I'm not worried about the raise. If you want to stay on, stay on." It helps I have both a hefty trust fund from my grandfather and a nice pension from the military.

"I know you don't need it, but you were promised a raise. You're getting a raise." He nods as if it would be a grave injustice.

As if.

Robbie saved me. He helped me find a way out of that old life before it killed me. I was only a week out of the military, at my parent's big Welcome Home reception at the Admiral's Club—their chance to show me off. I was still struggling and he pulled me aside, told me about this place, told me he was retiring in a year if I wanted the job.

I didn't hesitate. I was gone in less than 24 hours.

"If you give me a raise, I should do more to earn it." My smile is warm, full of gratitude, although I have no idea what more I can do. This place is like working in Mayberry. Still, I don't like handouts.

"I'm glad you said that." He circles back around to his desk, flipping open a different folder. "Part of the reason we've had such a nice influx of cash is certain celebrities I won't name have built houses up on Oceanside Cliffs."

"Those houses aren't new." They're also pretty much empty most of the year. I'm not sure why they're even here unless it's for tax purposes.

"No, but as property values continue to rise, our tax revenue increases."

"Right." Even with ibuprofen, my head's still a little achy.

I carried ten bottles of beer to the recycling bin this morning, and I'm pretty sure I drank nine of them. On top of tequila. No more drinking games.

We did get to know each other pretty well... Skinny dipping, phone sex.

The hangover's worth it.

I tune back in for the end of Robbie's monologue. "I want you to add checking on these places to your weekly rounds. Make sure bums aren't sleeping in the boat houses, make sure all the doors are locked."

"I'll head over there today." As soon as I grab breakfast at André's.

He'll want to know about last night as well—or at the least, he'll make that face and laugh.

Small-town living.

Shaking my head, I'm on my way out the door when it opens in front of me, and in storms a clearly pissed off Jimmy Rhodes.

"Sheriff Cole?" His voice is loud, and when he sees me, he skids to a stop, standing straighter, almost like he's puffing out his chest.

Jimmy is about five-nine or five-ten, and probably weighs about one hundred and forty pounds. I'm six-two, two hundred pounds, all muscle. I stop, curious to see what this is about.

Robbie doesn't look up from his paperwork. "What's on your mind, Jimmy?"

"Is it appropriate for a certain *deputy* to be getting so drunk on a Friday night he can't drive his date home?"

My jaw clenches, and I'm not sure if I want to laugh or snatch him up by the neck. "It's illegal to drive if you've been drinking, Jimmy." My voice is low, and his bravado wavers. He takes a few steps back and moves closer to Robbie's desk.

The sheriff leans back in his chair. He puts his hand over his mouth, and his blue eyes narrow, moving back and forth between Jimmy and me. "Your uncle told me you're driving for Uber now."

"Yes, and I got a call from upstairs just before midnight last night. Tabitha Green."

"Well, I bet that just made your night, now, didn't it."

I give Robbie a glance, and his hand is covering the curl of his lips, his eyes are twinkling with mischief.

"It did not. She was coming out of his apartment, dressed in nothing but an old tee and some boxers."

Robbie's brows shoot up, and I take a step toward Jimmy. "Her clothes had paint on them. Don't be talking about us around town."

"Probably too late for that," Robbie mutters through an exhale.

"Anyway, aren't you going to reprimand him or something?" Jimmy glares at me. "Strip him of his duties?"

Robbie sits forward in his chair, eyes on his desk. "That Uber service. That's to help people get home who might've... had a little too much fun to drive themselves, right?"

"Yes, sir." Jimmy steps closer to the desk.

"Odd name, Uber. Is that German for something?"

"I don't know." The boy's growing impatient.

"Never mind. It sounds like you did a good job last night, Jimmy." Robbie relaxes back in his chair. "What Chad does on his own time is none of my business. Or yours."

"That's it? That's all you're going to say to him?" Jimmy turns to face me, eyes blazing. "You'd better watch your step, Tucker. Tabby's not like what they say. You're not going to mess around with her like she's some kind of... Jacinda."

Robbie clears his throat. "Jezebel."

The kid nods. "That's right. Jezebel. Tabby's a lady. She should be treated like a lady."

"I agree." My voice is a low rumble, and Jimmy keeps a safe distance between us as he heads for the door.

"Remember this..." He steps forward slightly. "I'm watching you."

I straighten to my full height so he gets the picture. "That so?"

He fumbles with the door handle and heads out fast. I look back at Robbie, who's leaning over his desk again, grinning like a Cheshire cat.

"He's watching me."

Robbie nods. "That Tabby Green must be something pretty special."

Catching the door handle, I don't have to think about it. "She is."

Chapter 11

Tabby

The sun is making its way down the sky as I lock up the bakery, and Coco is skipping around on the front porch, Molly the Dolly safely in her arms.

"Don't leave her anywhere else, okay?" We had to make a special trip to Emberly's apartment over the store to retrieve the rag doll my little guest can't live without. "I'm surprised your mama didn't make sure you had it."

"She put her in my suitcase, but Molly doesn't like the dark. So I took her out."

"I see."

Emberly had packed Coco a tiny, pink suitcase with wheels monogrammed with a fancy *CCW* for Colette Corinne Warren. It contains a nightgown, tiny panties, a change of clothes, and more toys than any kid needs for a one-night sleepover... but no Molly the Dolly.

"Want a poboy for dinner?" I slip the key in the pocket of my black capris and straighten the hem of my tight red sweater.

It's short sleeved and light, just right for this warm night, and it matches my red lipstick perfectly. The black is fading out of my hair, and I'm trying to decide if I want to redo it or let it be brown for the first time in forever. My natural highlights are starting to show and my bangs are to my jaw now, taking the edge off my usual Bettie Page.

"Yes, yes, yes!" Coco hops in time with every *yes*, one little fist pumping over her head. "I want mac and cheese."

"Wait." I pause. "Mac and cheese or poboys?"

"Both!"

I give her a frown then decide to see what André can do with that order. He is the master, after all, and I'm all about keeping Princess Coco the Kangaroo happy while her mom's out of town.

I'm just turning to the bike when I slam into Daisy Sales. My heart plunges to my feet. We haven't spoken since Travis the Cheater left town last year.

"Oh!" Daisy steps back, nearly dropping the open catalog in her hands. "I didn't see you!" Her voice is loud and too high, and I think she might be as wigged out seeing me as I am seeing her.

"Melody!" Coco stops hopping and runs to grab Daisy's blonde toddler in a hug.

The little girl fusses, trying to push out of the embrace.

"Melly, give Coco a hug!" Daisy drops to a squat, catching her daughter's waving arms. "Sorry, Coco. She's been fussy all day."

"Mama says babies are fussy." Coco nods as if she's an expert. "She calls it the terrible twos."

I'd laugh if I weren't still getting over bumping into my nemesis. "Melody's three now, isn't she?"

Daisy stands, smoothing her hands down the front of the flowered sundress she's wearing. Her straw-colored hair is stick straight, and I can tell she tried to braid it to get some waves in there. A few telltale ripples are around her temples.

"Next week." Her hands shake, and now I know she's nervous. "I was going to talk to Emberly about a birthday cake. Is she out of town?"

Somehow, Daisy's nervousness cancels out mine. "Well, you picked the perfect time. She's at a cake decorating class in Brookhaven. She'll be back tomorrow."

"Oh... okay." She looks down at her feet again, tucking the catalog under her arm. "I'll check in with her then, I guess."

"What's your favorite cake, Melly?" Coco is holding the little girl's hand, trying to get her to talk. "Mine's mermaid."

I can't even imagine what her mom has come up with to make a mermaid cake. Returning to Daisy, I decide maybe it's time to bury the hatchet. I don't give a shit about Travis anymore anyway.

"I can take the order now if you want? I have the keys. Somebody left Molly the Dolly in her mom's apartment upstairs."

I tilt my head down to Miss Priss, who's holding Melody's hand and trying to walk her to the pack-n-save. Melody's fussing and twisting her arm, trying to get out of Coco's grip.

"Oh, no! I mean, that's okay. I can wait and call tomorrow. Or walk over on Monday. I don't have to bother you." Daisy looks up ahead to where her daughter has sat down on the porch in front of Wyatt's hardware store. "I'd better help Coco."

I look up to see Coco trying to get the baby to stand. Melody only waves her chubby arms and squeals.

"Hey," I catch Daisy's skinny arm. "It's okay for us to be friends again. I mean, we can say hi and stuff."

Daisy and I never really hung out together. In fact, you could've knocked my socks off when I found out Travis was sleeping around with her. The sleeping around part... well, I probably saw that coming a mile away, but not with Daisy.

She meets my eyes, and her brown ones are so sad. "Okay." She nods, looking down again. "Have you... Do you ever hear from him?"

"Are you kidding me? If that jackhole knows what's good for him, he'll stay far away from this town. I might go Lorena Bobbitt on his..." Catching myself, I remember I've got Coco, the Mouth of the South, with me. "You know."

Thin blonde eyebrows shoot up, and she looks away again fast, to the little girl who's squealing angrily and with more force at the persistent Coco. "I'd better get Melody before Wyatt comes out."

She scampers away, up the connected porches, and I put my hand on my hip. If I didn't know any better, I'd say Daisy Sales fell pretty hard for Travis "Cheater" Walker. I'm not sure what to make of it. With a shrug, I follow her. Nothing to make of it.

"Come on, Coo-coo. You've bothered this baby enough." I catch her hand, and give her a gentle tug. "Let's get some food."

She takes my hand and resumes skipping, swinging Molly as she sings. "Mac and cheese. If you please..."

"Tabb-ay!" André hollers out my name as I enter the store. "You're looking good for fresh off a night of debauchery."

I look around fast, but nobody's here but us. "Who told you that?"

"And Miss Coco Chanel!" He starts to laugh, looking up at me. "Who do you think? Our very own Uber hot line."

Jimmy Rhodes. I'm going to strangle him. "Isn't gossiping about your clients against some Uber rule?"

"You have to take that up with the management. Now what can I get for you ladies?"

"Mac and cheese... If you please!" Coco hops in place, doing her little cheer fist-pump over her head. I'm still trying to recover from the blaze of fury in my chest at Jimmy's big mouth.

"One mac and cheese poboy, coming right up! And what can I get for you?" André turns to me.

"That's a thing?" My eyebrows rise, and I peruse the menu, trying to decide. "I just had chicken salad last night..."

"I made it for you." He nods, still acting like he's in on some big secret.

Good grief. The last thing I want is to be the center of this goofy little town's attention. I can just see Betty Pepper and all her old church-lady friends going to town about this one. Me stealing their hunky hunky Eagle Scout and corrupting him... As if.

"I'll have—"

The bell above the door rings, cutting me off. André calls out again. "My boy Chad. Look who's here!"

Nerves fly through my insides, and I spin around to see Deputy Sex standing right there on the landing. *Damn*, he looks good even in clothes, especially when that friendly smile curls his lips, and that dimple appears. *Holy shit.*

"Hey, Tabby." He crosses to where I'm standing like a deer in headlights. "I was going to stop by later."

103

"Chad! Chad! Chad! Sher-riff Chad!" Coco hops around me to where he's standing, still pumping her fist.

He scoops her up so fast it takes my breath away. His muscles flex, Coco throws her arms around his neck in a hug, and that big hand sliding up and down her back so gently… His dimpled smile.

It's possible my ovaries exploded.

Wait—I don't want kids! *Shit!* Panic throws cold water on my lust-filled reaction. If Coco says anything about tequila or babies or the man you'll marry, I will drop dead.

Coco sits back on his arm. "I'm spending the night with Aunt Tabby tonight!"

"Is that right?" He bends forward to put her down. "Where's your mamma?"

"She's learning how to make roses."

A little wrinkle is between Chad's brows when he straightens, and those whiskey eyes do a quick scan from my head to my toes before locking his gaze with mine. I feel like I've been mentally undressed good and proper, and my panties are burning up.

Clearing my throat, I explain. "It's a cake decorating class."

"What's going on out here?" Betty Pepper's loud voice makes me cringe. "Tabby! Chad? Is that Coco with you?"

"I'm spending the night with Aunt Tabby!" Coco hops over to the bar and climbs on a stool. "Mr. André's making me mac and cheese."

"He most certainly is not!" Betty Pepper scolds her. "You know the Fall Festival for the church tonight. I expect you all to come right over and get some Boston Butt. André, that includes you."

"Ew!" Coco cries.

"Stop that fussing, Colette. We have a hayride and a dunking booth and games and cotton candy. You might win a goldfish!"

"Cotton candy!" Coco's entire attitude changes. "But I don't want to eat a butt. I want mac and cheese."

Betty's hand goes on her hip. "It's not a butt like your behind. Boston Butt is like... it's like brown chicken."

My nose wrinkles at that metaphor, and I try to rescue us from this hijacking. "Oh, thanks, BP. We're just going to take it easy tonight. I loaned Emberly my car and—"

"I could give you a ride." Chad is warm at my back, and I pivot, looking up at him.

His smile is still there, along with my favorite dimple, but something in his eyes has changed, it's grown hotter, panty-melting hot.

I go to where Coco's sitting so I can think straight. Church functions are not my thing, even if I am keeping a four year old. "You don't have to."

"We are not serving alcohol at this event, so you should be fine to drive." Betty's eyes narrow, and I swear, I am going to punch Jimmy Rhodes in the nuts next time I see him.

Chad exhales a chuckle. "See? I can even get you home as well."

"Yay! Brown chicken!" Coco pumps her little fist.

I catch it in my hand and lower it. "We'd planned to watch a movie... and I don't have any cash. Aren't these events cash only?" *Thank the Lord, I saved us.*

"We got a brand new credit card reader. One of those little white square things?" Betty's hand is on her hip, and she gives me a final nod. "I expect to see you all there in a half hour."

She stomps to the back of her store, headed to her office, and when I look at Chad again, he's still grinning. "I was actually planning to stop by this evening and see if you wanted to go out again." He closes the space between us, and my resistance melts in the presence of his hotness. "What do you say? It sounds fun."

"It sounds terrible. Brown chicken?"

"Cotton candy… I could win a goldfish!" Coco's hopping again, and I know I've lost. "Nevermind about the poboys, André. Looks like we have a change in plans."

Chapter 12

Chad

I follow Tabby in my truck to her place and wait as she parks the bike, gets Coco out, and removes her little helmet. Then she grabs a booster seat before joining me.

Scooting to the side, I help her position the chair and then fasten the little girl in the center of my truck's bench seat. "You're pretty good at this."

Her eyebrows furrow, but whatever bothered her is quickly dismissed. "Taking care of Coco is easy."

"Melody is not easy." Coco's eyes are big, and she shakes her head slowly. "She is a terrible two."

"She's almost three." Tabby taps her nose lightly, and I like their easy manner.

It's a short drive to the church grounds, and Coco sings some song about mac and cheese the whole way. I'm pretty sure it's made up, although I'm not up on all the kids' songs. As soon as we're parked, she's jumping in her seat, ready to ride the small Ferris wheel across the way.

"You stay where I can see you." Tabby's voice is stern as she gives this instruction. "What's the rule?"

"If I can't see you, you can't see me." The little girl says the words as if they're the Pledge of Allegiance.

"Now have fun, and no goldfish!"

That gets a little whine, but it's short-lived.

"Polly!" Coco waves to another little girl and takes off running.

"At least she won't have any trouble sleeping." Tabby's eyes roam around the semi-crowded field, where I know just about everyone, before turning to face me. "You were planning to come over tonight?"

Her red lips twitch, and a breeze pushes a long curl over her shoulder.

"I thought I'd be sure you were doing okay." Once again, I run my eyes over the skin-tight red sweater she's wearing with tight pants that stop at her calves.

In town she had on black flip-flops, but she traded them when she ditched the bike for the kitten heels she's wearing now.

"I'm doing okay."

She's doing more than okay. She's sending all the blood from my head to below my waist. "I found something you might like this afternoon. I thought we could check it out."

"Is it something Coco could do?" Her eyebrow arches, and I shake my head.

"It's something for next time."

"Impressive how you're already working on Date 3." Slim arms cross over her narrow waist, and damn, she's gorgeous. "Although, you might say Betty Pepper lured Coco here with promises of sugar and fish and brown chicken."

It makes me laugh, which causes her eyes to widen then flicker away. What's on her mind? Could it be the same thing on mine?

"We don't have to call this a date," I place my hand on her lower back as we slowly enter the festival grounds. "Betty trapped us all into coming here."

"I don't even know what they're raising money for," she sighs.

We walk slowly past a booth selling little sewn pictures with sayings on them like, *I cross-stitch so I don't kill people.* "Probably the youth in Asia."

"As opposed to euthanasia?" She caught the reference, and I laugh.

"You like David Sedaris?"

"Something about his little nasal-ey voice does it for me." Our eyes meet, and I like finding things we have in common.

"I might have to get this one for Emberly." She holds up one of the framed sewing pictures. It reads *Don't be afraid to take whisks.*

"Or this one." It has a rolling pin and the words *That's how we roll.*

"She'd love it!" Tabby laughs, and I see another one I like.

My hand is still on her lower back, and she's leaning into my chest. It feels great, but her uncle Bob interrupts us.

"Tabitha? I never expected to see you here."

Tabby stiffens and pulls away. "You should put Betty Pepper in charge of attendance."

"Is that so?" Her uncle chuckles and turns to me. "Good to see you here, and together?"

"Chad gave me a ride." Tabby answers for me. I don't like that reason, but after last night, I understand. I don't like it, but I understand. "I'm keeping Coco for Emberly. She wanted to come."

"Marjorie will like that. It's good to grow up in the faith."

Tabby's fur is bristling, and I try to think of a way to get us out of here before her uncle ruins our non-date. "Did you want to get this for Emberly?"

I hold up the rolling pin piece, but something flashes in Tabby's eyes.

"No, I think she'd like this one better."

She holds up a framed piece, more toward her uncle than me, but I can still read it. It says, *Whatever, bitch*. My lips tighten as I fight a smile.

Her uncle is unfazed. "You might wait until Colette is a little older."

"Look who made it!" Betty Pepper walks up, acting surprised to see us.

"Cut the crap, BP."

"Tabitha," her uncle says sharply, and I do laugh then.

"I have to say, Tabitha." The look on Betty's face is pure condescension. "It's nice to see you with someone who'll keep you on the right path."

"The only path I'm on is finding Coco." She storms off, leaving me behind with the two church leaders.

"You've got your work cut out for you." Betty nods, watching her go.

"Lord knows I tried." Her uncle concedes.

"I wouldn't change a thing." Both their mouths are open when I leave them to catch up to my date.

Damn straight, it's a date.

* * *

Coco's head is against my arm as I drive them home a few hours later. "I'm pretty sure she rode every ride out there ten times." I glance down at her and see she's sleeping.

"They were pretty short rides." Tabby still seems annoyed, which I don't like.

It doesn't take long to get to her house, and I put the truck in park. "Want me to carry her inside?"

"I can get her if you can handle all her crap." The cab is filled with three giant stuffed animals, an oversized unicorn, a teddy bear, and a monkey — but no goldfish.

I wait as she unbuckles the little girl and pulls her against her shoulder, walking slowly to the front door. I grab the booster seat as well and make my way carefully up the front walk.

Once inside, I see her coming out of what I assume is her bedroom and closing the door without a sound.

"I think you got the easier job." My voice is a whisper. "I can't see my feet."

That gets me a hint of a smile. It's gone in a blink, and she takes the booster seat and unwraps the monkey from my neck.

"It was sweet of you to win all these for her."

"It's kind of hard to tell her no when she wants something." I put the unicorn beside the couch and the teddy bear in front of the bookcase.

Tabby puts the monkey in her office chair, and for a moment she hesitates. My stomach is tight with anticipation. She's standing there in those tight black pants and that red sweater that accentuates her curves.

Desire heats my veins, and my fingers curl remembering the feel of her breasts. I'd wanted more tonight, but she hasn't been the same since that run-in with her uncle and Betty Pepper.

I felt her bristle every time a church lady nodded and smiled at us tonight. They meant well, but I feel like they killed Date #2.

Her hesitation disappears, and she steps to the door. "Thanks for giving us a ride tonight."

Shit. I follow her slowly. "It was my pleasure."

She pulls the door open, and I manage to smile. Her eyes don't meet mine — she seems to avoid looking at me altogether, and disappointment is a lead weight in my chest.

I want to touch her. I want to kiss her. Somehow I'm sure if our lips would meet just once more, everything would change.

I don't though.

My hands stay at my sides. I softly say goodnight a "Sleep well," and with that, she shuts me out again.

Chapter 13

Tabby

When I was thirteen, I got my period for the first time.

My stomach cramped and it was weird and scary. Uncle Bob didn't know what to tell me, and I started to cry because for the first time in a long time I wanted my mother. He brought me to the ladies Sunday school class for help, and Lurlene Woodruff told me I should be thankful the Lord gave me such a loving uncle to raise me after my Jezebel mother ran off when I was a baby.

It didn't make me feel better.

Betty Pepper took me aside and told me what was going on with my "menses," as she called it. She told me Lurlene meant well, then she gave me a little white Sunday school Bible and a piece of candy.

It was the day I realized while some ladies were cruel old meanies, even the nice ones had a plan for my life.

And it wasn't my plan.

As soon as I was old enough, I walked out of that church and never looked back.

Lurlene Woodruff died a few years ago, and I wanted to wear red to her funeral. Instead, I just went to the beach and hung out with some of the surfers who were in town for the weekend. I smoked pot and forgot why I even cared about those people.

Tonight I remembered why.

It's because while I'm not like my mother, I'm not like them either. I have my own dreams. I don't need a good influence, and I sure as hell don't need some man they all approve of showing me "the error of my ways."

It doesn't make me a Jezebel. It makes me smart and strong.

Hell, closing the door on Chad just now took the strength of Hercules, but I'm not losing my focus. I've been working on my plan too long.

Coco is a lump in the middle of my bed fast asleep, and I smile looking down at her angelic face. Soft brown curls are around her cheeks, and she is so much like her mom.

Emberly's strong, too, losing her dad when she was about Coco's age. She's been my best friend as long as I can remember, and she's always supported my dreams—just like I've always supported hers.

Slipping out of my pants and sweater, I pull on Chad's tee and boxers again. His scent is fading from the fabric, but I dip my nose inside and give it a hard sniff, searching for him. When I find it, my body relaxes.

Chad Tucker is sexy and hot and kisses like a rock star. He's like a chiseled boulder, and I won't lie—I want to climb him like a tree.

My phone lights up on the top of the dresser with a text. I walk over and pick it up, turning the face so I can read it. As much as I don't want to, my heart jumps when I see Chad's name on my screen.

Sorry things got weird tonight.

For a minute, I hesitate, trying to decide how much, if anything to say. *It's not your fault.*

BP is overbearing. Trust me, I get it.

Stepping over to the bed, I gently ease in beside my little guest before typing back. *She can be okay, but she uses God as a weapon.*

I understand.

My brow furrows and my defiant streak emerges. *You can't understand. When has anyone used the Bible to control you?*

I wait, watching the gray dots float as he types his reply. *Are you kidding? All the time.*

Example, please.

Masturbation?

Pressing my lips together, I swallow a laugh. *Everybody gets that one. Something just for men.*

Seconds tick past, and there are no gray dots. It's silent, and I'm feeling pretty smug about winning.

Finally he sends a reply. *What are you wearing right now?*

Air bursts through my nose as I laugh. *Are you changing the subject?*

Just trying to lighten the mood. Is it working?

Are you masturbating? What would the church ladies say?

I'm not like them, Tabby.

I'm not sure if I believe that statement, but I curl around Coco, my eyes heavy. *I'm going to sleep.*

Dream about me.

Clean your sheets.

I put my phone on the nightstand, and when I close my eyes, I see his smile, his whiskey eyes wrinkling at the corners, that deep dimple. A naughty memory of him in those sweatpants flickers across my mind. *Anaconda.* My stomach is tight and warm, fizzy with something...

My anger is gone.

What are you doing to me, Chad Tucker?

* * *

"I got back earlier than I expected." Emberly wakes me up, whispering from the opposite side of the bed.

Blinking my eyes open, I try to turn to face her, but my face is blocked by a foot against my cheek. Dawn is just breaking, and my room is filled with soft blue light.

"What time is it?" Sitting up, I rub my eyes, reaching for my phone.

A lone text is on the face. *Just for you.* It's from Chad, and I dismiss it, checking the time.

"You are early." It's only six o'clock, and Coco is sleeping soundly, upside down in the bed. "You sure you want to take her now?"

"I might as well let you get a few hours of sleep without a foot in your face." She giggles softly. "What did y'all do last night?"

"Church fair."

"Really…" Pure surprise is in her tone.

Two words. "Betty Pepper."

"Ahh." She lifts her chin and nods. "I don't know how I'm going to get those animals on my bike. They're as big as me!"

I wave her away. "Keep my car. I can ride the bike to work tomorrow, and we can trade back."

"Sure you don't need it?" She carefully picks up her sleeping baby.

Coco only lets out a little whine before snuggling into Emberly's neck and going right back to sleep.

"I gotta work all day. I'll call you if I need anything."

"Sleep some more." She disappears out the door, and I fall over on the pillow, spreading out like a big *X* in my now-empty bed.

I don't know how much time passes before loud knocking wakes me to white-yellow sunlight blasting through the blinds. Shielding my eyes with my hand, I look around the room trying to get my bearings.

The banging starts again. "Tabby, you awake?"

It's Chad, and I jump out of bed, throwing the blankets aside. I stop at the mirror, running my fingers through my hair and checking my eyes for crusties. Oh my god, my breath!

"Just a minute!" I yell, running to the bathroom and snatching up the Listerine.

A quick swish, and I check my face again. It'll have to do.

He's knocking again, and I race into the living room to open the door. "What are you doing here?"

Straightening, he looks me up and down, his gaze like a heat ray, sizzling my skin. "Good morning to you, too. Did you get my text?"

"What time is it?" I think back to the text. "I saw it, but I didn't understand it."

"You didn't understand 'Let's get breakfast'?"

His dark brow furrows, and *shit*, he's hot.

"I didn't see that one." My voice is quiet as I take him in.

He's standing here in front of me in jeans and a fatigue-green tee stretched tight across his chest. Aviator sunglasses cover his eyes, and his beard is a scratchy stubble I remember so well against my skin.

A grin ghosts across his lips, and he nods at me. "I like your pajamas."

I look down at myself all decked out in his clothes, and my face heats. "I... umm... I got dressed in the dark last night. Because of Coco. You know."

"Yeah, I just saw her in town with Emberly. It's why I knocked."

So thoughtful. "So you want to get breakfast?"

"Sort of. Remember how I wanted to show you something? It's my day off—come with me?"

"I have to work."

"On Sunday?"

"Yeah... Why aren't you in church?"

"I don't go to church every Sunday, Tabby." He takes off his sunglasses, and the look in his eye makes my stomach flip. It's hungry and a bit possessive, and it makes me very aware I'm not wearing a bra. Especially when my nipples tingle and tighten.

"Aren't you the rebel?" Crossing my arms over my chest, I shift from one bare foot to the other, fighting fantasies of him masturbating last night, tugging on that huge snake in his pants. "I have to change."

"Wear what you have on."

"I'm in boxer shorts and this shirt is humungous!"

"Tie it in a knot like last time."

"You're bossing me around again."

"It's time you started doing what I tell you."

Okay.

"Come inside and give me a second." Spinning on the ball of my foot, I hurry into my bedroom.

Leaving the tee on, I pull it tight at my waist and knot it, and I grab a pair of cutoffs. Then I dash into my bathroom and quickly brush my teeth, powder my nose, and apply a few coats of mascara. I grab my red lipstick and rub it across my top lip, pressing my mouth together and blotting it with a tissue. I scratch my fingers through my hair to activate the waves, then I dash back out to the living room.

"What type of shoes do I need?"

He straightens, and that look is back, hot and hungry. "Something you can slip off easily."

The suggestion almost makes me shiver. "Okay..." I grab my black flip-flops, and follow him out to the truck. Inside, a basket is on the seat between us.

"What's this?"

"Brunch."

"You made brunch?"

"Sure." He gives me a wink. "Eggs are my specialty."

Eggs. I don't make the obvious joke.

We're in the truck and the windows are down. Country music plays softly on the radio, and his sunglasses are back in place, his arm rests on the door, and I admire the lines in his muscles. Reaching out, I hold my hand in the breeze. The sun warms my skin, and it's toasty but not humid. Fall is creeping in, but it's still hot enough to wear shorts and be comfortable.

He drives in the direction of the strip, but just before we enter the tourist area, he takes the turn leading into the hills. I give him a curious glance, and that sexy muscle moves in his square jaw. I look out the window at the million-plus dollar homes passing as we rise higher into the bluffs. At the biggest one, he pulls in the driveway and enters a code on the keypad.

The iron gates slowly open, and my jaw drops. This place has to be worth several million dollars. "Do you know the owner?"

"No, but they asked us to keep an eye on it during the winter months. Thought you might want to help me check it out."

He parks the truck and grabs the basket before climbing out. I hesitate, unsure what to do. Chad doesn't give me a choice, coming around to open my door and extending his hand.

119

Chewing on my lip, I look from the house to him. "Isn't this sort of… illegal?"

He cocks his head like he's thinking about it. "Don't tell me you care about that."

I take a deep breath and his hand, following quietly along the path that circles the house and leads out to the bluff overlooking the ocean. It's breathtaking.

"Wow," I gasp, stopping to gaze at the blue waters below.

Chad steps up beside me and looks out as well. "That's exactly what I thought when I saw it yesterday. I wanted to show it to you."

His tone warms my chest. I like the idea of him thinking of me more than I should. "So we're not actually going inside the house?"

"Without a reason?" He gives me a disappointed look. "That would be breaking and entering. No, we're doing some run-of-the-mill grounds checking… and brunch… and whatever else we want."

My eyes narrow, and I wonder what that means. "Checking the grounds would be just looking around, not hanging out on their beach. Isn't that trespassing?"

"Only if we get caught." He takes my hand again and leads me down a long sandy path lined with soft sea grasses.

At the bottom it opens up to a wide, private beach, and he puts the basket down and pulls out a large towel, spreading it over the sand. In the basket are a bottle of prosecco wrapped in a cold sleeve, two silicone wine glasses, and a small carton of orange juice. Then he takes out a square container of what looks like frittata and two forks.

"Did you make this?"

"Yep." Lifting a glass, he holds it toward me. "Mimosa?"

"I'll just have the prosecco." Mimosas aren't my favorite.

I watch as he loosens the wire cage on the bottle and tosses it in the basket. Next he starts twisting it carefully.

Turning the glass in my hand, I can't help doing the math. "Three dates in three days? Isn't this a bit much, deputy?"

He frowns, using a bit more force on the cork. "I'd planned to do this yesterday evening, but you had company."

"And Betty Pepper had other plans for us." The cork finally releases with a loud pop. "Yay!" I clap. A cork popping is always a thrill.

"Only good things today."

Holding out my glass, I decide to agree. "Only good things." I take a sip, and it's cool and crisp, with a light pear taste. "That's nice."

He pours a glass for himself and gives mine a clink. "This can be our second date, since last night was sort of a bust."

My chin drops, and I fiddle with the stem of my flute. "You were very sweet to Coco, winning all those animals for her."

"She's a sweet little girl." I look up and he's studying me intently, as always.

I take another sip of bubbly wine. "And you're a closet bad boy."

He exhales a laugh, and takes a sip as well. I notice he doesn't contradict me. Picking up a fork, I take a small bite of frittata. A savory burst of cheese, tomatoes, onions, and meat makes me groan.

"It's so good! Where did you learn to cook?"

His smile widens, and he reaches out to wipe the side of my cheek. I touch his hand. "When I was traveling, I discovered eggs are about the easiest thing to cook. Once you have a few good recipes, you can make just about anything with them."

Nodding, I take another bite. "I want to travel. I'm saving up for a trip around the world."

He takes another drink, eyebrows rising. "Where do you want to go?"

"Everywhere. Australia, Thailand, Egypt, Asia…"

"I've been to some of those places. Maybe we could go together."

"Now you want us to travel together? You don't think that's moving too fast?"

"No." His voice is low, and his eyes are leveled on mine. My stomach squeezes, my heart beats faster. "Once I find something I want to do, I don't like to wait."

Shifting on the sand, I watch as he pulls out another container. Dark red watermelon quarters are in it, and I hold out my hand, doing grabby fingers. He chuckles, passing one to me.

Slugging my wine, I put the glass in the sand and take a big bite. "Oh!" Juice runs down my chin and onto my shirt. "Hand me a napkin, quick!"

He digs through the basket fast. "Shit, I didn't pack any."

"Chad!" I hop up, my face covered in watermelon juice. "Can I use the towel?"

"Use this." He stands beside me and pulls the tee over his head, putting his muscular torso on full display.

I forget my messy face when I see the lines cutting up his chest, the eight-pack disappearing into his low-slung, loose jeans. His arms are roped with muscles, and a chunky stainless watch is on his wrist.

"Oh my God," I whisper, and he grins stepping closer to me. One hand is on my waist and he touches the edge of the shirt to my chin.

"Good?"

I nod slowly. "Very good."

The breeze swirls around us, bringing his luscious scent to my nose, and when our eyes meet, it's a million volts of electricity. I'm not sure who moves first, but our mouths are together, lips pushing apart, tongues clashing in hungry, greedy kisses, fast and hot.

"Chad," I whisper as he lifts me off my feet.

My legs are around his waist, and I'm holding his face in both hands. The prosecco tingles in my stomach, and his kisses push me higher. My core is hot and wet, and I move my hands from his cheeks to the tops of his broad shoulders, sliding them around to his muscular back, loving the feel of his body.

His hands clutch my ass, squeezing and rocking me slowly against his growing erection. "You feel so good," he murmurs.

My chin lifts and warm lips trace my skin, his beard scuffs my neck, teeth nibbling. I'm dazzled by desire, and when I notice the waves breaking gently behind us, I have an idea.

"Skinny dipping," I say, and he stops. "You've never done it."

Leaning back, I catch his eyes. They're like mine — stormy whiskey meeting burning emerald. He lowers me to my feet, and I grab the hem of my shirt, pulling it over my head. I'm standing in front of him in cutoffs and a bright red push-up bra. He inhales with a hiss and steps forward, palming my breast.

"I've dreamed of these since Friday night."

Reaching around, I unhook my bra so it falls away. My nipples are tight, and he exhales a little groan. His thumbs slide over them, and he rolls them between his fingers, cupping and squeezing my breasts. I can't help making a little noise. I love his hands on me.

"You are so fine," he murmurs, and I'm about ready to ignite.

Placing my hands over his briefly, I go to the button on my shorts and unfasten them, shoving them down, so I'm only in my red lace thong. "Your turn."

I've been dreaming of that anaconda since Friday night.

Taking a step back, his eyes never leave my body, singeing me with the heat of his gaze. He reaches into his back pocket and takes out a small square. It's a condom, I realize, and I hold out my hand. He gives it to me, and yep. Magnum.

Shoving off his jeans, he straightens, and I almost fall to my knees. It's so big and thick and hard. I step forward and lightly touch him with my fingertips. It jumps, he groans. "Easy."

A little drop is on the tip, and I quickly dispose of my thong then take his hand, leading him to the water. The waves break gently and summer heat lingers in the surge. I turn once the waves reach my waist, and he's looking at me, eyes full of desire.

"Come here." Large hands circle my waist, and he pulls me flush against his chest, skin on skin.

We both let out a noise, and our mouths are together again, lips chasing, tongues circling and caressing. I reach down between us and grasp his thick erection. My fingers don't close completely around him as I slide my fist up and down, feeling him grow harder, longer.

"Jesus, Tabby." His voice is ragged. "Don't make me come in the water."

Leaning forward again, I press my body to his, my mouth to his. Large hands fumble along my ass, sliding up and down before reaching around to where I'm so wet with need. I let out a little noise then a loud moan as his thick fingers press inside me.

"Chad..." My mouth is at his ear, and I ride his hand, my eyes squeezed shut, lips parted.

"You're so wet." He strokes and pinches my clit until I'm on the edge. "I'm going to come," I gasp, and he takes his hand away quickly, finding the condom and ripping it open with his teeth.

The wrapper is a little ball in my fist, and I squeeze it tighter when I feel the head of his massive erection nudging at me. My stomach is tingly with anticipation.

"Is this okay?" he growls, as if he needs permission at this point, as if either of us could stop now.

"Yes, please." It's a purr right at his ear.

Then reaching down, I grasp his thick shaft, wrapping my legs around his waist. He catches my ass, and with a violent thrust, he's buried to the hilt inside.

"Ahh!" I let out a loud cry at the sensation of fullness, and he holds still.

"You okay?" His muscles are tense, vibrating with need.

"Just a second," I whisper, allowing my body to adjust to the biggest cock I've ever ridden. "Kiss me."

His hands move from my ass to my cheeks and he parts my lips with his. It happens just like I knew it would. When we kiss, my insides turn to molten lava, my body melts, and my hips start to rock, pulling him, massaging him with my core.

"Fuck... you feel so good." He groans against my mouth, moving his cheek to my cheek.

I'm riding fast now, flexing my thighs, grinding higher, and his hands are on my ass again, moving me up and down. He's so deep, so hard, he's hitting a place no one ever has. It makes little lights shoot behind my closed eyelids. It sends ripples of pleasure shooting through my inner thighs, centering in my core. My stomach flutters, and it's tightening, tightening...

Holy shit, this is going to be so good.

"You're hitting my spot..." It's all I get out before my insides clench irresistibly, then splinter with fireworks of the most intense orgasm I've ever had.

"Oh... oh!" I can't stop moaning, and I only barely notice Chad moving faster.

His face is at my temple, his lips are at my ear. His ragged breathing, his moans as his orgasm crests... It's all so fucking sexy, I come again in another round of clenching spasms.

"Tabby... holy—" He stiffens, and I feel him pulsing inside me, filling the condom.

His grip tightens, his muscles flex. It triggers another little burst in me. He pulses again, and a deep, sexy groan is in my ear.

It's incredible.

Salt is on my tongue. Warm waters swirl and fizz around us, lifting and rocking us as if we're in harmony with nature. We are... *we're doing what comes naturally*. The thought drifts through my mind. It makes me smile.

I'm a limp noodle, barely able to hold onto him, but it's okay because his strong arms are tight around my waist, holding me against his chest, kissing my neck, the side of my jaw, my lips. I turn my head and kiss him, and when our tongues caress, it's another little burst of pleasure.

We kiss, kiss, kiss, and I blink my eyes open to meet his satisfied grin. "Did you come more than once?"

"I think you found my G-spot."

He laughs, and it's a deep vibration against my chest. "I like skinny dipping. I think we should do it more often."

"You're a natural at it."

Chapter 14

Chad

Tabby's head tilts to the side, and she blinks those gorgeous green eyes up at me. "Is skinny dipping better than paintball?"

I'm holding her hand, leading us up the path to the top of the hill where my truck waits. "Yes. It's better than paintball."

She laughs, and I squeeze her hand. "Also better than church fairs." I add.

We stop when we reach the truck, and she waits with her back against the door while I put the basket in the bed behind her.

"And local busybodies." Her face tilts up, the setting sun covering it in gold.

I touch her chin with my thumb right before I lean forward and press my lips to hers. She exhales a sigh, melting into me.

I lift my head, looking deep into her eyes again. "So you liked my surprise?"

Nodding, she blinks slowly. "It was amazing."

On the drive back, she scoots to the center of the bench seat, leaning her head on my shoulder. The window is down, and I put my arm around her.

It feels kind of perfect.

I look out across the ocean as we wind down toward town, and the salt breeze twirls her hair around her shoulder. We don't talk. We just listen to soft music playing on the radio, relaxed and happy. When I pull into her driveway, it feels too soon.

Tabby exhales deeply as she sits up looking at her door. When she looks at me, a hint of sadness is in her eyes. I'm glad I'm not the only one sorry our day is over.

"I had fun today." I reach out and touch her cheek with my fingertips.

"Me too." She tilts her face into my hand. "You headed home?"

"I'll check in at the station first. File a report on the house."

A little smile curls her lips. "A partial report?"

"I don't have to include everything."

Her hand covers mine, and she turns her face to kiss my palm. "I guess I'd better go."

She starts to pull away, but I catch her cheeks for one more kiss. It's soft but hot, hungry, and only temporarily satisfying. Making love to this woman was better than I'd fantasized.

I put the truck in park, ready to go around and help her out, walk her to the door, kiss her again, but she stops me. "Better not. I do need to get some work done today."

"I'll call you."

"Text is good."

I watch as she walks to the door, dressed in my shirt and those cutoffs that show off the curve of her sassy little ass. She stops and waves before going inside, and I can't help a groan as I pull out of the driveway, headed back to my place.

* * *

130

Lying on my bed, I've eaten dinner, showered, and I have a glass of scotch on the side table. I hold up my phone and type out a text. *Still working?*

A few seconds pass, a few more, then I see the gray dots of her composing a reply. *Having a hard time concentrating.*

I smile, picturing her dark hair wrapped in a bun with a pencil stuck through it. It's what she always does when she's working at Emberly's store. *Something on your mind?*

A few seconds pass. *More like some body.*

I like the sound of that. *What are you supposed to be doing?*

Finishing up the travel agency site, adding pictures and linking blog reviews.

Interesting. What's the location?

Isle of Vin in Croatia. Supposedly the best beach in Europe.

I think about the places I've seen. *I was in Madagascar. It's supposedly Eden.*

Will we be naked?

I have no objection to that.

Is it legal?

I have no jurisdiction in Africa.

A few seconds pass, and I grin, wondering if I've stumped her. She finally replies, *I think I'm a bad influence on you.*

Just getting to know me better.

Another little pause, then the gray dots appear. *Want to see what I'm doing?*

My stomach tightens, and I glance at the clock. It's after ten, and I'm off the bed pulling on my jeans, a tee, putting a ball cap on my head. It doesn't take long to drive the truck the few miles to her house, especially at this time of night.

I ease the truck to parking then slide out as I'm texting my reply. *Sure.*

Took long enough.

Open the door.

I hear a little yelp followed by a scuffling of who knows what. The porch light flickers on just before her door flies open, and there she is, exactly as I pictured.

Nope, she's better.

Her dark hair is twisted on the top of her head with a pencil stuck in it, and she's wearing my old tee again. It's knotted at the waist like I like it, giving me a peek of her silky skin, her cute little navel ring. She's not wearing my boxers this time. She's in black bikini panties, and her shapely legs are bare down to red toenails.

Her green eyes sparkle when they meet mine, and her smile is beautiful. I don't hesitate. I lean forward, catching her waist and planting a kiss right on those pillow lips. Her hands are on my shoulders, and she exhales a sigh as our tongues touch. It's soft and warm and perfect, and when I lean up, her eyes blink open slowly.

Just as fast she grabs my arm, pulling me inside. "Get in here before everybody sees you."

I start to laugh. "They're going to know. My truck's out front."

Standing in front of me in her bare feet, she's so small. It's a direct contrast to her personality, which always seems larger than life. Still, I want to wrap her up in my arms and take care of her... something I know she'd hate.

Nope, this girl needs to be free.

"Show me what you're doing." I look to her computer.

She walks over to the chair. "I don't have a place for you to sit."

I sit in her chair and catch her waist, pulling her onto my lap.

She exhales a laugh, and I'm very aware of her sitting on my lap in only my t-shirt and panties.

Not yet.

I want to know what she does. I want to know what kept her so occupied for the last year while she avoided me. "Show me."

"Okay…" Reaching forward, she grabs the white mouse and wakes her enormous iMac. "So my clients—Rani and AJ—are travel agents who specialize in European and Caribbean tours. Their motto is 'Easy, safe, unforgettable.'"

"Safe." My voice is skeptical.

"People always think they're going to get robbed when they visit Europe."

"The pickpocket culture is strong." She moves around on my lap, and it's hard to keep my hands off her ass. I fight it though, clearing my throat and directing my mind back to what she's saying. "I thought travel agents went the way of the dinosaur."

"Have you seen the box office for *Jurassic Park*?"

"Yeah, but anybody can go online and book a trip to Europe or the Caribbean."

"Ahh…" She holds up a slim finger. "You're right. That's where Travel Time is different. It's all about perceived need and perceived value."

"Explain."

"Start at the homepage." She turns to the computer again and pulls up a clean, elegant website with the company name, the logo of a compass, and a search bar under the words, *Where do you want to go today?*

"But it's more than where. You can search by type of trip—girl's trip, wedding, anniversary, family vacation—and get recommendations of popular packages. You can enter the age of travelers, the duration, how long you want to stay in each place. You can pick the type of lodging you prefer, from hotels to hostels to B&Bs…"

She clicks fast and menus roll down.

"They've taken it a step further in that if you make an account and leave reviews, it can customize future trip recommendations based on your experiences. There's a chat function here." She clicks on a little dialog bubble, and a window pops up. "Rani and AJ are able to answer questions in real time during business hours, or they can take emails after hours. The last thing I'm adding are links to blog reviews, tips for overseas travel, pictures of popular attractions…"

"You did all this?"

"Yep." She looks over her shoulder. "It's my biggest job to date. They told me their vision, and I brought it to life. Then once it launches, I'll help maintain it."

"When does it launch?"

"Soft launch is Wednesday. We'll have it up and invite people to test it out, help us find all the bugs. Then they want to go live by the end of the month."

"Whoa, you really do need to work." I'm starting to feel bad distracting her.

"I invited you over, remember?" She grins. "I got a lot done this afternoon."

I feel bad. I took a nap. "You learned all this in one community college course?"

She's facing the computer again and shrugs. "I'd always been interested in websites and design. I'd been poking around for a while when I saw the billboard and decided to pull the trigger."

"I'm impressed. You're doing really well with this."

She clicks a few more photographs. "With clients like these, I can't help but do well. I send them big bills, and they pay them."

"Have you put together your own travel package?"

"Ha! In my dreams. They have a budget traveler option, but it's too limited for what I want to do."

"What's that?" My hands are on her thighs now, smoothing her silky skin.

She sighs and leans her back against my chest. "I want to see everything… Vis, New Zealand, Fiji… It seems silly to go from one beach to another, but I want to see them all."

My chin is on her shoulder, and she clicks to the different pictures. The mouse hovers over India, and I nod. "The golden triangle is unforgettable. I saw the Taj Mahal when I was in Agra."

She turns her head slightly. "Right—you've been there."

We're quiet, and I'm thinking about seeing it again with her. "It's a big tomb. The Shah Jahan had it built for a Persian princess he loved. She died having their fourteenth child."

"Oh!" Tabby sits up, her cute little nose wrinkled. "That's terrible!"

I chuckle and pull her against my chest again. "It's stunning in real life."

"An object lesson—how families are hazardous to your health."

"More like the importance of birth control. I imagine having fourteen kids can be hazardous to your health." My hands are under that tee now, and I'm sliding them up to her bare breasts. "Besides, they can't be all bad. You love Coco."

"I do love Coco," she sighs, melting into my chest as I tweak her hard nipples. "I'm just not sure it's the life for me."

Opening my mouth against her neck, I give her soft skin a gentle suck. "Life is long."

Her hips move, scrubbing that ass against my dick—which is now a steel rod in my pants. I take one hand from her breasts and smooth it down her flat stomach, inside the front of those panties, down to her clit, giving it a stroke. She moans, and I dip my fingers inside, to her dripping core.

"You're so wet." I kiss her ear.

She's fumbling behind her back, locating the button of my jeans, and I quickly help her unfasten them, lifting us briefly so I can slide them down my hips. She's still facing forward, but she grips my swollen cock, pumping it with her hand. It makes me groan low in her ear.

She shivers and laughs softly. "Big boy, big dick."

"It needs a condom." I start to rise, but she stops me.

Reaching down, she finds the pocket of my jeans, my wallet. "In here?"

I pull her panties down as she leans forward, and my cock grows harder at the sight of her bare ass on my lap. "Yeah." My voice is thick with need. "Hurry up."

As soon as she has it out, I take it from her, ripping it open with my teeth. She's leaning forward, her forearms on her desk, looking at me over her shoulder.

"What do you want, big boy?"

"I want you to ride my big dick until you're screaming my name. Then I want to bend you over that desk and fuck you from behind until your knees give out."

"Holy shit," she whispers, slipping her hand between her legs.

The condom's on, and I grip her waist, lifting her and positioning it at her core before letting her drop, sheathing me hot and wet.

"Oh, yeah," I groan, leaning back to watch.

She leans forward, lifting her ass up and down, bouncing on my cock as her hand massages her clit. "Oh, she gasps... it's so big."

She's so tight, and I slide my hand over her round backside. I want to slap it, leave my mark... Instead, I grip her hips, moving her faster, trying not to blow. She's the sexiest thing I've ever seen.

Catching the hem of her shirt, I lift it higher. She quickly jerks it over her head, and the pencil falls. I get a quick peek at a tiny mermaid tattoo on her shoulder blade before long, dark curls cascade down, covering it.

Pulling off my own shirt, I lean forward, kissing a line up the center of her back, reaching around to squeeze and pinch her nipples.

"Yes," she whimpers when I bite the side of her neck, moving my lips into her hair. "Keep doing that... keep... Oh!"

I feel the moment she breaks, shuddering and squeezing my cock deep inside her body.

It's time.

Holding her waist, I lift us to standing, pushing her forward onto her hands. Our thighs are flush, and gripping her hips, I jerk her ass against my pelvis while I thrust hard and fast, chasing my own orgasm.

Tabby's legs wobble, her feet stagger further apart, and she moans my name. It's the fucking best thing I've ever heard.

"I'm so close," I groan. "You feel so good."

The desk bangs against the wall, lifting off the floor with the force of my thrusts. I'd be worried, but Tabby cries out, "That's it! Don't stop... Oh—" Her knees actually give out, as she collapses forward with a loud wail.

She comes so hard, my own orgasm breaks. It snakes up my legs like electricity, tingling in my balls, in my pelvis, blanking my mind. My eyes squeeze shut, and I have to hold steady or we might both go down.

The sensation is intense, mind-altering.

With every pulse, I groan, deep and low.

Tabby pushes off the desk, arching her back against my bare chest. I wrap my arms around her waist and hold her, pressing my forehead against her neck, still buried deep in her warm body.

She lifts a hand, threading her fingers in the side of my hair. "I think you broke me."

"You're not broken." I lift my head to kiss her neck. "You're mine."

"Hmm..." She exhales softly, her fingers still moving in my hair.

It was a risk saying it, but she doesn't pull away. I reach down and hold the condom as I pull out, tying it off and disposing of it in the small trash by her desk. I'll take care of that tomorrow.

Stepping out of my jeans, I lift her in my arms and carry her to the bedroom. Her cheek is against my shoulder, and her hand is on my neck, her thumb tracing my jaw.

"Want to spend the night?" she asks softly.
"I'm one step ahead of you."

Chapter 15

Tabby

When I open my eyes again, it's dark. Two strong arms and the clean, masculine scent of Chad Tucker surround me, and I'm sweating. He generates heat like an oven.

Wiggling forward carefully, I scoot to the other side of the bed where it's cooler. Then I turn and study his profile asleep with the moonlight streaming across his skin.

Chad Tucker is some kind of sex god with a magic snake in his pants. Andy the Anaconda. I seriously can't believe the way he gets me off every time. It's throwing a wrench in my plan to keep it casual.

Okay, that's not true. *He* is making it hard, with the way he asks about everything I'm doing, the way he's so interested and wants all the details. The way he keeps coming up with plans to help me do what I want to do. Then he surprises me by being so unexpectedly dirty. I shiver thinking about how savage he is when he takes me. It's possessive and fierce, and his massive dick hitting my G-spot is a bonus.

But he wants peace and quiet, a family, babies…

My stubborn brain is right there reminding me how different we are. Our conversation about the Taj Mahal is a perfect example. Maybe he doesn't want fourteen kids, but he definitely wants one. I'd expect more than one.

You love Coco…

He's right, I do love that little girl, and Emberly's always saying how much better her life is because she had her. I lower my cheek to the pillow, studying his sexy square jaw, his full lips, that dimpled chin.

You're mine…

A little shiver moves through me at the thought, surprising me with how much I like the sound of that. Can peace and quiet, babies, a family co-exist with wanderlust and websites?

Could it possibly ever work?

* * *

The second time I open my eyes, I'm alone. The sun streams through the blinds, and I sit up quickly, looking all around.

"Chad?" I call loudly.

No answer.

It's quiet in the house, and I see a slip of paper sitting on my bedside table. I wonder why he didn't send me a text. Snatching it up, I read his perfectly neat, block handwriting, and I'm so glad he didn't send me a text.

You're beautiful when you sleep, I hated leaving for work. I'll see you when I check in the store later. Until then, I'll be thinking of how sexy you are when you come on my cock, screaming my name. And that little mermaid… I want to see her again.

–C.

"Such a dirty boy, Deputy Tucker." I hold the note against my lips and grin, warm waves of happiness vibrating through my insides.

142

For a few minutes, all I want to do is stay in bed reliving last night, maybe rubbing one out as I remember the details—until my phone starts buzzing with a text.

My heart jumps, and I wonder if…

Lifting it up, I see it's only Emberly. *Coco stayed with me last night. Think you could come in a little early? I promised André scones.*

I'm not sure what the last sentence has to do with anything, but I quickly text back. *Sure.* Then I'm out of bed and heading to the shower.

When I arrive at the bakery, I understand. Several trays of large, round biscuit-looking cakes are all around the place. Emberly is in the back, a lock of dark hair falling out of her messy bun, and she's running the mixer while she reads a book. She looks frazzled.

"Aunt Tabby!" Coco jumps off the chair beside her mother and races to meet me. "Mama's having a terrible morning."

"Tabby! Thank God you're here."

I scoop Coco up onto my hip and cross to her mother. "What's happening?"

"Why the eff did I tell André I would do this? I've never made a scone in my life, and they're not coming out right. True scones are supposed to be light and fluffy. These are like dense little hole-less cake doughnuts."

"How many have you made?" I look around the room at all the trays. It looks like a hundred.

"I don't know."

Coco's eyes are round and she leans into my ear. "*Eff* means a bad word."

"Coco!" Emberly cries, lifting the beaters out of the mixing bowl. "Stop repeating everything I say."

"What does it mean?" I whisper, positive she has no idea.

"Tabby…" My best friend warns.

I look at my friend then back to her daughter's round eyes. "Whisper it to me."

Emberly waves us away, shaking her head.

Coco's eyes widen again, and she gets close, whispering, "Fart."

I do not laugh. It takes all my strength, but I do not laugh. Instead I nod seriously.

"Mama's under a lot of pressure right now." Walking over to the nearest tray, I lift a beige little biscuit with dark purple blueberries in it. "It looks good to me!"

"I'm almost out of blueberries." Emberly's spooning another batch onto a tray. "This is my last cookie sheet."

I take a bite and thick, buttery goodness fills my mouth. "Hey!" I nod, bending to put Coco on her feet. "These are delicious!"

"Which ones?" My best friend's head snaps up. "Ugh, those are too buttery!"

"Is there such a thing?" I stuff the rest of the little cake in my mouth. "Stop making scones. Nobody in Oceanside will know the difference, and we're going to have to feed the rest of these to the ducks."

"I want to feed the ducks!" Coco jumps up, holding her hands over her head.

"Sorry, that was a joke." She frowns and does a little whine. "We'll wait until they're stale and throw them at people."

That makes her laugh, but Emberly scowls. "We're not throwing scones at anybody. Would you help me box those up? They'll have to do, I guess. André's waiting."

"These will do fine. They're delicious." I grab a rectangular plastic bin and line it with parchment. "Coco, come help me."

The little girl hops over to where I'm filling the bin with scones and climbs on the stool. "Mommy says scones are for tea time."

"Only if you're British." I've emptied two trays. "Take these trays to the sink."

The pastries are quickly packaged, and I'm heading out the door for André's when I skip a step. Chad is right outside, looking like sex in a uniform and grinning so I can see that dimple.

"Well, hello, there." I give him a radiant smile. "Scone?"

I lift the lid of the container to show him the small biscuits. This morning I put on a silky red wrap-dress, but I left my hair hanging down in dark chocolate waves around my shoulders. I've noticed Chad seems to dig a more natural look, so I smoothed some coconut gloss on my lips and went with mascara and powder.

His eyes stay on me. "You look good enough to eat."

"Hmm…" My eyes slide to the side. "Something for later, perhaps?"

He leans against the side of the building, that sexy smile firmly in place. "Seems like I promised to use my handcuffs on you."

Lowering the lid, I act casual, not like his words are making my panties wet. "You might need to work on keeping those promises."

"Maybe I can work on it tonight."

"I have an hour lunch break at noon."

"Is that so?" Our bodies have somehow drifted closer together with only the plastic box between us.

"Yep."

Whiskey eyes hold mine, and he's leaning closer. I feel pretty sure I'm about to get one of those toe-curling kisses when Emberly sticks her head out the door. "Tabby! André just called about the scones!"

"Oh, shit." I straighten. "I guess I'll see you later."

"I know where you live."

Giggling, I trot the rest of the way to Betty Pepper's pack and save, running inside to deliver the goods.

"Café au lait." André has my usual morning order waiting for me.

"And one hundred scones for you!" I hand over the plastic container, and his eyes go wide.

"A hundred?"

That makes me laugh. "Just kidding! It's only like twenty or thirty."

He looks inside the bin. "That's still a lot."

"I told her she made too many." I grin up at him, and he gives me the squint eye.

"What's going on with you? You haven't been this perky in the morning since that idiot Travis left town."

"Travis who?" I widen my eyes as if I don't know what in the world he's talking about.

André crosses his arms, sizing me up. "This have something to do with Deputy Tucker's truck parked outside your house all night."

My eyebrows rise, and I take a sip of coffee. "Mmm... Perfect. Have a great day!" I prance to the door without another word.

He only laughs, and my stomach is fizzy and bubbly thinking about bumping into Chad just now, almost kissing him, our potential nooner.

Emberly's pulling the last batch of scones from the oven when I return to the store. "I'll let these cool then

146

box up half and take them to André when I run Coco to preschool."

"Here," I open my laptop and logon to the Oceanside Village website I designed as my class final. "I'll put an update on the main page and do a little email blast about 'Emberly's famous British scones.' That might help to move some freight."

"Famously inauthentic," she quips. "Speaking of, how's the travel site going?"

"Soft launch on Wednesday." An additional flutter is in my stomach at that announcement. "Just a few final tweaks and it's ready."

"You seem really peppy today." She puts a hand on her hip and studies me. "And you're glowing. What's going on?"

"Just happy." I do my best to look innocent as I add the update on the website. "I've been making a list of where I want to go on my personal around the world adventure. It's probably that."

I give my best friend a quick glance, and I can see she's not convinced. With a shrug, she returns to drying the baking supplies. "What's on your list?"

"New stuff since we last talked." Shifting in my seat, I think about the new additions. "I found this island in Croatia called Vis that looks amazing."

"Ooo," she coos, leaning a hip against the counter. "I want to see it."

"Let me finish this."

"Where else?" She walks across the room to put the glass bowl on its stand under the mixer.

"The Taj Mahal…"

"Wait… I thought you'd crossed India off the list?"

I think back to when Emberly was my original partner in seeing the world. "They do have that human

147

rights problem." My lips twist. "If you were still going with me, I guess we'd skip it."

"Are you trying to say it's safer for you to go there alone?" Her brow furrows, and she grabs a smaller plastic bin and puts half the scones inside.

"I don't know." I am not about to say Chad wants to go with me. I'm not even a hundred percent sure how I feel about that. Everything with Chad is moving so fast. It could flame out as fast as it started. Instead, I just say, "It was fun planning with you."

She smiles. "I wish I could go, but having Coco kind of nixed that idea for a while."

"Yeah…" I think about my internal debate last night and the conundrum of having a family and going through with my plan. "Kids change everything."

"Not just that, I'm building my business, taking classes… I can't leave before this bakery gets up and running. Not to mention it's eating all my money fixing up the upstairs so Coco and I can live there."

Emberly inherited this old storefront when her aunt died, and she's spent every dollar and every day painting and scrubbing and cleaning out so she can live upstairs, over the shop.

I hit save on the business website, then pull up the email alert tool. "Did you know they think Madagascar is where Eden used to be?"

"Is it a nudist colony?"

I start to laugh. "I swear, our brains are just alike."

"What's a nudist colony?" Coco hops back into the room.

"Something to learn about when you're older." Emberly grabs the plastic bin. "Come on. Time for school."

Our little kangaroo's shoulders slump, and she groans. "I want to stay and eat more cake."

Sliding off my stool, I grab a napkin and wrap up one of the fresh scones from the tray. Then I slip it into a Ziploc and tuck it in her backpack when Emberly isn't looking.

"For later," I whisper, kissing her cute little nose.

She hugs me, and the two of them head out the door. I look up at the clock, wondering how I'm going to get through three more hours without climbing the walls.

The email alert is sent in a few clicks. I putter around the shop a little while, arranging and rearranging the ingredients, making sure the orders are organized, and checking our supplies.

Finally, with an hour left, I jot a note to Emberly that I'm running errands and will be back after lunch.

Chapter 16

Tabby

It's straight up noon when the knock comes on my door. My heart thuds in my chest, and I run to open it, catching my breath when our eyes meet.

"Hey, beautiful." Chad's low voice sends a zing right to my core, and I pull him inside quickly.

He's on me at once, cupping my face in his hands and kissing me hard, forcing my lips apart and plunging his tongue into my mouth. I let out a little whimper. He's so demanding and aggressive.

"I've been going crazy all day thinking about your tight, wet pussy," he groans against my skin. "Don't tease me like that again."

My stomach flips at his dirty mouth. "Stop bossing me around."

"I'll boss you around." Stepping back, he unfastens the top two buttons of his uniform shirt before pulling it over his head, leaving his thick brown hair a sexy mess. His white undershirt is next, until he's standing in front of me, heaving muscles and raw sex wearing only his boots and pants.

I pull the tie on my wrap dress, ready to be naked immediately and all over that. It falls open, exposing the black lace bra and thong I'm wearing. I'm about to reach around and unclasp it when he catches my hand.

"Not yet." Pulling my body against his chest, he scans my small house. "I've been thinking about this for months."

"Months?" I lean forward, running my nose along the side of his neck, inhaling his scent, slipping out my tongue to taste his salty skin. "We haven't been together that long."

"You think I wasn't watching your sexy ass?" He backs me toward the bedroom. "I wanted to do this standing up. I guess the bed will have to do."

Out come the handcuffs, and my heart beats so fast. "I've never been handcuffed before."

His brown eyes darken. "I'll have to make it memorable."

"We don't have much time."

"It doesn't take long to have you screaming my name."

"So arrogant." *But it's true...* Bring out the snake!

Holding my waist, he helps me scoot up the bed on my back, then taking both my hands, he puts the handcuffs around one of the iron rods in my headboard before loosely locking them around my wrists. They're cold metal and a little uncomfortable, but I'm distracted by him stepping back from the bed and slowly unfastening his pants.

I'm completely at his mercy, handcuffed to the headboard in only my bra and panties, and I'm nervous and thrilled at the same time.

I roll onto my side, and the way my hands are tied presses my breasts together. His eyes don't leave them as he shoves his pants down and off, allowing that massive erection to spring free.

A little whimper escapes from my throat, and I instinctively rub my thighs together as he grasps his cock, tugging it slowly and moving his hand over the tip.

"So fucking sexy," he hisses. "Are you wet for me?"

"Yes." I answer fast. I'm burning up inside, wondering what he's about to do next.

He tosses a condom on the bed beside me before stepping forward and hooking his thumbs in the sides of my thong. Pulling it slowly down my legs, his eyes trace their path until he stands back again, leaving me bare. He watches me squirm a moment before dropping to his knees and wrapping my thighs around his upper arms.

"Look at you." His eyes are on my pussy, and it's electric and a little embarrassing.

"What are you… Oh!" My eyes flutter shut when he covers me with his mouth and starts to lick and suck hungrily.

He kisses my outer lips, my inner thigh, then goes right back to my core, sliding his tongue up and down and over my clit, using just the right amount of pressure, again and again.

Holy shit… It's my mantra with this man. I can't believe how crazy he makes me.

Instinctively, I jerk against the cuffs. I want to thread my fingers through his hair. His beard scrapes my inner thighs, and I jump, moaning. His teeth lightly touch me, and my breath disappears. My legs go rigid with orgasm, as if I've been struck by lightning.

"Chad…" I struggle to catch my breath. My body shudders, and with every pass of his tongue, an irresistible jolt grabs my stomach. "Stop… You have to stop… It's too much."

He grins up at me, moving his mouth to my stomach, circling his tongue around my navel. "Cute little navel," he murmurs, scuffing my hyper sensitive skin with his beard. "Now I want to see that mermaid."

I'm breathing so hard, I can only nod.

"How are you feeling?" I'm on my side, and he's behind me, nudging my legs apart with his knee as he tears open the condom.

His erection is a steel rod against my ass, and I know what's coming. "Good... so good."

"Ready to feel better?" He catches my hips and with one firm thrust, he's balls-deep inside, stretching me so wide, I cry out.

This time, he doesn't hesitate. He continues pumping, holding my hips and fucking me hard. The pressure, the friction, oh, God, it's so good until...

The handcuffs jerk against the bed, pinching and rubbing my wrists. All at once, they tighten so fast, the pain is unbearable.

"Chad," I gasp. "The cuffs... Stop... They're hurting me."

He pauses, slowing down, and waiting for a second. He's breathing hard, and I know he's on the edge. Still, he holds the condom, slipping out and fumbling for the keys in his pants.

"Shit." He unlocks them and frees my hands, cradling them in his, inspecting the damage. "Why didn't you say something sooner?"

I look at my wrists. Bright red marks stripe across them right at the bones, and they feel slightly numb. "It happened so fast... It wasn't like that before."

His brow furrows, and he kisses the marks, wrapping his large hands around them. "I'm sorry. The skin isn't broken, but it'll probably bruise."

Taking my hands from his, I lift them to his neck. His erection is against my thigh, and I kiss his lips softly, taking a little nip between words. "Can we finish?"

"You sure you want to?"

Reaching back, I unfasten my bra and smile. "You can't go back to work like this."

He finally stops frowning and gives me a little smile, cupping my breast. Raking my fingernails across his cheeks, I pull his face to mine and we kiss gently, mouths opening, tongues finding each other. They curl and caress, and it only takes a few passes for us to heat up again. It always happens when we kiss.

My arms are around his neck, and he scoops me off the bed, standing and carrying me to the wall. My legs are around his waist as he puts my back against it and sinks deep into my core once more, moving his hips, thrusting in and out so deep my thighs begin to quiver.

Closing my eyes, I lean my head back, riding this crazy wave. He moves my hips in time to give him the deepest penetration. I hold his broad shoulders, gripping them as I grind my hips, when I feel his fingers tracing my crack, moving between my cheeks and…

"Oh!" I gasp when his finger sinks into my ass.

My eyes go wide, but he whispers, "Shh…"

Covering my mouth with his, he plunges his tongue inside as his finger works that little hole, in and out, rocking me into him as he thrusts faster, more feverish.

All the sensations, the position, his kiss, his finger, take me higher. My orgasm builds, and I'm lost in a haze when it breaks, flying through space, calling out his name.

He holds me steady, bracing me with his legs, as he pulses. His mouth is right at my ear, and I love the sound of his moans, his deep groans, his swears, as he comes. It's amazing, and so unexpected.

His chest is against my breasts, the fine scattering of hair tickling my nipples. We're breathing fast when he kisses my jaw, giving it a little nibble. "I'm going to be late getting back to work."

My eyes go to the clock. "It's one."

"Shit." He kisses me fast, grabbing the condom as he pulls out, lowering me to my feet.

He moves fast, tying off the condom, and dashing over to his discarded pants, his boots. Then it hits me.

"You cleaned up this morning."

He frowns, stepping into his boots and tying them. I go to where he's standing, placing my hand on his bare back, sliding it up to his shoulder as I kiss his cheek. "My little trash can was empty."

"Of course, I did." He stands, gives me a quick kiss on the mouth, then leaves me naked in my bedroom.

I follow him into the living room, watching as he pulls on the undershirt then his uniform shirt, jamming it into his pants. "I might see you again this afternoon, depending on what Robbie needs me to do."

Stepping back, I get one more rough kiss, and he's out the door, smoothing his hair and jogging around the corner. I didn't even think about the cruiser. He must've parked it down at the church.

"Dirty Deputy Tucker," I muse, thinking about all those nosey church folks. "Aren't you something?"

My legs are weak, my insides deliciously aching and ravaged. Echoes of his presence linger in both my holes. My body feels like someone thoroughly enjoyed it. I'm pretty sure he did. I know I did.

Still, they'll call me the bad influence.

Chad says I'm just getting to know him better.

I wonder who's right.

Emberly's squinting at a diagram when I get back to the shop a few minutes later.

I took a quick shower, smoothed my hair, and did my best to cover the red marks on my wrists with body makeup. Every time I move, I'm reminded Chad was here... Andy was there, finger was there. It heats me right up again.

"Getting some work done?" she asks without even looking up.

"Umm... Sort of." I don't want to lie to my best friend, but I seriously can't tell Emberly what I did for lunch... What Chad ate for lunch.

Not yet.

She'd be cool with it, of course, but telling Emberly makes everything so real somehow. I have to sort out my feelings first, make sure this isn't some ultra-hot *Nine and a Half Weeks* kind of thing.

The thought of Chad eating food off my naked body makes me flush.

"Why are you blushing?" Emberly straightens, frowning at me. "What have you done?"

Dude, I'm so busted. "What are you talking about?"

"Were you looking at porn instead of building the website?"

"I would never do that!" I pretend to be offended, but the whole reason she said it is because I told her I did it sometimes after Travis left.

"Okay..." She narrows her eyes at me before returning to her book.

I walk over to where she's standing, pulling out a stool beside her.

"Working on something new for André?" I keep waiting for her to mention Chad's truck being at my house last night, but she hasn't. Has she somehow missed the hot gossip of the day?

"Hm? Oh, no—I think we're set for now. I barely even had a chance to say hi before I had to get Coco to school."

I guess that explains it... "What are you looking at?"

"Daisy came by a little while ago. Looks like I'll get to try out my new skills sooner rather than later. She ordered a birthday cake for Melody—"

"Oh, yeah. I meant to tell you I bumped into her on Saturday, and she mentioned it."

Emberly's chin drops, and she straightens. "You talked to Daisy?"

"What's that supposed to mean?"

"It means you've avoided her like the plague ever since that idiot drove out of here on the piece of crap motorcycle he rode in on leaving both of you devastated and hurt."

I exhale with a huff. "I just didn't feel like reliving it is all."

Emberly's lips press into a line, and she nods. "Well, good. I'm glad you're burying the hatchet. Travis was a dirt bag, but I think Daisy really fell for him."

My hand is on my hip. "Thanks for caring about my feelings."

"Oh, stop it. You would've gotten over Travis in six months or less. He wasn't half smart enough for you. All he had going on was that cocky grin and a few tattoos."

And that dimple... I seem to have a thing for dimples. "What makes you think Daisy was different?"

Emberly leans against the back counter crossing her arms as she thinks. "I don't know, but she actually cried for him. You got pissed off and tried to sleep with a sixteen-year-old."

"Seventeen!" I try to defend myself while cringing on the inside.

My best friend starts to laugh, and I soften a little bit. "Why would Daisy cry over idiot Travis? Why would she even give him the time of day? She's so quiet... and straight laced... and traditional."

Emberly returns to her book. "Just because she has a baby doesn't mean she doesn't have a wild side."

"Daisy Sales does not have a wild side."

A moment passes as my friend thinks. "I don't know. Maybe he was different with her. All I know is she was a mess."

"Well, it's her own damn fault. She knew he and I were together when she let that wolf in the door."

"I agree." My best friend shakes her head. "I'm still glad you're talking again. Especially since she ordered the most complex birthday cake. It's Alice in Wonderland, and it's huge. She must've made a big commission. When I told her how much it would cost, she didn't bat an eye."

"What is it?" I walk over to look at the design when the bell above the door rings.

"Good afternoon, ladies." That deep voice makes my stomach flip.

Emberly leaves me at the table. "Chad! I haven't seen you all day. Where have you been? You didn't stop by at lunch."

"I had business. An old promise to keep." To his credit, he doesn't look at me, still my whole body, including my face, is red hot.

"That's nice." Emberly looks over her shoulder to me. "It's nice to hear some men do keep their promises."

It certainly is... I think, but I only smile and nod, turning on my heel and picking up the clean pans from the drying rack.

"Were you out of town?" She continues. "I didn't see you in church Sunday either."

"Robbie had a new place he needed me to check out. I'm sure I missed a good one."

"Just more shouting about depravity." Emberly shakes her head. "I wish Mamma would get off that kick."

"Your mother?" Chad is confused, but he's probably the only person in town who doesn't know Emberly's mother provides my uncle with the texts for all his sermons.

My best friend stumbled upon the emails right after her daughter started preschool. It only reinforced my decision never to step foot in that tiny house of worship again. Money money money. It even makes the religious world go round.

What would Jesus do?

Start flipping tables if I remember correctly.

Yes, I went to Sunday school.

I tune in just in time to catch Emberly's next question. "That's right! You were in Africa and Asia. You should get with Tabby. You know she's working on a travel site right now. She just said something about Madagascar."

160

Supposed to be working on it. I stretch and return the final pan to it's cabinet. "I might leave a little early to finish up," I say, but she's not listening.

Chad however never takes his eyes off me. I might have lingered a bit longer, stretching to put the pan away before looking over my shoulder and giving him a wink.

A hint of a grin curls his lips, and he answers her absent-mindedly. "They think it's where Eden used to be."

My best friend is not a slow learner. "Is that so?" She turns to give me a piercing glare. "I just heard that somewhere today..."

"Umm... Yeah." If I wasn't busted before, I sure as hell am now. Clearing my throat, I dust off my hands. "So I need to leave early. To finish up the site."

"To finish up the site. Right..." Emberly gives me a knowing look. "No problem! You came in early after all."

"See you tomorrow." I'm out the door quicker than anybody can say *gotcha*.

Chapter 17

Chad

The scent of Tabitha Green has been on me all day, making me crazy. I see her cuffed on that bed, breasts heaving, legs rubbing together slowly. I taste her, sweet and rich on my tongue.

Standing in my kitchen, I lean on the scrubbed metal counter holding my scotch and remembering her sitting here, kissing me. I tilt my glass back and forth, watching the amber liquid move side to side. Kissing her is like a fever in my brain. It's hot and fast and hungry.

She's so fucking sexy and so damn smart. When I first saw her, I admit, I fell for her looks. Of course, I did. She was standing in a transparent bra and panties at the side of an ancient pool looking embarrassed and angry and defiant... and so damn tempting. I was curious, yeah, but I had come here to get myself back together, to stop ignoring the past and trying to outrun it. I had to put her on hold.

But she never left my mind.

How could she?

I would see her every day, and every day she was the same—embarrassed and angry and defiant. She thinks she knows who I am, but she doesn't. She thinks she can put me in a neat box, but she can't—just like she can't be fit into a box, categorized like a fish or a bird.

We're complex and more alike than she realizes.

She skipped out of Emberly's bakery like a rabbit, but I don't think she's scared. It's been a fast three days, but she doesn't seem like the type to spook easily. She turned her back on me for a year... until she didn't. Now I can't get enough of her, and I'm pretty sure she feels the same way.

Am I wrong?

I want to know the answer.

I want my hands on her.

I want to kiss her again.

Lowering the glass to the counter, I jog down the steps, shove my feet in a pair of tennis shoes, and I'm out the door. My head is on fire, and I'm walking fast. Almost like I'm being driven.

It takes a few minutes to walk the mile separating her house from my apartment. The lights are on inside, and I see the shadow of her sitting in front of that huge computer screen. Lifting my phone, I quickly text her.

You busy?

She doesn't move at first, and I wonder how long it takes for a text to make it into space and back down to where her device waits beside her... Not long.

I watch as she straightens then lifts the phone. She holds it a minute, and my stomach tightens. Will she answer? Will she tell me yes?

Her reply makes me smile. *Can't concentrate again.*

Are your wrists okay?

They don't hurt, but they look bad.

My stomach tightens. I never want to hurt her. *Can I see them?*

I'll send a photo.

Open the door.

Her shadow quickly turns in the chair. I wonder if she can see me through the window, standing here in my gray sweats, my white undershirt, and my old tennis shoes. She stands, briefly disappearing from my sight before opening her door a crack.

Her pretty, pretty face appears in the moonlight, and she hesitates a moment. I take a step closer, tense, anxious, feverish. Will she be angry I showed up on her doorstep? Will she tell me to go away?

She smiles, and my muscles relax. "What are you doing here?"

I jog the few steps separating us and stop in front of her. Her eyes are wide, moving quickly from my waist to my shoulders to my lips then all the way to meet my gaze. It's electric.

"I had to see you again." My voice is low, a little hoarse.

Without a word, she reaches out, taking my hand and guiding me into the room, closing the door behind me. We stand face to face, breathing quickly, anticipation so high. Does she feel it, too? I know she does when she puts her palm flat against my chest, right over my beating heart.

I cover her hand with mine, lifting it out so I can see the dark bruise on the side of her wrist. It's just below her little Believe tattoo, and it makes me wince.

"I'm sorry that happened." Lifting her arms, I kiss one, then the other.

When our eyes meet, she reaches her hands around my neck, placing her thumb on my chin. Green eyes hold mine, and she rises onto her tiptoes, lifting her face. I don't hesitate.

Our mouths collide, and it's passionate, needy, hungry. Tongues caress, and she's in my arms.

I want her, and I want her to know how much.

I'm not holding back anymore…

* * *

Tabby's cheek is against my chest, and she's spread across the bed when I open my eyes again. The sun floods the room with bright white light, and I lift my head, looking for a clock.

She doesn't have one.

Her breath is a whisper against my skin, and I don't want to move. I smooth her hair away from her cheek, thinking about last night. Even with the fever driving me here, it was different.

We weren't starving.

We took our time, touching, observing, holding. She straddled my lap, and my hands roamed the length of her back, my palms fitting into her curves as she rode me, as we climbed higher together.

When she came, it was waves crashing, galaxies soaring, showers of fireworks. Yet, at the same time, it was the two of us together, hearts beating in time, exchanging our breath. I curled her in my arms, and we slept… then sometime in the night, we made love again.

Rubbing my palm over my eyes, I realize with a jolt I didn't use a condom. *Shit.* Was I even awake when I slid inside her from behind last night? All I know is I wanted her, and I reached for her. It was like a dream I've had so many times—the two of us together, no barriers, rocking gently, eyes closed.

I have to tell her I'm clean. Apologize.

A breath and she exhales a little sound. She stirs, lifting her head off my chest, and her brown hair hangs to the side in a silky curtain, green eyes finding mine.

"What time is it?" she whispers. "I can't believe I slept all night."

"You don't seem to have a clock."

We both sit up, and she's beside me, her chin down as she rubs her forehead.

Her hand drifts down to her mouth, and she blinks up to me. "You spent the night again."

"I did." I take a moment, waiting.

Tabby's stubborn, but even she has to feel what's happening here. I know she does, but will she acknowledge it?

She drops her hand to her lap, twisting her fingers together. "We had sex without a condom. I never do that."

"I never do that."

Both our voices are quiet, and she blinks up to me once more. "I went and got tested after Travis cheated on me. I'm always careful, but I just needed to be sure."

"I get tested every year because of my job. People can get violent—biting, scratching, whatever—I never know."

"So we're good?" Her eyes are on mine again, and I nod.

"I am if you are."

She nods, and her lips press into a line... which slowly becomes a smile. The tension evaporates, and I reach out to put my hand on her neck, my thumb on her bottom lip. Leaning forward I try to kiss her, but she arches back.

"Oh, no. I know exactly where that leads, and I have to get to work." Swinging her legs around, she hops out of the bed completely naked and goes into the bathroom. "We're really going to be the talk of the town today."

"How so?" I stand, walking over to where I stripped off my clothes last night.

The toilet flushes, and she returns wrapped in a lavender silk robe. "How did you get here last night?"

My grey sweats are on my hips, and I lower the tank top over my head. I don't miss her lusty gaze on me as I straighten the fabric over my body. It makes me grin. *I know you like what you see, beautiful. The feeling's mutual.*

She shakes her head, clearing her throat. "What was I saying? Oh! How did you get here last night?" She walks to the window as I slip in the bathroom to use it and splash some water on my face. "Is your truck parked out front again?"

"I walked." As soon as I'm finished, I go to where she stands, lowering my face to her neck and sliding her hair off her shoulder.

She ducks and spins away. "I'll drive you home. What time are you supposed to be at the station?"

"Probably now." I lean my back against the wall, arms crossed over my chest as I watch her opening and closing doors, pulling out leggings and a tee before disappearing into the bathroom again. "If you owned a clock, I could tell you."

She's out just as fast, her hair up on her head in a messy bun, dressed in black leggings and a gray tee falling off one shoulder that reads *I love Jesus, but I cuss a little.*

"Nice." I nod to her shirt, and she catches my hand.

"I'll drive you home real quick. Maybe they won't see us."

Holding her hand, I give it a gentle pull, stopping her. "I don't care if they do. Now, give me a kiss."

"Chad, I—"

168

Her protest is lost in my lips covering hers, pushing them apart, sliding my tongue along hers. She melts almost at once, and I feel her hand touching my lower back. The other one is on my cheek, and it makes me smile. Our eyes blink open, meeting, and she sighs, smiles.

"I like spending the night with you. I liked fucking you without a condom. I like where this is going, and I don't give a fuck who knows."

Maybe it's too fast. Maybe it's too strong, but I'm not interested in that. I've watched her, waited for her to open the door. She let me in, and I won't have her spooked by small-town gossip.

"So bossy." She touches my stomach, and I know she's into it. "We still have to work today."

I catch her hand and kiss her fist. "I'll jog home, and I'll see you at lunch."

Not waiting for another word, I take off out the door, glad I shoved my feet in tennis shoes before I left my place last night with one thing on my mind.

* * *

Lunch finds Tabby straddling my lap in the cruiser. We're parked off a narrow road leading to a small beach, behind a tree and two thick bushes, far enough from the main road to be hidden.

My hand is in the back of her panties, cupping her ass, and I slip my finger in that little hole, using it to guide her forward and up as she rides my dick.

"Oh!" She jumps and her inner walls grip me tighter at the sensation. I almost blow.

We're soft and slippery, skin against skin, no barriers. Her breath is laced with little moans as her orgasm builds, and it's so fucking hot.

Too eager to wait, we're both still partially dressed. Her skirt is up, shirt unbuttoned, and I jerked her bra down so her soft breasts bounce right at my chin. She exhales a whimper of pleasure with every thrust. Dipping my head, I catch a hard nipple, giving it a firm tug, a gentle bite, and her orgasm explodes all around my cock.

"Yes..." Her head tilts back, and I lean up, loving the feel of her coming on me. Two more upward thrusts and I let go with my own blistering orgasm. It blanks my mind.

"Tabby..." I hold her, filling her, realizing every time we do this, it gets harder to stop, harder to imagine ever letting her go.

She sighs, relaxing into me. Her elbows are on the tops of my shoulders, and she traces a finger along my hairline. "Two weeks, and I've not only ridden in a cop car, I've ridden *you* in a cop car."

"They warned me you were a bad girl."

"You're a bad boy, Chad Tucker."

That makes me chuckle. I'm still deep inside her. Her shirt is still open, soft breasts against my chin. Our lips are a breath apart, and I hold her, sliding my hands along her soft body. "You bring out the best in me."

"The best or the beast?" It's a sassy purr, and I kiss her again.

"What do you think?"

"I think lunch is over, and I've got to get back to town." She hops off my lap to the other side of the car, straightening her panties under her black skirt.

My uniform pants were only shoved partially down my ass, and I jerk them back into place, looking down for any signs of what we just did. Somehow, I don't see any.

Tabby's murmuring on the other side of the car. "Andy ruined these." Her stretched and misshapen panties are on her finger, and anger rises in my chest.

"Who's Andy?"

Her face flames red, and she covers her mouth with her hand. "Did I say that out loud?"

"Tabby?"

"Are you acting jealous?" Her eyes widen, and she starts to laugh more.

"Who's Andy." My voice is level, and she leans toward me.

"The anaconda in your pants." She gives me a quick kiss on the lips, and I snatch the panties off her finger. They're in my pocket before she can protest.

"Andy…" I shake my head.

She hops to her seat again, flipping down the visor and touching up her makeup. "I need to shower. I'll have to make do in the bathroom."

"You're beautiful, you know?"

That gets me a sly look from the corner of her eye, and a sexy little grin. "You're trying to spoil me."

"I'd love to spoil you." Reaching out, I smooth her hair off her cheek, resting my hand behind her neck. "I'll make you forget all the assholes who came before me."

Her lips press together, and she blinks a minute, thinking about my promise. Something changes in her face, a softness is there, a thoughtful expression.

She tilts her head to the side, and when she looks at me her tone is quiet, serious. "I think you would."

"So let me."

He brow furrows, and her eyes flicker away.

I want her to say yes, but instead, she grabs the door handle.

———

171

She's out so fast, I only catch the hem of her skirt as it flicks past the bumper. I turn in my seat to see her jogging up the trail back to town, leaving me with the scent of her all over my clothes, and a promise hanging in the air.

Chapter 18

Tabby

"Tomorrow's the big day, right?" Emberly holds a bowl of jet-black batter as she stands in front of a large sketch of the queen of hearts and different sized cake pans. "Or is it tonight? Does it happen at midnight?"

I'm coming out of the bathroom after having spent a few minutes cleaning up. Andy the Anaconda leaves a big mess when he's happy.

"What are you talking about?" I've tied my hair up in a messy bun again, and even after washing my hands, I'm still convinced I smell like Sex with Chad Tucker.

My stomach tingles remembering all of it... riding his big dick, kissing his soft lips... *I'd love to spoil you.*

The man is so fine. He's perfect...

Nobody's perfect, I remind myself.

"The website?" Emberly stops stirring and gives me a frown. "You said the soft open for Travel Time is tomorrow. You are so distracted these days! Is Chad Tucker so good in bed you can't think?"

My jaw drops, and I feel my cheeks get hot.

It makes her burst out laughing. "I knew it. You've been fucking Deputy Tucker."

"Emberly!" I look all around the empty store. "Shh! They'll hear you."

"Nobody's here but us. Anyway, *they* already seem to know. André said a familiar truck was parked outside your house all night on Sunday. I guess my scone disaster had me too distracted. I'm not even going to start on how mad I am at you for not telling me."

Excitement mixes with dread mixes with nerves mixes with cautious glee — it's all churning in my guts.

"It's happening so fast." I walk slowly to the table, thinking. "It's happening too fast. I don't know what to make of it. I didn't want to tell you until I knew what I thought about it."

A vase of dried flowers is on the enormous, weathered wood table where Emberly does all her prep work. Sunlight streams through the big glass windows, and the place is empty except for the little register at the front and empty glass cases we hope to fill one day with a selection of large, specialty cakes and cookies.

"And you're worried about that *why*?" She goes back to mixing, taking a moment to pour the black batter into one large round and three smaller square pans.

I lean against the table, trying to find the right words to express how I feel. "Remember how we used to say we were going to backpack around Europe together?"

"It wasn't just Europe." She walks over and puts the glass bowl in the sink, running water to rinse it. "We were going to go to Australia, Thailand, New Zealand, Fiji..."

"And then everything changed when your aunt died and you inherited this place... and Coco and the cakes..." She nods, and I hold my breath, hoping she isn't taking this wrong. "I don't want to change. I still want to do all the things we said we would do. The things I've been working toward."

"So who says you can't?"

My lips twitch, and I think about it. "It's a fair question. I guess maybe I'm just worried if I get too attached, I'll never leave."

"Afraid you'll want to settle down in Oceanside and start having babies?"

One of Coco's toys is on the table in front of me. It's one of the play-dough molds she uses when she pretends to be making cakes like her mother. With a little flash of surprise, I realize my best friend is exactly right. Only it's not something I'm afraid of. It's a real thought I've had the last few times Chad and I have been together, starting with last night when he slipped between my thighs condom-free.

I'm on birth control, of course, but I still had the thought of a chubby, dark-haired baby in my arms—and I liked it. A lot.

This morning it freaked me out.

It freaked me out again in his cruiser.

I'm falling for him.

Majorly.

"It's way too soon for that." My voice is a firm protest, a wake-up call. "I said no more relationships after Travis, and I meant it. Besides, I barely even know the guy."

"Oh, please." Emberly's mixing up a deep red batter now. "He's been in Oceanside a year. Robbie trusts him more than anybody. He's André's best friend. He checks on Daisy and me every day. We all know him. Chad is not Travis, Tabby. He's a great guy."

He is.

"Still…" I turn the toy over in my hand. "Even the perfect ones can break their promises, break your heart, go off and leave you. Then where are your dreams?"

The room is quiet. She stops stirring, and I'm afraid to look up.

I'm talking about Jackson. Her first love, who she thought she would marry. I remember vividly how they looked at each other, how serious they were. They couldn't keep their hands off each other. I thought it was real.

Then he left and never came back. No word. No explanation. It almost broke her completely.

My voice is so quiet, it's barely above a whisper. "I can't let that happen to me."

Emberly begins to stir again, still not speaking. I brave a glance at her face, and I see her cheeks are pink. I feel like a dog, and I hop off the stool, rushing over to where she is and putting my hands on her waist, my chin on her shoulder.

"I'm sorry. I didn't say it to hurt you."

She gives the batter a few more stirs before setting the bowl down with a thud. "You've never hurt me."

Her hands are on my wrists, and she takes them off her waist, turning so she can meet my eyes. "Chad is also not Jackson. Don't borrow my pain as an excuse to be alone. Anyway, my dream is right here. Look at it." She opens her hands in an arc, gesturing to the shabby-chic old place she's slowly turning into a legitimate small business. "I'm almost there. All we need is more customers."

Nodding I look down. "You're right. You've never given up, and it's going to happen."

"I believe it will." She reaches for my hand, turning it so she can see my wrist — only today I've got layers of bracelets covering both.

"What's this?" Her brow furrows, and she looks up at me. "You never cover your tattoo... Oh! What happened?"

Her voice goes loud, her eyes huge, and I cringe as I try to ease my bruised wrists out of her hands. "It's nothing. Just a little accident."

"It looks like... handcuffs?" Her expression morphs into excited surprise, and her voice goes louder. "Did Chad put handcuffs on you? Tabitha Green! You kinky hooker!"

"Stop. It's really nothing—"

The bell over the door dings, and we both spin around like we've been busted doing something wrong. As if by cosmic fate it's my uncle walking in with Wyatt Jones right behind him.

"Oh, good gravy." Emberly hops over to the table and scooping up the bowl, stirring rapidly.

"That's not suspicious," I mutter, readjusting my bracelets.

She ignores me, calling out, "Good afternoon, Reverend Green! Wyatt. What brings you here?"

"Good afternoon, Emberly. Tabitha." Uncle Bob nods and gives us his signature pious smile. *Gag.* "I'm glad you're here, Tabitha," he continues, walking slowly to where I'm standing. "I've been meaning to speak with you."

Here we go. "What's new, fam?"

He lifts his chin. "I want you to know I've noticed some things."

"Is that so?"

Yes, I'm sure he's noticed Chad's truck parked in my driveway all night. Did he also see Chad's cruiser violently rocking behind a bush today at lunch? If this cruiser's a-rockin, it means don't come a-knockin.

I almost burst out laughing — but I control myself.

"You've been making a real effort this year, Tabitha. I want you to know I've noticed. Emberly's mother has noticed, and I'm sure God has noticed as well."

Not what I expected. Of course, my mouth goes off. "Did God tell you that himself?"

Bob continues unfazed. "I was so pleased to see you with little Colette at the church festival on Friday." He delivers these words like one of his Sunday homilies. "I can't tell you what a relief it is to know you're getting your life right with the Lord and making good decisions for a change."

"I've been working a lot." His tone, his words, the way he looks down his nose at me, all of it is tightening my stomach into an angry little ball.

"I also approve of you seeing Deputy Tucker." He rocks back on his heels, nodding. "Chad Tucker is an asset to our community, and I'm sure he'll be a force for good in your life."

My jaw is clenched, and I flash a look at Wyatt standing beside him rubbing his chin. "Is Wyatt on the approval committee, as well?"

Emberly coughs a laugh, and I know she of all people is very aware the effect my uncle's words are having on me. I might have to find some pot to smoke or set something on fire.

"Er, no." Wyatt cuts in. "Emberly, I was on my way over to tell you I posted a job notice for somebody to paint these old storefronts. Hopefully, I can get a crew in here before too long. Give us all a good facelift."

"Well, Hallelujah!" I glance at my best friend. "I was beginning to think you were pocketing that money."

Emberly's been sending fifty bucks a month to Wyatt for "beautification" of these old buildings since she moved in here, and it's the first time he's made any signs of using it.

"Emberly Warren!" Wyatt straightens up fast, pressing his palm against his chest over his heart. "That would be dishonest!"

"It's been two years." I jump in, riled up and ready to fight. "That means between Daisy, Em, BP and you, you should have close to five thousand dollars now."

"It'll take most of that to pay for the labor and supplies." He's still offended, and my uncle is standing back with his hand on his stomach watching it all unfold. "It takes time for things to happen."

"There's a sermon in those words, Wyatt." Uncle Bob is still giving us that holier than thou smile. "Perhaps this painter will be a blessing in disguise. God brings people into our lives for a reason."

I don't have time for this.

Snatching my purse off the table, I step over and give my friend a quick kiss on the cheek. "You good here? I need to make sure Travel Time is ready for tonight."

"I'm good." She knows I'll go off if I stay here much longer, but she catches my arm before I run out the door, lowering her voice. "Don't let that speech freak you out. From what I've seen, Chad might be perfect for you."

My jaw is still tight, and I cast a glance toward my uncle. "We'll see."

Chad is definitely perfect at keeping me off my computer. I've got to work double-time if I'm going to be ready for midnight. My focus needs to be on Rani and AJ—not Chad and Andy... and these condescending, *approving* townies.

* * *

"How's it looking?" My headset is on, and I'm sharing a screen with my two clients in Seattle.

"We really can't tell you how much we love it, Tab." Rani's smile is bright white, lifting her smooth brown cheeks. Her dark hair is cut short, and she keeps a lock tucked behind her ear. "The articles you added about Vis and The Great Blue Hole really set us apart. I doubt many people have even heard of those places."

"That's what our adventurous travelers want." AJ bends down to wave at me from behind her shoulder.

I wave back. "I did my best to ask questions and dig deep. The only thing left is to go there in person and take pictures of our own."

I'm only half-teasing when I say it, but Rani clears her throat, sitting a little straighter in her chair. "That's actually something we wanted to discuss with you."

My eyebrows perk up. "It is?"

AJ rolls up a chair beside Rani. "How would you feel about being sort-of a field scout for us?"

"You want me to be your field scout?" I'm going to have to pick up my jaw off the floor. "What does that mean?"

"Basically, you'd take our planned trips, give us firsthand feedback on what works and what doesn't, whether the accommodations are as good as they say, if there are sites we haven't included people should see or vice versa…"

"So you'd be paying me to travel?"

"Not very much," Rani's dark brows pull together. "We could arrange the accommodations, even get you decent fights. The only thing that would leave is your meals and drink, clothes, incidentals…"

"We know this means you'd probably have to sacrifice other work." AJ adds. "And we're not quite in a position yet to pay you for that loss of revenue. Our hope is the adventure would make up for it."

I rock back in my chair, thinking about what they're saying. I'd be going to the places they tell me for the stories they want. It's not exactly my dream of freedom to travel wherever I want to go, but hell, it's pretty damn close.

"My work is pretty portable." I study my calendar, looking at the open dates ahead. "It's possible I wouldn't have to give up too many other jobs."

AJ rests his chin on his hands. "I guess what we're trying to say is we'd want you to prioritize us. There might be times when you're in remote locations, poor connectivity. Something might have to give. We don't want you to be surprised. We want everyone to go in with clear expectations."

"Okay... Umm... I guess I'll need to think about it. Is that okay?"

"Of course!" They both cry at once. "Take your time. We're confident in the material we have for the launch, and it's not like we need something new right away. We're more concerned the stuff we're pushing is as good as we say it is, being able to answer questions."

Nodding, I look over the packages on the site. "I get that. I won't take too long."

"Great!" They both smile, but I feel tense. I'm anxious and uncomfortable, and I'm not really sure why.

"I think we're ready for tonight," I say, attempting to calm my anxiety. "But I'll run through everything again one more time to be sure. Then we'll just wait on family and friends to pull all the levers and press all the buttons."

They laugh, and from behind, I hear a knock on my door. "Tabby, it's me!"

It's Chad, and my insides are on edge. "I just have someone at my door."

"No worries! We'll say goodbye for now."

I disconnect the call and close the window before I hurry to answer it. Chad's dimpled grin on the other side only adds to my swirling emotions. My stomach is in knots from my uncle's dumb speech at Emberly's, now the job offer from Rani and AJ is hanging over my head. I'm all mixed up. I should be thrilled by their offer. What's wrong with me?

"What are you doing here?" I sound irritated.

I guess I am.

His brow lowers, and he reaches for me "I came to see you. I missed you." He leans down to capture my lips in one of his schedule-altering kisses, but at the last minute I turn my face, pulling away.

"No…" I grasp his wrist, exhaling a frustrated groan. I step outside, turning him on the threshold, and closing the door behind me. "I can't do this tonight."

His frown deepens. "Why not? What's going on?"

"I have to be focused on the soft launch for Travel Time." I release his hand, twisting my fingers and pacing. "I have commitments and responsibilities. In the last four days, since we had our date on Friday, I haven't done anything!"

"You said you'd gotten a lot done on Sunday."

"Yes, I worked Sunday, but that's it!" My voice rises. "I usually work every day for hours and hours!"

"That doesn't sound good for you. What's the old saying about all work and no play?"

His cocky smile only increases my stress.

"It's what made Jack Nicholson lose his shit and axe murder everyone in the Shining!" The tension in my chest is almost more than I can bear. "I'm going to need you to give me some space, okay?"

His smile dissolves into more of a crooked grin, and his eyebrows rise. "I'm saying for the next couple days, you can't just show up here for a booty call."

"I never thought of you as a booty call." His voice is low, possibly a touch defensive.

Trickles of pain begin to filter into the sides of my stomach. These words are coming out, but they're not really how I feel.

"I just need a little space, okay? I need to get this job done and think about it. Think about what I want to do. Can you let me do that?"

His hands go up, palms facing me as if I'm holding a gun on him. "You got it. I'll leave you alone."

"Thank you." Cramps are in my sides now, and I'm pretty sure I'm going to cry. "I'll talk to you later."

"Later." He nods and hesitates for a moment before leaning in to kiss me on the cheek. "Goodnight, Tab. I was just thinking about you."

His clean, Chad-scent drifts all around me, but he pulls back, turning without another word and heading to his waiting truck in my driveway. My lips press together to stop the trembling, and I grab the door, hurrying inside before he can see me cry.

Why the fuck am I crying? I'm just being honest. For almost a week we've been together nonstop. I've neglected my work. I've neglected my friends. Now I've been offered my dream job and I'm not even sure if I want to take it... What the hell?

Now would be a really great, fucking time to have a mother to talk too. Oh, right, she ditched me when I

183

was a baby. I walk across the room and kick the small trashcan under my desk so hard it hits the opposite wall and falls over.

Nothing spills out, and I hiccup a breath. Chad emptied it the last time he was here. He's so thoughtful… he pays attention to everything. *He's kind of perfect…*

Collapsing to sit on the spot, I bend my knees and rest my forehead on the backs of my hands as tears pour from my eyes. I used to have it all figured out. Now I have no idea what the fuck is going on.

Chapter 19

Chad

I should've walked to Tabby's place. I'm too pissed to sit in my truck, driving back to mine.

Space? Are you kidding me? This afternoon she was riding my cock and screaming my name, less than eight hours later, she's asking for space. What the fuck happened?

The minute I'm in my drive, I throw it in park and get out, leaving the keys in the visor. I don't even want to go inside. I step out and start to run. I don't have a plan in mind. I'm just blowing off steam.

I jog up the short drive until I'm at the cross section leading either left, down into town, or right, up into the old garden district. I take a right and follow the streets past the old houses. It's darker here because the live oak trees line the path with their heavy, thick limbs filled with thick green leaves hang low, blocking the light.

When I get to Marjorie Warren's giant mansion in the center of the oldest part, I take another right, heading down to the dead end road. It only ends for cars. A bike path leads into the trees, down the hill, past the scrub bushes, following the narrow road I'd been on earlier today.

Bearing to the right, I jog across a wooden bridge, my feet making dull thudding noises as I cross. The water trickles under it. So many little streams and creeks run through these woods. None of them are big enough for boating, but they keep this land from being developed. It's too wet with all these small capillaries running out to the ocean.

The path drops down, still following the narrow road above. They both circle around, and if you know what you're doing, if you're a local, you know it leads to a secluded beach hidden by a cove. It's pretty and private, and not many people come out here. They prefer the beach bars and social life out on the strip.

When my feet hit sand, I stop. I'm breathing hard and slick with sweat. The edge of my anger is slightly dulled by the exertion but not completely gone. Toeing off my shoes, I leave them at the top of the path and walk straight into the crashing waves, going under and letting it all wash away. This place is beautiful.

The sun is just creeping down the horizon when I emerge from the water. I start to walk along the shore, allowing the breeze to dry my skin and hair. It's only about seven-thirty. I was anxious to see Tabby, and I headed over to her place right after dinner. The memory fans the smolder of anger in my chest—until the happy squeal of a little girl catches me off guard.

I trot forward and see a familiar sight hopping like a kangaroo all along the water's edge. I look around, scanning the beach until I see Emberly following along behind her.

"Mister Chad!" Coco squeals and takes off running toward me. "Is Aunt Tabby here?"

As soon as she gets close enough, I scoop her up in my arms. Coco is such a funny little girl. Nothing bad ever happens in her world—unless you count Melody not wanting to be bossed around by her.

Emberly waves, and we slowly close the space between us. When we're all together, I put Coco on her feet. "What are you doing out here?" I ask.

Emberly's smile is a little sad, and she looks out at the breaking waves. "I try to get out here at least once a month." Something wistful is in her tone. "It's sort of a special place for me."

"I'm sorry. I didn't mean to intrude." I don't know her story or why this place might be special, but I understand going somewhere to feel safe or to remember.

"You don't have to apologize. I don't own this beach," she laughs. She studies my face a second. "What's wrong?"

"Nothing." I try to laugh, but it comes out weird.

Emberly's too smart for that. "I've seen you every day for almost a year now, Chad Tucker. You look like you're about to rip somebody's throat out or put your fist through a wall. Which is it?"

"Am I that transparent?" Her mouth presses into a frown, and I know I'm not getting out of this.

Coco takes off after a tiny sandpiper, and the two of us walk along the shore behind her. "I hate going out on limbs," Emberly starts. "So stop me if I'm going too far. Is this about Tabby?"

"So the answer is yes, I am that transparent." She gives me an empathetic smile, and I do a little shrug. "Things were going pretty great. At least I thought they were."

"From what I could tell they were... then her uncle dropped by the store today." She sighs, crossing her arms over her chest. "I never can tell if the man is really that clueless or if he likes pressing her buttons."

"What does that mean?"

"Oh, he just basically told her how proud he was of her for finally making good life choices and getting her life right and how much he approves of you."

"Jesus." It's like a punch in the gut. My jaw tightens, and I shake my head. "Why the hell did he say all that?"

Emberly starts to laugh, but I feel sick. I know my girl, and I bet that was like rubbing a cat's fur backwards.

"Yeah, he really fucked everything up."

I rub the back of my neck trying to figure this one out. "What am I going to do?"

The waves swirl in around our bare feet, and the water is getting colder. Fall is coming.

She exhales a heavy sigh. "Bob Green approving of you is just about the kiss of death. But… I think you still have a really good chance."

Tilting my head, I give her a little frustrated smile. "You think so? Why?"

"For starters, that right there." She points at my face, and I don't understand.

"What do you mean?"

"Have you looked in the mirror lately? You're a good-looking man, Chad Tucker, and that dimple. Shew." The wind swirls her hair around, and she grabs it, wrapping it into a coil at her neck. "I'm pretty sure my best friend has fallen for you. Tabby doesn't get emotionally involved… Seriously, I can't even remember the last time I saw her sacrificing work for a guy."

I think about what she's saying for a few steps. If anybody knows Tabby, it's Emberly. "So what do suggest I do?"

"What did she say the last time you talked to her?"

"She said she wanted space. She said I thought of her as a booty call… she said she'd call me later."

"That's good." Emberly nods quickly. "If she said she'd call you, she will. Tabby's not shitty. She won't ghost you out."

I'm not sure I like the sound of that. "So the next time I hear from her, she's going to break it off?"

"I don't think so." She keeps walking, looking down at her feet, watching the waves swirl around them. "I think if you're really interested, you'll wait."

"I don't know about waiting." I don't like being put off.

"You waited a year. What's a little while longer?"

"That wasn't exactly waiting. I was dealing with my own shit."

"And giving Tabby's ass really hot looks whenever she'd walk away." Emberly winks, and I can't deny it. I might not have been waiting for her, but I sure as hell was noticing her.

For a minute we don't say anything, then Emberly looks out at the sun sitting right on the ocean now. "When Tabby and I were Coco's age, she used to cry a lot for her mom. Not crying like a baby." She shakes her head and waves her hand. "She would hide and cry, like when she thought no one would see."

My chest aches thinking of her hiding away to cry. "Why did she leave?"

"I'm not sure anybody knows, but it really messed with Tabby's head." Emberly crosses her arms over her waist. "It took a long time before she finally stopped crying. Then it was like she decided she wouldn't let anyone make her cry that way again."

"I would never make her cry."

Emberly nods, giving me a smile. "I believe you. Tabby's just been protecting herself a long time. She wants to believe. Can you be patient and help her get there?"

I think of the tattoo on her wrist. She said it was to remind her...

189

Reaching out, I catch her small hand and give it a squeeze. "Thanks, Ember."

"Take care of my girl, Deputy Tucker." She gives me a playful, stern glare.

"I intend to do just that."

* * *

I'm frustrated and, I confess, a bit of a dick the rest of the week. The days are too long, the nights are too long, and Jimmy Rhodes had better watch his mouth.

"Noticed you've been by yourself a lot lately." The little punk actually walks over to greet me with a smug look on his face. "Has our girl realized there's better fish in the sea."

I give him a tight smile. I know he's pushing my buttons because of his crush on Tabby, but his use of the phrase *our girl* annoys me.

Crossing my arms, I straighten to my full height, which is a head and shoulders over him. "I got a call last night about a break-in down around one of the beach houses on Oceanside Cliffs. Where you around eleven p.m.?"

"I don't know what you're talking about." I'm only jerking his chain, but he gets nervous enough to make me suspicious. "I was doing my Uber rounds last night."

"Not much activity in Oceanside on a Wednesday an hour before midnight. Who did you drive?"

"He actually was doing a run," Wyatt walks up laughing, patting Jimmy on the shoulder. "I needed him to take my mamma home after prayer meeting."

"That's pretty late for a prayer meeting."

"Yeah, she came over to the house after. That woman can talk!"

"I'll take your word for it." I nod to Wyatt, backing down. I am just messing with the kid anyway. Robbie thinks it was a deer or possibly a raccoon set off the house alarm. Still, I give the kid a stern look. "You keep your nose clean."

Punk-assed kid has the nerve to call back to me. "Afraid I'm going to steal her out from under you?"

"There's been some petty theft at the gas station as well. Not too many kids out of school to cause mischief."

Jimmy juts his chin out. "Probably old Mabel Collier. Dre says she's developed sticky fingers now that she's got dementia."

He's right. I forgot Lance Collier told us he kept finding her pilfered loot in her mattress. He's always very apologetic and embarrassed when he returns it, even offers to pay damages. Nobody takes him up on it.

I give up. "Leave Tabby alone."

With a smug look, he goes to the other side of the hardware store, leaving me even more annoyed than when I walked in.

Nothing takes her off my mind. She hasn't been in the bakery all week, and Emberly says it's because she's working on the Travel Time site. Their official launch date is right around the corner, and she's double-checking everything.

I understand that.

It doesn't make me feel better.

At night, back at my place, after I've showered, I stand with my arms propped on the bar thinking about having her here, sitting her up on this bar, kissing her. I should have kissed her that night out on her porch. Everything changes when we kiss.

Instead, I let her tell me she needed space.

My phone is in my hand, and I'm thinking about sending her a text when it starts to ring and vibrate. Turning it over, I internally wince when I see it's my mother calling. I tap the accept button.

"Hey, mom. What's up? Haven't heard from you in a while." I try to sound casual and not tired and sexually frustrated.

"It has been a while. I wish you'd remember to call me at least once a month."

Great, here we go. "Sorry. It's been pretty busy the last couple of weeks."

"I'm sure a real crime spree has broken out. Someone steal Farmer Ted's prize pig?"

It sounds like she's making a joke, but I know my mother. She's right there with Dad on being completely confused as to why I'm here in this small town working as a sheriff's deputy when I could be running one of their multi-billion dollar logistics firms, playing golf with Charleston's richest assholes.

"Actually, Petunia's doing just fine. It was Maggie Sue's turnip patch. Some local kids broke in it, and… well, the damage they did was shocking."

"Be serious. When are you going to give up this absurd obsession with rural living and come home? Your father needs your help. The trucking line out of Burlington lost their manager, and you're the best judge of character—"

"It's not an absurd obsession. I have a nice place here. I've made friends, and I like it."

"I refuse to believe that. You have never enjoyed small towns."

"I guess I've changed."

She's quiet a moment, and I vaguely hear the clinking of ice against crystal. "I'm coming to see you."

I sit up on the couch. "Don't you have a ball or a ladies auxiliary function to attend?"

"I'll drive down tomorrow. Is there somewhere I can stay?"

Standing, I walk around my place. It's only one bedroom, but I could sleep on the couch for a night. It's not too dirty. "You can stay here with me."

"I can't wait. Have your intriguing little hamlet roll out the red carpet. I want to see for myself how happy you are in Podunk by the Sea."

That doesn't sound very good. "I'll see you tomorrow."

We disconnect, and I stand in the middle of my living room thinking about what she said. She doesn't believe I'm happy here. She doesn't believe anyone can be happy outside her world... but she's wrong.

My hand is on my stomach, and I'm thinking about Oceanside on a Friday night. Before I even consider it, I send her a text.

Are you busy tomorrow night? I haven't seen Tabby all week. Emberly said she's been working on that website, and I know she's on a deadline. Still, she's the first person I think of when I want to show my mother how happy I am here.

It's probably a mistake.

I shouldn't have texted her.

Seconds tick past, and she's not going to answer. It's almost worse than not seeing her.

The device buzzes in my hand. It's her. *No time for paintball, sorry.*

I smile at her words. I can almost hear her saying them. *Can you get away for a quick dinner?*

Another few seconds, gray dots floating on the screen. *I suppose I have to eat.*

Full disclosure — my mom is in town.

Your mom? Are you kidding?

Tightness is in my chest. *She wants to know about Oceanside. You know it better than me.*

Your mother and me sounds like a bad idea.

Rubbing my chin, I can't let her back out. I can keep things light. *Just give it a shot. Tomorrow, seven, Blue Crab?*

I never pass up an expensive dinner. Meet you there.

I hesitate a moment, then just fucking type it. *I've missed you.*

A few moments pass. I think she's done. She's not going to respond. I'm about to put my phone down when it buzzes. *I've missed you, too.*

That's all I needed to know.

Chapter 20

Tabby

My third ad is up on the job boards for website developers. I haven't stopped thinking about Rani and AJ's offer since they made it.

Most of the week I've been focused on streamlining Travel Time. My sleep habits have been irregular. I go to sleep with my laptop in my bed, then I wake up and stagger into the living room to work on my desktop.

The soft launch went off without a hitch, thanks to me busting my ass then staying up all night Wednesday while friends and family trickled onto the site to poke around, build trips, customize, test out chat functions, watch videos, read reviews.

We only had a few glitches with the reservation search function. The website wouldn't hold dates, and visitors had to keep re-entering them.

I spent the last two days ironing out annoying problems that would ultimately lose customers. Today's tech users expect speed and ease.

Now, three days later, we're still getting raves. Everyone's talking about how much fun the site is to use. How they can't wait to book their next trip with us. How excited they are about making their travel dreams come true.

It's exactly what we want to hear, and as soon as I logged off, ready to put the site to bed, I started updating my résumé. If I'm going to say yes to Travel Time, I have to be sure it's what I want. I have to be sure I'm not giving up a chance at another offer, a better offer…

My brain has been like a computer with programs running in the background all week. Only the program running in the background is my life. Three days have gone by, and no one has responded to my job posting. Logically, I can't tell Rani and AJ no if nobody else wants to hire me.

Logically…

Illogically, my stomach is in knots and I'm not sure I can say yes even if I don't get another offer.

As much as I've tried, I can't stop thinking about Chad and how he fits into all of this. I shouldn't. It doesn't make sense. We barely know each other. I can't make important life decisions based on something that could end up being a fling.

I'd be like one of those girls who follows her high school boyfriend off to college then breaks up in the first month. Then she's left wondering why she's in Alaska majoring in Wilderness Studies when she really wants to be in New York majoring in Fashion Design.

This is my life, my career, the dream I've been working on for a year. I can't let some guy derail it, no matter how thoughtful he is or how good he is in bed.

Ugh! No matter how many excuses I throw at it, the truth patiently waits to be acknowledged. Despite my annoying uncle's speech, I really miss Chad.

Sitting on the floor of my cottage with my knees bent in front of me, I allow the feelings I've been holding back to rush in on me like a tidal wave.

I miss him so much.

I miss his strong arms around me, that deep dimple in his cheek, those whiskey eyes. I miss being naked with him. I miss kissing him. I miss his lips on my body and that beard scuffing my skin. I miss chatting about work and Coco and traveling and dreams. I miss Andy…

My hand goes over my eyes, and I exhale a laugh as tears fill my eyes.

"Oh my God." My voice cracks. "What am I going to do?"

As if by some divine, immediate answer to prayer, my phone goes off. I'm holding it in my hand, and I turn the face to see a text from Chad asking if I'm busy Friday.

That's how I ended up here, at the Blue Crab in a navy long-sleeved, silk V-neck romper with gold chains and my hair styled over my shoulder. I toned down the Bettie Page routine for Chad's mom, although I have no idea what to expect.

I don't know anything about his family, other than they live in Charleston, they lost a daughter, and they sent a son to military school. Still, something tells me she's a formal lady.

I'm standing in the foyer holding my beige clutch, when I look up and see him coming through the glass front doors. My hand goes out to catch the side of the hostess stand. I didn't anticipate my body's response to seeing him for the first time in nearly a week.

An exhale hisses through my lips, and my stomach does a flip. Chad in a suit is even sexier than Chad in his uniform. He's actually not in a suit, now that I look closer. He's in dark jeans, a white shirt with navy stripes, and a blue blazer. It all looks amazing with his dark hair and those eyes holding mine.

That's when I see his mother, and I shift in my heels. It's clear where Chad's elegant features come from. His mother is tall with swept back, shoulder-length white hair and high cheekbones. Her nose is small, and her eyes are the exact same color as her son's—only hers are like lasers, focused on me.

Striding through the door, she's dressed in beige pants, a cream silk shirt with a dark blazer on top. She's kind of amazing... and a lot scary.

Chad escorts her to where I'm holding on for dear life to the hostess stand, my heart beating too fast in my chest.

Yes, I did miss you, Chad Tucker...

"You look very elegant," he whispers, leaning forward to kiss my cheek.

Holy shit. My eyes close, and my panties ignite when his soft lips touch my skin. I catch his arm as a seductive wave of clean, manly Chad-scent surrounds me.

He straightens just as fast. "Mother, I'd like you to meet Tabitha Green. Tabby, this is my mom. Evelyn Tucker."

"How do you do, Mrs. Tucker?" I get it together and hold out my hand, remembering the tiny bit of etiquette we were taught in grade school.

"How do you do." She shakes my hand, running her cool eyes over my outfit, my hair. "It's nice to meet you."

"Table for three? Or are you expecting one more?" I don't know the perky hostess, and I guess she must be a college kid.

"Three," Chad answers, and she leads us through the sparsely filled restaurant to a table by the window.

I can't help thinking it's too bad the sun has already set. The Blue Crab has amazing views of the ocean. I worked here for about four months last year while I was going to community college.

"Tabitha." His mom studies me once we're all seated and have our menus. "That's an interesting name. Are you from around this area?"

"Yes, ma'am. I grew up in Oceanside."

Thankfully the waiter walks up at that moment. "Welcome to the Blue Crab. My name is Kyle. Can I start you off with some drinks tonight?"

Chad answers first. "I'll have a scotch on the rocks. Mom, a martini?"

"Yes, dry please with an olive."

"Vodka or gin?" Perky Kyle is looking at his pad, so he doesn't see the withering glare Chad's mom gives him.

"It's not a martini if it's made with vodka. It's a kangaroo cocktail."

"I'm sorry?" He finally looks at her, and his eyes widen slightly.

"She'll have gin," Chad cuts in. "Brooklyn, or Beefeater if you don't have it."

"I'll have the same." I nod, wishing I could make it a double.

I've never been afraid of an adult in my life, but Chad's mother scares the shit out of me. Does Chad care about her opinion? If so, how much?

"Thank you, Charles, it is so hard to find a decent waiter these days." She sighs, looking at the menu. "Your father and I have just about given up dining out unless we can get a table at Circa."

Charles? That's something he didn't tell me.

Chad's eyes briefly meet my surprised ones before he looks away. "What's dad up to this weekend?"

"Oh, he's at our house in Kiawah." She shakes her head in disapproval. "Can't get that man off the golf course. I told you we have that issue in Burlington needing attention. I suppose I'll have to get Darren to handle it."

"He'll handle it fine. Darren's been with the business since I was in high school." Chad returns to me. "Sorry, my parents own some shipping companies—"

"Logistics." His mother corrects him.

"Sorry, my family is in *logistics*. My father insists we use the correct terminology." His smile is already exhausted, and I really want to slip my hand in his.

I'm kind of starting to understand why Chad wanted to move to Oceanside. He left his overbearing relatives in Charleston. Sadly, mine are right here hanging over me—or one of them, at least.

"Here you go." Kyle is back, handing out the drinks. "And are we ready to order?"

"I haven't even looked at this. Charles, would you mind ordering for me?" His mother hands him her folded menu.

"I can help if you want." I lean forward, smiling. "I used to work here… a couple years ago."

I realize my error as the words leave my mouth.

"Is that so?" His mother gives me a look I know means trouble. "Were you the manager?"

"Um, no." I shift in my seat wishing I'd never opened my mouth. "I was a waitress."

"Ah." She smiles, but I know a fake smile when I see it. "A waitress."

The way she says it, you'd think I was a hooker.

Her eyes go to her son, but Chad looks at the menu instead. "What do you suggest, Tabby?"

I look down and give my best opinion based on two years ago. "Well, their blue crab bisque is delicious for a start, and as a main course, you can't go wrong with the surf and turf. They serve it with grilled shrimp. Or if you don't want a steak, you would probably love the crab claws du jour. They're usually grilled and served with a light butter sauce and blanched asparagus."

His mother turns to me with her eyebrows raised. "Sounds like you were very good at your job."

She's being condescending, and I shrug, flipping my menu closed. "It paid the bills."

"That all sounds great." Chad, by contrast, is not being condescending. He returns my smile, and it calms my stomach a bit. "I'll have the surf and turf. Mom, you want the crab claws?"

"Whatever you think dear." She pats his hand, and I barf a little in my mouth.

He moves his hand away, taking her menu and handing both to the waiter. Then he looks at me with something like an apology in his expression. I'm wondering why he invited me tonight. His mom's a judgy bitch. He should've known she'd hate me. I guess he needed a buffer?

"I'll have the bisque to start and a crab salad." Kyle makes a note.

"A bottle of sauvignon blanc for the table." Chad adds at the last minute.

More alcohol might not be a good idea. I'm still working on my martini, doing my best not to slug it.

"How did—" Chad starts, but his mother's laser eyes are on me again.

She interrupts. "So Tabitha, who are your people?"

My martini is halfway to my lips. "My people?" I take a quick sip as I try to figure out how in the world to answer that question. "I'm not really sure."

"Tabby's uncle is the Reverend Green. He's pastor of the church in Oceanside."

"Her uncle? And what about your mother and father? Let her speak, Charles."

While the martini is still at my mouth, I just go ahead and take another, bigger sip. No point being something I'm not.

"I have no idea who my father is, but my mother ran off and left me when I'd just turned three. Uncle Bob raised me after that, but I didn't care for his nonstop God talk. I moved into the old parson's cottage when I turned sixteen, and I've been taking care of myself ever since."

Chad's lips press into a grin, and his mother leans back in her chair crossing her arms. "Is that so? And how does a sixteen year-old girl take care of herself?"

I don't like how she asks that question. "Turning tricks, of course."

Take that, Evelyn Tucker. I've been handling bitches like you all my life.

A loud laugh explodes from across the table, and I drink a little more gin. "She's only joking, Mom."

"About which part?" His mother glares at me, and I don't even crack a smile.

"Tabby's a small business woman. She's an entrepreneur like you and dad."

The woman's eyes narrow. "What's the business?"

I'm about to say prostitutes when Chad answers first. "Website design. She's pretty damn good at it, too."

"Language, Charles. Please."

Oh, smell the roses. Thankfully our starters are here.

Kyle puts the soup in front of me and two small salads in front of Chad and his mother. "Shredded parmesan? Cracked pepper?"

"No." His mother is curt, but Kyle is doing a great job in my opinion.

I put on my friendliest manner. "I'll have some pepper."

He takes care of us and then he's gone again. Back to the inquisition.

"So you design websites." His mother nods, taking another bite of salad. "Anything I've seen?"

"Have you ever visited Pornhub?"

Evelyn's lips tighten, and our eyes clash. I've had it with her bullshit.

Chad only shakes his head. "She just launched a major travel site called Travel Time."

I'm surprised he remembered the name. I break the ice-cold staring match I'm having with his mother and give him a warm smile. "You remembered."

"Of course I did."

That little exchange gets her attention. She puts her napkin beside her plate. "I don't care for coarse humor. Perhaps I should return to your apartment, Charles."

Chad's expression is startled, and now I feel like an ass. I'm ruining the evening, and I don't mean to. It's just my mouth...

"I'm sorry, Mrs. Tucker," I say quickly. "I didn't mean to offend you. Please stay for your dinner. I can leave if you'd prefer."

"Tabby, no." Chad reaches out to catch my hand.

I love feeling his warm hand around mine. His mother's eyes go to that connection, and she pauses. I see the change in her expression, and I'm not sure if it's a good thing or a bad thing.

Kyle is back with a busboy and all our food, and she takes the napkin, returning it to her lap. We're all served, the wine opening ritual is performed, and finally we're alone again with our entrées and glasses of wine. I kind of hope we can eat in silence, but I'm pretty sure that won't happen.

Chad takes a bite of his steak and sits back, giving me a wink. "This is delicious. Great call, Tabby." He smiles, and that dimple I love appears.

Evelyn seems to get her second wind. "Nan asked about you the other day."

Chad's brow furrows and he shifts in his seat, clearing his throat. "Okay."

I'd taken a few bites of salad, but the way Chad is acting now makes my stomach tight.

I know I shouldn't ask, but I can't help myself. "Is Nan your grandmother?"

His mother laughs, and it sounds a little like breaking crystal. "Nan is from one of the oldest families in Charleston."

"Cool." I put my fork down and lift my wine glass.

"It's just someone I dated." Chad's fork is on his plate as well, and my favorite dimple is gone. Now the muscle in his jaw is moving.

"Dated!" Evelyn picks up her wine glass and takes a sip. "Why, she and Charles were engaged to be married before he left for Africa."

Oh. Nodding, I put my hands in my lap. Of course, he was. The star quarterback, captain of the football team, Mr. Graduated with Honors. I can just imagine the blonde Barbie type in a St. John suit and pearls holding his arm. I bet she was perfect for him, too.

"That's nice." I don't know what else to say.

Chad acts disinterested, but engaged? That's kind of major. "Tell her I hope she's well."

"She's not well. She's as confused as all of us are about what you're doing here being a sheriff's deputy." Evelyn takes another sip of wine. "I'll be glad when you get this nonsense out of your system and come home where you belong."

Poor Kyle ventures up to the table at that moment. "Can I get you anything else?"

"Just the check, please." An edge is in Chad's voice now.

"What?" His mother cries. "So soon?"

"I'm ready." I can't look at him.

My eyes are hot, and I feel small and foolish. I wonder when he'll wake up and realize she's right. Why would anybody give up all the money and prestige she's describing to stay in this silly town with me?

No one ever has before.

I really should accept Rani and AJ's offer and get the hell out of here.

"You're awfully quiet, Tabitha." Why is this woman talking to me again? "Thinking about your web designs?"

Blinking fast, that strength in me rears her head. I might be a nobody bastard-orphan with no pedigree or prestige, but I've never liked bullies. And I've never backed down from one.

"Actually, I was thinking about my next job. I think I just made a decision about it."

Chad's eyes meet mine. "What is it?"

I blink away from him, focusing on Evelyn. "Travel Time offered a job as a sort-of quality-control travel-scout for their company. They liked the website so much, they want me to be their woman in the field, testing existing packages and finding new ones."

"When does it start?" Chad's expression is even darker now, but my eyes are focused on the stem of my wine glass.

"They're just waiting on me to make a decision.

It's sort of a dream come true for me. They'll send me to the most exotic locations... The Great Blue Hole in Belize or Blue Lake, which is a true mystery. Divers have never found the bottom."

"That sounds terrifying," Chad's mother exclaims, and I don't miss the change in her voice. She sounds almost thrilled to learn I'm headed to the far corners of the Earth.

"I think it sounds amazing." My voice is quieter. "And it's a great deal. All I have to pay for are my meals."

"When did this happen?" Chad is not thrilled. He sounds really mad.

"It just came up this week. After the soft launch."

"Here's your check!" Kyle puts a little black tray on the table. "Thank you for joining us tonight at the Blue Crab! I hope you'll come back again soon!"

"We had a delightful time, thank you, Carl. You were a delight." Evelyn touches our waiter's arm, and I slide my chair back.

"Thanks so much for dinner." I'm talking fast, needing to go before I get pulled into anything more involving Chad's mother. "I'm so sorry, but I have to get back to my place. I have some work to finish tonight."

"Oh, I'm sorry to hear that." Evelyn's voice sounds the exact opposite of sorry. "It was nice meeting you, Tabitha."

"Nice meeting you." I dare a glance at Chad, but he's signing the check. "Thanks again."

Turning on my heel, I head for the door before anyone can stop me. My hand is on the glass when I hear his voice calling for me to wait. I can't do that. I've got to get back to my place and call Rani and AJ before I change my mind.

Chapter 21

Chad

I hustle my mother out of the restaurant and into her Lexus. The only thing on my mind is getting her back to my apartment and getting to Tabby's place. Tonight did not go how I'd expected at all. I'm not sure what I expected, but it wasn't Tabby dropping a bombshell like that and walking out.

The Blue Crab is all the way at the end of the strip, but since it's the off-season, traffic is light. I fight the urge to speed home, only because I know I can't. I'm sure Jimmy fucking Rhodes would be waiting in his Uber to let Robbie know.

And I guess I am supposed to be setting a good example in the community.

My mother hasn't stopped talking even though my mind is miles away. Returning my focus to what she's saying, I catch the last part.

"...and after everything we've been through. I don't know how you could get involved with a girl like that." Her voice is sharp.

My fists tighten on the steering wheel, and my jaw clenches. "A girl like what?"

In my peripheral, I see her head snap toward me. "A girl just like Charity. She's out of control. Did you hear the way she spoke to me?"

I heard her.

At the time, I thought it was pretty fucking funny. Now my stomach is in knots at the thought I might lose her, and I don't have patience for my mom's bullshit.

Clearing my throat, I manage to speak calmly. "Tabby is nothing like Charity."

My sister acted out because she was desperately unhappy and not strong enough to stand up for herself. I'm beginning to understand her more.

"That's what you think." My mother continues in her superior tone. "I know a wild girl when I see one."

"Tabby's not wild." I was wrong to listen to the gossip and pre-judge her that way. "Tabby doesn't take shit from anybody. She stands up for herself. Cherry would never do that. She would only make bad choices." *Or do more drugs.*

"Don't talk about your sister that way." My mother's voice goes shrill. "How could you say bad things about her now that she's gone? Are you deliberately trying to hurt me?"

She looks down, and I glance over at her. I can't tell if she's crying, and I'm not trying to hurt her. I can't understand what it would be like to lose a child, but I do know her overbearing nature ultimately was too much for my sister.

"I'm not trying to hurt you." I take a breath and adjust my tone.

I don't want to fight with my mother or make her cry. I just want her to stop trying to manipulate me. Cherry is gone, and I'm not looking to take her place.

"What made you decide to come for a visit? Was it really to see me or was it to try and make me come back to Charleston?"

208

She sniffs and shakes her hair back. "A little of both, I guess. I wanted to see you, to know you're okay."

"I'm okay. I'm actually better than okay. I really like living here. I like my job..." I like Tabitha Green. Maybe a little too much too soon.

"I don't believe that. You're a Charleston man, and it's time for you to act like it. You have a place in society and a responsibility to your family. We need you at home. I want my son back." Her chin goes down again, and my brows furrow.

What new line of bullshit is this? "I haven't been home in almost ten years."

"That doesn't mean you can't come home now. Nan is still available. She understands you broke things off because you were upset about Cherry."

"Did you tell her that?" Now my hackles really are up.

"Only because it's true. If you came back now, everything could be like it was before you left."

It's taking all my effort not to go off on her. I'm holding back because I know she'll just shut down, and I want her to hear me for once. "Mom, I don't want that life. It's why I left."

We're back at my place, and I put her car in park. Fuck trying to reason with a crazy person. I hustle around to help her out. She moves at her own pace, and I exhale a little growl.

"I'm sorry I don't move as fast as I used to," she grumbles.

I don't answer. I walk her to the top of the stairs then dash to my room to change into a dark gray tee while she gets herself settled on the couch. I offered her my bed, but she refused — something about not wanting to intrude. *Irony.*

"I'll see you in the morning." I grab the keys to my truck and lean down to kiss the top of her head. "Help yourself to anything."

"Where are you going?" Her voice rises.

"I have to talk to Tabby."

"Charles! Do not go over there!"

She's still yelling, but I'm out the door and in my truck, again doing my best not to break all the rules of the road as I cover the distance between us.

When I finally get to Tabby's place, the lights are off, but I see the glow of her computer screen in the living room. I throw the truck in park and jump out, jogging up to her door.

"Tabby?" I knock… a little too hard. "Tabby, it's me. Open up."

She says something on the other side, and the door opens fast, causing me to lean forward slightly. She's standing in front of me in that same silk romper, but the jewelry is gone. Her feet are bare, and her long hair is gathered into a messy bun on her head with a pencil stuck through it. I know what that means.

"Sorry to bother you while you're working." I try giving her my signature grin.

Slender arms cross over her waist, and she's not smiling. "What are you doing here? Don't you have a house guest?"

"Ahh, yeah. About that." I rub my chin. "My mom can be a bit much."

"Ya think?"

"She wanted to know why I like it here." *I wanted to show her my top reason.* "I didn't think it through."

I wanted to see her so much tonight, I'd have done anything.

Dropping my arm off the doorjamb, I hesitate. I want to pull her to my chest and kiss her. I want to bury my face in her neck and inhale the sweet scent of her perfume. Somehow, I get the feeling that might not go over so well.

I clear my throat. "Anyway, I was curious about the job you mentioned. What's that about?"

Her lips press together, and she frowns. "That's none of your business."

"It's not? I thought we were going to those places together." I motion between the two of us.

"That was all just pillow talk."

"It was more than that."

"Who's Nan?" Her eyes flash.

Straightening, I clear my throat. "Nan is... Nancy Miller."

"Why is she waiting for you?"

I exhale a growl. "She is not waiting for me."

Tabby steps out onto the front porch and closes the door behind her. "But you were engaged to her?"

"It was a long time ago."

"How long?"

"A year? More than a year. As long as I've been here."

Her arms are still crossed, and she's showing no signs of thawing. "So like right before you came here?"

"Yes, but to be fair, I'd just gotten out of the service. I'd been gone, and when I came back, I ended it with her."

Tabby's lips tighten, and I can see her mind working. "So you came home and broke her heart after being engaged to her for at least four years?"

"I didn't break her heart."

"No one stays engaged that long and doesn't have her heart broken."

"We never saw each other. It should've ended long ago." Stepping to the side, I rub the back of my neck. "Why does this even matter?"

"Because you were engaged for more than four years." She takes a step to the other side, away from me. "I told you about Travis, and he was just a douchebag I wasted six weeks on. You were with a girl you wanted to marry, to spend your life with. What other secrets are you keeping, *Charles*?"

"Nobody calls me that but my mother." *Who I'd like to strangle...*

Her voice grows louder. "It's another thing I didn't know."

"I'm sure it would've come up eventually. Tabby, listen to me. Nan and I were high school sweethearts. I felt like I had to propose to her before I went overseas because it's what they all expected of us. Not because we were in love. It was because that's what they wanted."

"Are you so sure that's how she felt? You were off on a boat."

"I'm sure."

She shakes her head. "You have this whole other life in Charleston—"

"A life I don't want. I never wanted it. The pressure, the expectations... I hated it."

It killed my sister... The unwelcome thought drifts through my mind.

Tabby's voice is quiet. "You say that, but it's all still back there waiting, unresolved. What happens when you realize one day that's where you belong?"

"Nothing. Because it's not going to happen!" Now I'm shouting.

This whole fucking night is pissing me off—this argument included.

Tabby's eyes widen slightly and she returns to her door. "I need to think about it."

"A million miles away?" My voice is still raised. "Do you know how dangerous blue holes are? They're called diver cemeteries. And you're going to go there alone?"

"They're not all like that." Her voice gets louder, matching mine. "Anyway, I've never let fear stop me from doing anything."

"Fear can be a healthy emotion if it's telling you not to do something that could get you killed."

"Stop bossing me around!"

We're standing on her front porch shouting at each other.

I take a step back, take a few breaths, lower my voice. "You're doing this because of your uncle. Emberly told me what he said."

"Bob Green's approval is usually a red flag in my experience. Seems it still is."

"Don't do this." My jaw is clenched again. "Don't shut us down because of what he said. You know what we have is special."

"I thought it was. Then I found out how much I didn't know."

"You know everything that matters." I take a step toward her. I want to hold her, kiss her. Everything would change if I could just kiss her.

Her back is to the door, and she shakes her head. "I don't like secrets. I don't like feeling like you're living a double life. I don't like feeling like you have all these unresolved feelings and one day you could just leave. I can't let you..."

"Tabby, all I want is you." My hands are on the door, one palm on each side of her head, and I have her caged. "I want you."

Leaning down, I'm just about to take her lips when she opens the door and goes inside. It slams in my face, and I place my forehead against the wood. I know she's right on the other side, and my chest aches at this barrier between us.

"Tabby..." My voice is loud enough for her to hear me if she's there.

She doesn't answer, and I have to walk away.

* * *

The Tuna Tiki is crowded for the off-season, but I don't care. I don't even look around at the Friday night revelers. I lean on the bar and order another whiskey. It's my fourth.

"You know Jimmy Rhodes is the only Uber driver in Oceanside County right now." Robbie Cole's familiar voice pulls me away from my drink. He's smiling gently. "What's on your mind, cowboy?"

"Women." I lean heavily on the bar.

He chuckles and sits next to me, signaling the bartender. "I'll have a Coke."

The bartender nods and turns away.

I give him a glance. He's dressed in jeans and a Hawaiian shirt. "What are you doing here on a Friday night? I thought you were on duty."

"Just finished having dinner with my family. I told them to head on back to the house when I saw you." He takes a sip of Coke, and I take a sip of whiskey. "Did you drive your truck up here?"

I nod and he nods in response. "Figured I could give you a ride home. Then check in at the station."

I don't answer. I'm feeling the alcohol, although it's not taking the edge off my anger.

He gives me a wink. "You don't look like you're up for a ride home from Jimmy."

My jaw clenches, and a growl is in my throat. "You ever wish you could stop being a sheriff... just for five minutes?"

That gets me a real laugh. "All the time, friend. All the time." He puts a hand on my shoulder. "It'll pass the longer you're here."

We're quiet a moment. Music filters around us. I can't stop thinking about tonight, all that went down.

"How'd dinner with your mom and Tabby go?"

"About like you'd expect." I rest my elbow on the bar, rubbing my eyes with one hand.

"That good?" He chuckles again. "Tabby Green is something else. She always has been. I saw your mom earlier today. She hasn't changed much."

"Never truer words..."

He looks down at his drink. "How's your dad doing?"

"I don't know. The same I guess."

Robbie sits back, holding his soft drink. "Your family's been dealt a heavy blow. I can't imagine losing a child. Be patient with your folks. If you can."

"Mom's trying to get me to move back to Charleston." My eyes are on the half-full tumbler.

"How do you feel about that?"

"Nothing interests me less."

Robbie rests both arms on the bar and exhales deeply. "You went into the service right after it happened. Then you came straight here after getting out... If you need to take a few days, go back there and check on things, see how you feel, we could arrange that."

Tabby's words are in my head. *It's all still back there unresolved...*

And she is right here unresolved.

———

"This isn't like you, Chad." Robbie's hand is on my shoulder again. "You've come a long way this year, and you're always in control. It's impressive."

"I'm in love with her." I can't believe I said it out loud. Clearly, I'm drunk. *Fuck*.

"With Tabby?" He sits back.

"I'm an idiot. It'll never work."

"Hm... I don't know." He rubs his chin as he thinks. "Why not?"

My stomach is tight, and I don't know how to answer him. I want Tabby more than I've ever wanted any woman. It has to work. I'll make it work.

I realize he's waiting, and I clear my throat. "I don't know. Maybe it will."

"Okay, then." Robbie grins, sliding off his stool. "Now that that's off your chest. Let's head on home. I need to check in at the station, and you need to get some rest."

He's right. I've had too much to drink. My head's a mess, and now that I've said it, I'm ready to sleep. I'm also ready to make this right, and I'm going to start by going back to Charleston.

Then I'm coming back for what's mine.

Chapter 22

Tabby

I shut the door in Chad's face, sat on the floor in my living room with my back to it, and cried. It felt like somebody had pulled the thread on our relationship and all the guts had fallen out. All these things had been waiting to come crashing down, and boy did they.

From Uncle Bob's speech to Chad's horrible mom to the discovery of all the things… I feel like the rug got pulled out from under me.

Maybe it's unfair, since I kept trying to keep it casual between us — not too serious. We're oil and vinegar, right? We don't mix. We can't get serious.

Only I did. I seriously fell for him in a major way.

But we were playing different versions of the game, and somehow the tables turned when I wasn't looking. I fell in love, while he kept it casual. I told him everything, and he told me nothing. He simply went along for the ride…

And it hurts like hell.

I did not spend Saturday in bed.

Not all day, anyway.

Emberly texted me a few times, but I told her I was too busy working to chat, which was the truth. As a responsible businesswoman, I checked in with Travel Time to be sure everything was up and running properly—it was. Then I took a shower and washed my hair…

Then I wrapped it in a towel and lay in bed watching sad Nicolas Sparks movies all day. I started with *Safe Harbor* then *The Longest Ride*, *Dear John*… finishing with the ultimate cry into your ice cream film, *The Notebook*.

I'm wearing cooling eye pads when I call Emberly this morning.

"Why are you calling me so early on a Sunday?" Her voice is muffled, and I hear the noise of the mixer in the background. "Where were you all day yesterday? I tried to call… How did your date with Chad and his mom go?"

"Can you kill the twenty questions?" I flop on my bed staring at my closet. "His mother is a controlling shrew. Chad's real name is Charles, and he was engaged to some fem-bot named Nan right before he moved here."

"Shut the front door! You are kidding me." The whirring noise stops. "I can't see him as a Charles."

"He said only his mom calls him that. Are you going to church this morning?"

"Are *you* going to church this morning?" The shock in her voice makes me roll my eyes.

"It's time for one of my tithe Sundays, but I'm not going if you're not there."

"Yeah, explain that to me again? You go ten Sundays a year?"

"Good lord, did you fail math? Five. I go five Sundays a year."

"Because of the tithe." Her voice is muffled again. "I still don't understand."

"There's fifty two weeks in a year. Ten percent is five, so I go five Sundays a year."

"Technically, you should round up and go six."

"Did Uncle Bob put you on the payroll? Are you in league with Betty Pepper? Five is plenty." I step over to my closet, moving hangers as I inspect my dresses. "Are you going? It sounds like you're baking."

"I'm making white monster number two cupcakes." Her voice is warm with pride.

"What the hell is a white monster number two cupcake?"

"Coco has the best preschool teacher this year. She's teaching them colors, numbers, and even Spanish with these monsters every week. Last week it was green monster number one, *uno*. This week it's *dos*, and I told her I'd make a cupcake for it. I'm making coconut cream with white chocolate frosting and a big two."

"Coco is the only kid I've ever heard of who eats coconut." I settle on a demure, fitted beige dress that hangs mid-calf. I have no idea if Chad will be there or his mother.

"I liked coconut when I was a child."

"So are you going?"

"I'll see you in an hour! I'll need to run these by Mamma's first so they don't melt."

An hour later, I'm waiting at the door to the sanctuary for Emberly to show up. Everyone's inside, and I don't miss Chad's truck parked down the lane in one of the spaces. I can only guess that means Evelyn went home, as I doubt she'd ride in an old silver step-side.

"Sorry. The door was locked, and I had to climb the tree into my old bedroom. I was a mess. I ended up having to scrub my knees…"

"We almost missed the song service." I grab her hand just as I pull the heavy, squeaky door open.

"Why they don't oil this thing." I murmur under my breath as everyone in the sanctuary turns to stare at us.

"And not shame the latecomers?" She murmurs back.

Looking down, away from their shocked eyes, I scoot into the closest empty seats just as the final hymn ends. Emberly and I sit, but right before my butt hits the cushion, my eyes land on Chad—sitting with Daisy Sales!

"Oh!" It's like the word jumps right out of my mouth on its own.

My eyes are locked on her hand touching his forearm. He's holding her program and her Bible, and it looks exactly like they're here together.

I can't move. All the blood drains from my face, and in the space of two seconds, my heart feels like it shrivels inside my chest. It goes to the size of a prune, then it shrivels tighter to the size of a raisin.

Chad's eyes are confused as they hold mine, and something's violently jerking on my arm. I snap out of it when I realize I'm the only one still standing with Emberly trying to get me to sit.

I drop into my seat, tucking my chin and blinking fast. I mouth the words, *Oh my God*, without saying them out loud, Emberly's hand goes into mine, and I know she heard me even if I didn't speak.

Even my uncle's shouting isn't loud enough to cut through the roaring in my ears. I just have to get through thirty more minutes and the final prayer, then I can run out the door, all the way back to my house.

In my mind, it's like Travis all over again. It's walking around behind Emberly's bakery and seeing Daisy up against the wall with Travis between her legs sticking his tongue down her throat.

Okay, it's not as bad as that, but it sure feels that way. What the hell is he doing holding her shit and helping her take her seat in church? Why is she touching his arm like there's something between them? What the fuck is up with that girl going after my man?

Emberly nudges my arm with her elbow, and I look down to see she's written in the margin of her program. *I'm sure there's a logical explanation.*

My lips tighten, and my nose gets hot. I take the tiny pencil and scribble back, *So I'm not crazy to be upset?*

I press my elbow into her ribs and slide the program back. She looks down and reads then slowly shakes her head no.

I take it back and add one more question, *Does he sit with her every Sunday?*

Her lips press together, and she takes the little pencil out of my hands. *I haven't really noticed. I'm sorry.*

A painful knot is in my throat, and it has never taken my uncle this long to make us all feel like hellbound sinners. Finally, he instructs us to bow our heads while God examines our hearts for secret sins.

I don't even care anymore. I stand and slip out of the pew in front of my best friend. Then I walk to the back door and push it open. It lets out a loud screech, and when I step out the door, a warm breeze pushes past my shoulders. I keep on walking, all the way home.

Chapter 23

Chad

The minute Bob Green says Amen, I'm ready to bolt.

Daisy stands, holding my arm like we're on some kind of date. *We're not.*

She called the station this morning saying her car wouldn't start. Since I was standing outside after seeing my mother off, Robbie asked if I'd swing by and pick her up on my way.

I wasn't planning to attend the service. I'd told my mother I'd be home tonight for supper. As I expected, she was thrilled—and a bit smug, as if she'd won some sort of victory. She offered to wait for me, but I'd already rented a car. I made an excuse that I needed to be sure Robbie had everything under control.

There's no way in hell I'd go back to Charleston without my own transportation. I need to be able to leave when it's time to come back, and I don't intend to be gone more than a few days. I know my mother and her ways—she'd invent excuse after excuse to keep me there for good.

So I hung around a bit longer to drive Daisy to church. I also wanted to try and see my girl one more time before I left.

Not like this.

What the hell was she doing in church this morning?

"I don't think I've ever enjoyed a service more." Daisy's soft voice is at my shoulder. I turn from straining my eyes down the road after Tabby to studying the young woman holding my arm. "We just have to wait for Melody to be let out of Sunday school. Penelope usually gets her and her little sister Polly and Coco for us."

"Sure." We're down the short flight of steps, heading to where Emberly is glaring daggers at me from beside Betty Pepper. *It's not what you think!*

"Would you like to stay for lunch? I'm just having chicken, but—"

"Hey, would you mind if I let Bucky drive you home?"

We both speak at the same time, and her nose immediately curls. I know—Bucky Pepper smells like formaldehyde. He's a taxidermist. He's also a bit odd.

"I just need to run a quick errand—"

"It's true, isn't it." She looks down at her hands. "You're really serious about Tabby Green."

"You didn't know?" I thought the whole town knew after my truck was parked outside her house that night.

"I guess I don't get out much." She glances up at me. Round hazel eyes, hair the color of straw. Daisy's sweet, but she's not my Tabby. "Jimmy Rhodes keeps saying how you're trying to steal his girl."

"Jimmy Rhodes." It's a part-growl, part-annoyed response.

"Tabby's so quirky, I thought... well, you always check in on Melody and me, making sure we're okay. It seemed like..."

My shoulders drop, and I do my best to say this as kindly as possible. "Did you think this was a date?"

Her cheeks flame pink. "Of course not! You're just being neighborly... Or a good Samaritan or officer of the law. Or—"

"Robbie asked me if I'd give you a ride this morning." I put a hand on her arms. "I do check on you and Melody. I also check on Emberly and Coco. I didn't mean to give you the wrong idea. I'm sorry—"

Her lips press together, and she nods fast. "Thank you so much for your help this morning, Deputy Tucker. I'll see if Donna White can give me a ride. I'm sure she can."

She trots off across the church lawn before I can finish apologizing, and I don't have time to feel bad about it. I hustle to my truck and take off in the direction of Tabby's house.

When I arrive, everything is just like it's been the whole last week—locked up tight as Fort Knox.

Lifting my fist, I knock loudly. "Tabby, open up. It's me. I need to talk to you."

I'm getting to know the outside of this door too well.

"What do you want?" It opens fast, and I take a surprised step back when I see her. Mascara is smeared at her eyes, and her nose is pink from crying.

Panic hits my chest. "What's wrong? Are you okay?"

She sniffs loudly, but anger flashes at me. "Why do you keep coming here? Go sniff around some other girl's door."

Even with her anger, her tears are like shards of glass in my stomach. I can't believe she's crying. I've never seen her cry. "I wanted to talk to you. I have to go—"

She holds up a finger. "I'm just going to stop you right there, Chad Tucker, because I have something to say to you."

"Okay…"

"I don't know what the hell is going on between you and Daisy Sales, but I think she's just perfect for you." That slim finger is pointing at my chest now.

"You do?"

"You want some law-abiding family girl, someone who's meek and easy to control? Well, she's it. You can keep her barefoot and pregnant right here in this crummy little town, and I'm sure the two of you will be very happy."

"Tabby, that's not what—"

"I'm not finished!" Her voice gets louder, and I hold up my hands. "You are not to come here anymore. I don't want to see you. I don't want to hear the seductive words coming out of your mouth. I don't want to smell your…" She waves a hand between us. "Whatever that smell is that smells so good."

"You like how I smell?" For the first time in a week, the tension in my chest breaks. She likes the way I smell… My words are seductive? It's like the sun rising over the ocean. She's in love with me, and I'm a fucking blind-assed idiot.

"Don't change the subject!"

"Are you finished?" My voice is gentler now, and she crosses her arms, glaring at me with watery eyes. She's so beautiful when she's feisty like this. "Stop crying."

I reach out to wipe her eyes, and she pushes my hand away. "Stop bossing me around."

"I can't help it. It's who I am." I want to gather her to my chest and kiss those tears away. My arms ache for her. "Seems like you used to like me bossing you around."

She lets that pass. "Why are you here?"

"For starters, I'm sorry I raised my voice Friday night. I overreacted."

Her fury softens a notch. "We were both yelling."

"Still…" I think about what I'm about to say. "Tell me about your job. When does it start?"

"I told you it's none of your business."

I want to say everything about her is my business. I don't.

"Just tell me—how soon do they want you to start?"

Her arms uncross, and she looks away. "I don't know. It was pretty out of the blue. They liked the website so much, they asked if I'd like to join their team. I told them I'd have to think about it."

"So you haven't told them yes?" I take a step closer.

"No, but I'm going to." Green eyes flash at me. "I just haven't had a chance to get back to them."

"You said they offered you the job after the soft launch. That was on Wednesday. Why didn't you say yes to them then?"

She shrugs and looks away again. "It's not good business to say yes that fast. It makes you seem too eager."

The warmth in my chest grows stronger. I'm not buying a word she just said. She didn't tell them yes because she's going to those places with me.

But I'll play along. "How long will they wait for an answer?"

Her brow furrows, and she pinches those full lips together. "I don't know. Why are you asking so many questions?"

"Don't tell them anything until I talk to you again. Will you do that for me?"

"Are you trying to control me? Trying to put me in handcuffs again? It didn't work, remember? It was a sign."

"A sign I need better handcuffs." Her eyes narrow, and I put my hands on her waist, holding her closer.

I don't care if she's mad at me, I want to touch her, make her stop being so damn stubborn. Only… it's her stubbornness I love.

"Will you just do this for me? Wait until I see you again before making any permanent decisions?"

"What does that even mean?"

Leaning down, I steal a kiss. It's a quick one—just a parting hit off those sweet, sweet lips, no tongue. I know I'm supposed to ask permission first, but the little whimper in her exhale lets me know she isn't offended.

When I lean up, her eyes blink open slowly, and I give her a grin. "It means wait for me."

Chapter 24

Tabby

Just like that, Chad Tucker leaves town without a word.

It takes me a few days of holding my breath to realize he isn't checking in at the bakery like he usually does. Emberly doesn't bring him up. I won't say his name, and I'm sure as hell not about to text him. I have my pride.

The bruises on my wrists are almost completely faded, and every time I see those pale yellow marks, my insides ache. I miss Chad. I miss Andy.

I make it to Wednesday until I finally break down and ask.

"Robbie said he went back to Charleston." Emberly's rolling out fondant to cover the Queen of Heart's dress for Melody's birthday cake.

Me and my big mouth. "Did he say for how long?"

"I'm not sure he knows."

"He has to know." I mutter, standing back to look at the Alice in Wonderland masterpiece my friend has created. "Daisy's lucky I don't stab this cake right through the middle."

"Don't you dare!" Emberly cries. "That would be hurting me and Melody, not her."

"I know, I'm only fantasizing." My arms are crossed and I walk back to the table where she's working. "What is her deal, anyway? I tried to bury the hatchet, and she goes after my man again."

Emberly leans down to cut diamond shapes all over the now-flat white paste. "Technically, you had broken things off with Chad." She straightens and holds her lower back a minute. "Were you ever even officially together?"

"Yes!" I answer fast, although Emberly has a point.

We only went on two official dates—the church fair was sort-of forced by Betty Pepper, and it ended up being annoying as hell. Then after our brunch, it pretty much turned into a week-long fuck-fest. My elbow is on the table, and I rest my chin on my hand, remembering those days. We were insatiable, stealing every moment we could get. In the ocean, in his cruiser, on my desk…

"What impure thoughts are you having right now?" Emberly is leaning over the diamond pattern again, but she's looking up at me with a grin. "Your cheeks have gone all pink."

I sit up straight on my stool. "I'm not thinking about anything!" It's a lie. I was daydreaming about riding Andy and how good it feels.

The bell over the door rings, and as if it couldn't get worse, Jimmy Rhodes saunters in wearing that black leather jacket and jeans with his motorcycle boots. He walks right up to where I'm sitting and stops, doing a bangs swish.

"What's wrong with you?" I ask, crossing my arms just in case he has any ideas.

"I came to tell you goodbye, girl. I'm heading out."

Emberly straightens and hurries over to where he's standing. "Jimmy! Did you get the money? Are you going to Glendale?"

He straightens, swagger gone, and gives my best friend a big smile. "I got it. I'm heading out today. Just finished packing."

Frowning, I look back and forth between them. "Get what? What's in Glendale?"

Jimmy whips his face around and gives me a smolder. "College. Will you miss me?"

"Eh..." I don't want to be mean, but my nose wrinkles involuntarily. "I think it's really great that you're continuing your education."

"I helped him write a grant," Emberly explains. "He's studying auto mechanics so he can start his own small business one day."

My eyebrows shoot up, and I nod. "Cool. Good work, Jimmy."

"You can call me Blade." He does a little head twitch. "Sorry we never got the timing right, boo."

"Not your boo."

Emberly pats his arm in a motherly way. "I'm really proud of you. I bet you'll make a great mechanic one day."

"Maybe I'll come back here and open a garage." He walks slowly to the door. "Maybe down by the filling station."

"That sounds like a great idea!" Emberly is too encouraging in my opinion.

"Oh, and Tabby." He points at me, and my eyebrows rise. "I give you my blessing to see the deputy."

"Your blessing?"

He nods. "I think he really likes you. I'm sure he'll be a better man once he gets a handle on that drinking problem."

"Chad does not have a drinking problem!"

"Whatever you say, girl. Just remember, denial is more than a river in Egypt." He pulls the door open and does a little finger salute at us. "Later, hot potatoes."

The door closes, and Emberly and I explode with laughing.

"What the hell was he doing? Poor man's James Dean?" I give her a finger salute. "Later, hot putater."

"He gives you his blessing," she calls, returning to the fondant.

"I'm so relieved." The truth is I'm antsy as hell.

Ever since yesterday, all I can think about is Chad's last visit. The stolen kiss that curled my toes and melted my panties. The dimple in his cheek when he grinned, and the heat radiating from his eyes. It was pure possession, and no matter what I said, he knew he had me.

Wait for me…

Jesus, my butterflies have butterflies remembering the way he said those words.

"If you can take a break from daydreaming, come help me lift this fondant over the queen's skirt."

I hop off the stool and walk over to lift the opposite side of the soft, white pastry covering. I hold up my side as she quickly wraps it around the upside down triangle that formed the skirt.

Stepping back, I watch as she smooths and cuts it, careful not to ruin the perfect diamond design she made all over it. "I'll just go back and paint the diamonds red and black."

"This really is an amazing cake. Let me take pictures of it for the website."

"Of course!" She looks over her shoulder at me, then her eyes go wide. "Oh, hell, look what time it is! Would you mind picking up Coco from preschool for me?"

I glance up at the clock to see it's almost three. "Sure. Want me to bring her back here?"

"No, she's staying with Mamma a few more weeks. It still gets too hot at night for her to be comfortable here with me."

"I don't know how you stand it." Emberly's loft apartment over our heads gets hot as blazes by the end of the day with no air conditioning. "You know you can come and crash with me if you need to."

"I know." She takes a step back and looks around, over her head. "But I turn the ceiling fans on high and leave the French doors open. The heat breaks eventually, and I like being here, even when it's the dog days. Makes me feel one step closer to having it all."

"You'll get there."

She gives me a warm smile as she takes down the small glass bowl she uses to mix colors. "Better hurry. Mamma wants to go to prayer meeting tonight."

"I swear, that woman has Coco in church every time the door is open, poor thing."

"She doesn't want her to turn out like us."

"What's wrong with us?"

"Oh! Hang on." Emberly puts the black mixture down and hops over to the refrigerator. "While you're out, run this down to the Blue Crab. They ordered a cheesecake for desserts." She takes out an oversized box.

"Hey, that's awesome! Only… I was thinking I'd just take the bike."

I was secretly hoping a little exercise would ease the pain of missing Chad.

"So take the bike! I do it all the time." She picks up the bowl of black food coloring and a paintbrush and returns to the queen.

"It's like two miles! Come get me if I'm passed out on the side of the road."

She laughs, and I pull the door shut, balancing the cake box. Just as I turn, here comes Daisy Sales walking up the hill towards me.

When our eyes meet, her face goes white.

I put a hand on my hip. "Hello, Daisy."

She only hesitates a moment before she starts walking again. "Hi, Tabby. Is Emberly still inside?"

"Of course." I wait at the door until Daisy's reaches it, wondering if she'll try to say something for herself.

She only stands there, blinking down to her shoes. "You know…" She's speaking carefully, as if she's choosing her words. "Jimmy Rhodes has been my delivery boy for the last year."

"I know." I shift my position. "And Wyatt's and Betty's. What's the point?"

"He used to always talk about how you were his girl." She gives me a weak little smile. "He'd say, 'That Deputy Tucker keeps trying to steal my girl!'" She imitates his voice and exhales a little laugh when she finishes.

"Did you really believe I'd date a seventeen-year-old?" I'm not buying it.

"I thought he was eighteen." She shakes her head. "Anyway, between taking care of Melody and trying to run the shop, I don't get out much. Deputy Tucker would stop by every day and chat for a little while. He'd hold Melody and say how big she was getting, how cute she was."

"He stops in and chats with everybody—André, Betty, Wyatt, Emberly, Coco. He's getting to know the community, making sure everybody knows him and feels safe."

She nods. "I understand that now. I guess I was just feeling lonely, and he's so handsome…"

Damn you, Daisy Sales. "Look, I get feeling lonely, and I get you don't go out much. Stop going after my guys."

She blinks down fast again and nods. "I'm sorry. I really didn't know he was yours."

My lips tighten. I guess technically he wasn't… Still.

Our eyes meet, and hers are pleading. "Besides, Chad isn't like Travis. It didn't matter that I didn't know. He doesn't want anyone but you."

A pain twists in the middle of my stomach at her words. Now he's gone, and I don't even know for how long.

"Whatever, I have to go." I hurry down the steps to where Emberly's bike is chained in the alley. Before she leaves, I call back, "Now you know."

Our eyes meet, and she nods. I pull out the bike and push it towards the lane, standing in the pedals so I can pick up speed to get to Coco before her teacher charges me a dollar for being late.

* * *

It's after six when I return with Emberly's bike. I park it in the alley and put the chain on, carrying Coco's little helmet under my arm as I enter the shop. Instead of sugar and vanilla, the place smells like hair spray and Shalimar.

I know what that means.

Betty Pepper is standing by Emberly's table with a pimped-out Roxanne Philpot at her side. When Emberly sees me, she gives me a look that screams *Help!*

"Hey, BP, hey, Roxanne! What's new in the world of swinging singles?"

"Tabitha," Betty barks like a drill sergeant. "Come over here and get in on this. Roxanne has the best idea for getting more business in the store, and Emberly's dragging her feet."

"I don't know if I'd call it the best idea..." Emberly's voice sounds defeated.

"Stop being a prude, Emberly Rose. Your mother doesn't have to know everything you do. Besides, how often does she come in here anyway?"

As much as I don't like Marjorie Warren, BP has a point. Emberly's mom rarely visits, and it makes me sad, considering Emberly is my best friend and all. I know not having your mother's approval hurts. Even if your mother is the queen of all the judgy old biddies and constantly makes you feel like you're not living up to your "full potential." I wish Marjorie would get her head out of her ass.

At least she's sweet to Coco.

"So what's this great idea?" I look from Betty to Roxanne.

Roxanne Philpot stands with one hip cocked to the side. She's wearing hot pink pants and a white shirt with matching hot pink palm trees all over it. Her platinum hair is teased into a perfect bouffant around her head, and her glasses are purple frames with rose tinted lenses.

The only thing she's missing is a foot-long cigarette holder and a pink poodle.

"Well, as you know I just got back from my trip *abroad*." She says the word like it's code.

Betty leans in to me. "You should talk to Roxanne about getting her sex club island up on your travel site. Suggest that to your friends in Seattle."

"Sure, I'll suggest it." I have no intention of suggesting it.

Roxanne flashes her sparkling white veneers at me. "Oh, yes, honey. I have pictures and everything if you need them."

I also have no plans to mentally scar myself looking at pictures of a bunch of old people naked.

"You know, the clients really prefer to use stock photos—unless it's something I've taken myself. For legal reasons. Otherwise, we'd have to track everybody down, get them all to sign releases. Or blur out their faces, which makes it seem like we're hiding something…"

Hot pink lips twist into a frown. "Good lord, I don't know how all that stuff works. Anyway, so I was telling Emberly here one night while we were on the island, we were celebrating Antonio's birthday. Let me tell you, it was *wild*. We were all drinking champagne in our birthday suits, and when they carried out his cake, it was a giant penis!"

I almost swallow my gum. "A penis."

"Yes!" Roxanne starts to laugh. "It was the funniest thing I'd ever seen. I mean, it was perfectly decorated and very appropriate, if you know what I'm saying."

I'm almost afraid to ask. "So you're suggesting Emberly should start making penis cakes… for Hedonism?"

"No! Pfft. You silly girl." She waves her hand, rolling those heavily lashed eyes. "I'm talking about doing them here! For bachelorette parties or anniversary parties or girls' nights. Or hell, do we have any of *the gays* in Oceanside? I'm sure they'd just love a penis cake. The boy ones anyway."

Jesus, take the wheel. "You know, they always forget to wear their rainbow badges when they go out. Those silly gays."

Emberly snorts, but I'm holding my face steady. I've never met anybody so utterly clueless... Okay, that's not true. I look at the old lady salivating next to Roxanne.

"Never mind them. What do you think?" Betty Pepper is practically jumping up and down with glee.

"I think it's up to Emberly to decide if she wants to make penis cakes. Right here in town."

My best friend is shaking her head, and I just shake my head right back at her.

"I tell you what," she finally says. "If I get an order for a penis cake, I'll see if I can figure out how to make one. Until then, I'm not putting it on the regular list of options."

"Ha ha! There you go!" Betty slaps her hand on the table. "I told you she'd be open to the idea. Now we'll get you a little side business going, bringing in more money for you and Coco. You can charge extra for adult items."

"Thanks." Emberly's voice is the opposite of grateful. "Y'all have a good night now. Thanks for stopping by."

"Come on, Roxie, now that that's settled, we have to hurry. We're going to be late for church." Betty hurries to the door, but Roxanne stays beside me.

"You know, Tabitha," She places a manicured hand on my arm. "I've always thought you and I are a lot alike."

"Is that so?" I'm not sure where this is going.

She continues unfazed by my hesitance. "We're both independent ladies. Some might call us *bad girls* or

Jezebels, but they're small-minded twerps." She leans a little closer, surrounding me with Aqua-Net and Shalimar. "If you'd ever like to tag along with me on one of my trips, just say the word. I'd love a companion."

I can't even imagine. "Thank you, Ms. Roxanne. I'll remember that."

"Call me Roxie!" She straightens and heads to the door. "Goodnight, girls. Glad I could help out your business, Emberly."

The door closes, and Emberly snorts a laugh. "Next stop, Hedonism!"

"You'd better start shopping for new cake pans. I have the feeling a rash of penis cakes is headed your way."

"No!" Emberly's hands fly up to her face. "Don't say *rash* and *penis* in the same sentence."

That makes me laugh. "You know Betty Pepper is sitting in church dreaming of hers right now. I've never seen that old lady's eyes so bright."

"I confess, I'm intrigued." Emberly puts a hand on her hip. "I'd like to see if my skills are up to the challenge."

"You can do anything you set your mind to!" I hand over Coco's helmet and hug her goodnight. "See you tomorrow."

The exercise, the time with my best friend, even the suggestion I join the over-fifty crowd at Hedonism have all lifted my spirits.

As soon as I get home, though, it all evaporates.

I walk into my lonely cottage. It's quiet and my computer screen glows in the darkness. The Travel Time site is done, tested, debugged, and ready for its big launch tomorrow at midnight.

I have to make a decision about whether or not to take Rani and AJ's offer. Chad's words are on my mind. Hell, Chad is on my mind. He never leaves my mind. *What is he doing?*

Dropping onto my couch, I pull out my phone and stare at the blank face. Roxanne Philpot's offer echoes in my brain, and as much as my inner travel goddess recoils at the suggestion she and I are alike, it's kind of true.

She's thirty years older than me, but she has a unique sense of style. She's independent and free spirited... And she's alone.

Is that how I want to be?

It used to be. Granted, my destination choices are a little different, but I always dreamed of taking off, seeing the world. I never cared if I did it alone. Now everything feels hollow and empty. The trips that were so exciting before feel half as exciting now. It's like I've lost part of the thing that made me want to go.

Have I lost it?

Turning my wrist over, I trace my finger along the lines of my tattoo. The bruises are gone, but the word is there bold and dark. *Believe.*

My throat is tight, but I reach for my phone. Touching the buttons quickly, I tap out a message. Every muscle in my body is tense as I stare at the words, my thumb hovering over the blue *send* arrow.

Before I can change my mind, I tap it.

Chapter 25

Chad

The Admiral's Club is filled with Charleston's elite, and my mother holds my arm as we circle the room. I feel like a prized stallion being taken out for a walk.

"Buffy, your eyes look amazing." She kisses the cheek of an older woman I've known since I was a child.

"I don't know what you're talking about, Evelyn," Buffy, short for Elizabeth, shakes her helmet of hair. Her newly lifted eyes turn to me. "My goodness, Charles, you look just like your father in that suit. If I'd glanced, I'd have thought you were him."

"Thank you, Mrs. Hatcher." She leans forward to kiss my cheek, and her expensive perfume fills my nose. I do my best not to cough.

Once *Buffy the Vampire Slayer* was on television, Charity started calling her Mrs. Hatchett.

An older man joins us—Mr. Beau Hatchett. Yep, Buffy and Beau. It's like that here.

He extends a hand, and I give it a firm shake. "Good to see you, son. How's that golf game holding up?"

I smile, giving the expected reply. "Can't seem to get below a 92."

He slaps me on the back. "You need to join your father and I on the course. Get in more green time."

"I'm not sure I'll ever be up to your standards." It's a double entendre, and I know it. These old guys live in a different world — one I am not here to join.

I'm here for one reason only, and I haven't seen her yet.

"What's this I hear about you working as a sheriff's deputy?" Beau's voice lowers, and he catches my elbow, pulling me away from my mother's grasp.

I feel her fingers tighten, but Buffy takes her arm. "Let the boys talk. Have you tried the pâté? It's vegan walnut. You know Charlene is on a cruelty free food campaign. It's actually quite delicious…"

They drift away, and Beau guides us into a more secluded area of the hall. He's holding a tumbler of scotch, as am I, but he's also clutching a large cigar.

"What's all this business about?" He smiles, but I know he's been sent to ask the questions my father never will. "Still got the urge to serve and protect? I bet we could find you something more prestigious right here at home."

"I'm sure you could." I take a sip of my drink. "I appreciate the offer, but I enjoy being in Oceanside."

"Oceanside… that's the little town on the coast. The one Randall Lockwood tried to develop." He takes a pull off his cigar and blue smoke curls around our heads.

"From the looks of things, he did more than try. Oceanside Beach is thriving. Several celebrities have recently built mansions on the cliffs."

"Is that what you want? A cliffside mansion?"

"No." My eyes drift to the room, searching.

"What do you want then?" The words are just leaving his mouth when I spot her.

I look back at him, ready to end this conversation. "I want to live my life on my own terms."

He coughs a laugh. "None of us are able to do that, Charles, it's a fairytale. We all have roles to fill. It's time you came back and took your place at your father's side."

"According to whom?" I'm too old to be intimidated by these people anymore. I have too much to lose now.

"Your father would never say it, but you broke his heart when you ran off less than a week after getting out of the service."

"Robbie made me an offer I couldn't refuse."

"Robbie Cole is an outlier. His mother was an artist, a hippie." Beau shakes his head and takes another sip of his drink. "You're not. You've got a good head on your shoulders. We'd discussed grooming you for a place in the senate. Now that you're a veteran, it's practically a given."

My brow furrows. This is news to me. It makes sense now that I think about it. Having me in a position with the government could yield all sorts of useful tax breaks and incentives for business in Charleston.

"I don't have any interest in running for senate. Now if you'll excuse me. It was… interesting to see you again, sir."

I grip his elbow then make my way through the crowd to where a tall blonde is standing beside the champagne table.

Beau's voice is just loud enough for me to hear him over the low murmur of voices and modern jazz. "Maybe Nan can talk some sense into you."

My ex-fiancée is wearing a floor-length sand-colored gown with clear beads all over it. I'm sure my mother would say it's *blush* or *greige*. Some made-up color. It's times like these when Charity's absence feels particularly acute.

She turns as if she feels me approaching and her slim brows rise. Her platinum hair is chin-length and curled in two perfect waves at her cheeks, and her lips are the color of her dress.

"I heard you were here." She steps forward and places both hands on my chest, kissing my cheek. Nan always smells like vanilla or some type of pastry, and her tone is always like she's telling a joke. "As tall, dark, and handsome as ever. What the hell are you doing back in Charleston?"

"Looking for you." My voice is low and serious by contrast.

"Lucky me." Her blue eyes narrow. "Only, I don't think you mean what I hoped you meant."

"Can we go somewhere to talk?"

"It's too late to worry about setting off the gossip hounds. The moment I touched you, they all declared us back together and are now preparing for a December wedding. I'm sure my mother is picking out fur-lined bridal gowns as we speak."

She takes a sip of champagne, and I remember why I stayed with her for as long as I did. If I were going to be forced into marriage with one of their pedigreed young ladies, at least Nan had a biting sense of humor.

"Even so." I take her arm and lead her to the wall of French doors separating the dining room from the balcony overlooking the grounds. "I'd rather have this conversation where I'm sure no one's listening."

"Someone's always listening, *Charles*." When we reach the low stone walls of the balcony, Nan sits, crossing a leg and looking up at me. "I thought you said you were never coming back here."

"My mother came for a visit last weekend. She said some things that bothered me."

Nan starts to laugh. "If I took a trip every time my mother said something that bothered me—"

"I'm sorry I left the way I did." Her brow furrows with confusion. "I know you were probably expecting more from me, and I came back and ended it. I felt like I needed to apologize to you."

She stands and steps closer, putting her hand in mine. "Is this why you came all the way back here? We talked about all that. We agreed it was the right thing to do. You weren't in love with me, and Lord knows, I'd have just driven you crazy."

Our eyes meet and hers are warm. She stretches up on her toes and kisses my cheek once more. "Oh, Chad," she sighs. "Underneath that brooding façade and shield of brawn, you still have a soft heart."

She lets me go and walks over to pick up her champagne flute. I watch her a moment, wanting to be sure. "And you've always been the sweetheart of Sigma Chi. Why aren't you dating someone? Why would my mother say you're waiting for me?"

Her head snaps up, eyes flashing. "Your mother said…" Just as fast she nods. "Right. Of course she said that. That's how they're spinning it."

"I don't understand."

"I'm afraid you've been pulled into the fiction of why I'm, quote, not seeing anyone, darling." She moves her fingers in little curly motions.

"What the hell is that supposed to mean?"

"It means you made the trip all the way out here to check on me for nothing." She slips her hand in mine again and starts to walk toward the enormous ballroom. "I am seeing someone. I'm very happily seeing someone. His name is Trevor Johnson."

Pulling her hand, I stop our progress, turning her to face me. "Trevor Johnson?" She nods waiting as I mentally run through everybody I know. "I don't recognize that name."

"You wouldn't. He's a musician... and hold onto your hat." A mischievous light is in her eyes, and she smiles, stepping closer to my ear. "He's the wrong shade of beige, if you get my drift. Too much pigment for the old guard."

"He's black?"

"Black as ebony and so gorgeous!" She does a little shiver. "You should see him. I think I really might be in love for the first time in my life."

I have to hand it to her. I only walked away from this scene. She's taking a sledgehammer to it.

"That's great news." I squeeze her hand. "I hope you're very happy together."

She cocks an eyebrow at me. "You're seeing someone, too." She lifts her chin and nods. "You are! I can tell. And... it looks like you're in love."

I try to act confused, but I can't help smiling. I kind of wish Tabby were here to meet Nan. She'd like her a lot. "What makes you say that?"

"For starters, you haven't told me how beautiful I look tonight." She holds out her arms and turns as if she's modeling her dress for me.

Relief bubbles up in my chest, and I laugh. For the first time in a year, this weight is off my shoulders. "You are very beautiful tonight. I thought it the moment I saw you."

"And you're as wonderful as ever. Now, escort me inside and let's get some food." Her hand goes in the crook of my arm, and she leans her head against my shoulder. "As grandma always said, you're more fortunate to be rich in love than rich in money."

My hand covers hers, and I couldn't agree more.

* * *

Walking along the manicured lawn of the cemetery the next day, I think about Robbie and Nan and me. It's good to know I'm not alone in feeling suffocated by this place. I worry for my friend. She's venturing into sticky territory. Still, if anyone is strong enough to brave those waters, it's Nan.

Strength and bravery. My sister's headstone is a large angel holding both hands up to the sky. It's an unexpected tribute, knowing her, but I'm sure it's the story my parents want to believe.

My memory is slightly different, although I like their version better. I want to think of her as a strong warrior who reached up to heaven and flew to something better.

A fine mist fills the air, and gray fog has rolled in off the ocean. I'm wearing a dark wool topcoat, and I look down at the bouquet of white lilies in my hand. They have deep green stems and leaves, and they're wrapped in paper.

I lean forward to put the flowers in the vase at the feet of the angel.

Charity Yvette Tucker is engraved in all caps on the base of the monument. *Beloved daughter and sister*, is next. *Heaven needed you sooner than we were ready.*

The quote has never felt right to me, even now as I stand reading it over and over in the damp air as the mist slowly turns to rain.

I remember a young girl with swirling brown hair. I remember her being playful and careless, climbing out of windows and running all over town in the dead of night. I remember her holding hands with girls and kissing them. I remember thinking she was playing a dangerous game…

"I'm sorry I was too young to understand." My throat aches as I say the words. "I'm sorry I was too ignorant to help you."

I remember my father shutting us out. I remember my mother clutching her chest and crying. I remember Cherry just wanting to be free.

"I hope you're happy wherever you are."

My hands are in my pockets, and I wait for something to happen, a feeling to come, something.

Last night, talking to Nan, I felt a release. I knew that part of my life was closed. I'm not sure I'll ever get closure on this one.

When someone you love dies, it's like everything stops making sense. The little things that used to matter so much seem silly. I wasn't sure I'd ever feel normal again. I wasn't sure I could ever believe in anything again.

Believe…

It's raining more, and I have to go.

Reaching out, I put my hand on the angel representing my sister. "If you're flying, remember not to get too close to the sun." My dry throat aches at the thought of her falling. "I hope you see the galaxies and stars and all the beautiful things. I hope you're as beautiful now as you always were then."

I hold my hand on the statue a few seconds longer. I still don't feel a change, my chest is tight and I feel like I'm bracing for impact. After a while, all I want is Tabby. I miss her, and I want to hold her in my arms.

I know what I believe, and I'm ready to make it happen.

* * *

My mother stands at the foot of my bed watching me pack the few things I left at her house. "You came all this way just to pack up and leave again?"

"I only came for a visit. I've stayed a week. Now it's time to get back."

"Beau said he told you about the senate seat. Your father spent years building a network for you to take over when you were discharged. It's ready and waiting for you."

"Nothing is waiting for me here." I glance up at her and smile as I tuck my socks into my shoes. "Dad and his friends can find another fortunate son to fill that role."

"Don't say it like that. Your father wanted you in that role. He sees you as a leader."

"I am a leader. Just not in this community."

"You're going back to that girl." Her voice is sharp. "No matter what you think, she's not good for you."

"She's the best thing that's ever happened to me. She taught me how to believe again, and I'm in love with her."

My mother drops her hand and exhales a heavy sigh. "I'll see you off in the morning. Don't stay up too late."

Stepping away from the bed, I catch her hand. "Mom?" She turns, her eyes tired. "It's going to be okay. "

She doesn't agree, but she doesn't argue with me. She only leaves, closing the door behind her. I move the suitcase to the floor and pick up my phone. I have one more commitment to fulfill tomorrow, then I can get on the road for Oceanside.

I haven't tried to text Tabby since I've been gone. I wanted to give her what she asked for—time, space, what's that saying about if you love someone, set them free? I felt pretty confident when I left her on Sunday, but what if I misunderstood her tears? Can I go back there and continue my daily routine without her?

I wonder if she did what I asked and waited to give Travel Time an answer? The phone is in my hand, I'm staring at the face, when it goes off. Her name appears as if she felt me thinking about her, wondering, and wanted to give me an answer.

Warm satisfaction unfurls in my stomach as I read her words. *Things aren't the same without you here. I miss you so much. I want to see you again. The door is open. Please come home.*

I don't waste time responding. *On my way.*

Chapter 26

Tabby

Friday is the official launch day of Travel Time, and I'm bouncing off the walls. Not only have I been awake since midnight, drinking Red Bull, checking periodically to be sure no servers have crashed or reservations systems bugged up, I can't stop thinking about Chad and wondering when he'll be here.

I told him I needed time to think, and boy, did he ever give me what I asked for. This week has been more than enough time… and space. I want to see him. I want to touch him. I want to kiss him, and then I want to do all the things that always come after that.

When 10 a.m. finally rolls around, Rani and AJ are ready for my answer. Even though I told Chad I wouldn't make a decision before he got back, I'm pretty sure he meant not to tell them yes, and I've decided I could never do that anyway.

As much as I love the idea of being a permanent explorer, I don't want to go alone. Roxanne has been hanging around the pack-n-save all week, and she made some additional points about traveling alone — no one to share your excitement when you see something cool, but most of all, having to put up with all the couples on vacation together and what a drag it is after a while.

I don't intend to be in that situation ever.

"The site looks amazing. It performs amazingly well… I just can't tell you how happy we are." Rani is smiling, and my chest is so full.

"Thank you, Rani. I enjoyed every minute working on it. Really." I'm beaming with pride in a job well done.

"Have you made up your mind about our offer?" AJ joins her on Skype, lifting her out of the chair and sitting behind her.

Rani lets out a little squeal, and I can't help remembering when it was like that with Chad and me, sitting on his lap, showing him all the bells and whistles of my job. Then kissing, riding Andy... I feel my face getting hot and shut down those steamy memories.

"Does that smile mean yes?" Rani's voice is so excited, I feel bad.

"You know, guys, it's such a generous offer. I've pretty much been thinking about it 24-7 since last week…"

"But?" I can tell by AJ's expression he knows what I'm going to say.

"But I can't. As much as I'd love to travel full-time, I have too many commitments here. I don't want to have to turn down other work. I still want to travel, and I'm happy to use your service and take pictures we can use. I just can't do it full-time."

"We thought you might say that." Rani leans to the side so I can see them both.

"I'm sorry. It really is the most generous offer."

"Since we were anticipating your decision, we went back and looked at our original payment agreement." AJ slides a sheet of paper in front of him, and my eyebrows rise.

"Okay…"

"So our original agreement was the flat fee to cover the website design and development, the plugins and support." He's going down the list, and I'm nodding. "We included bonuses for hitting our launch dates, which you did easily."

Again, I nod. They don't have to know how close I cut it on the soft launch. "Were you wanting to change something?" I honestly have no idea where this is going.

"We reported a glitch in one of the airlines' reservations tools we were using. The fault was theirs. Basically, it was overbooking flights, causing delays and super pissed off customers…"

"What? That's horrible!"

"Yeah, it was a mess." Rani jumps in at this point. "They were so happy, they gave us a dozen travel vouchers. It's way more than we can use in the time allowed… so we thought we'd give some to you as a bonus to thank you for all your hard work—"

"And in the hopes you might use it to try out a few of our packages, see if they're as good as we're claiming, and take pictures."

My heart jumps. "But not as a job?"

They look at each other, and Rani's brow furrows. She asks a question I can't hear, and AJ shrugs then nods. "I'm sure we can get you some comps if you use our recommended places."

"It's a deal!" I say it fast before they can change their minds, then I start to laugh. "It's an amazing deal. Thank you so much."

"Aw, thank you." Rani tilts her head to the side, and we laugh some more. "We're so excited to get this off the ground. It's our dream come true, you know?"

"I do, and I'm excited to be working with you on it."

We spend a few more minutes basking in the excitement of their new business venture before saying goodbye and ending the call. AJ says the final payment and vouchers should be in my online accounts by the end of the day.

Running to my bedroom, I quickly change out of Chad's old tee, which has completely lost his scent—thanks in part because I finally broke down and washed it. Now it just smells like me. I slip into a short red print dress with spaghetti straps and large, tropical flowers all over it.

My hair is on my head with a pencil stuck through it. Pencil out, and it falls around my shoulders. I smooth it with my fingers, add some mascara, lip gloss, and I'm out the door, headed to town. I can't wait to tell Emberly what just happened.

I have no idea how many vouchers they'll give me or how much they're worth, but depending on what happens, maybe I can give her enough to take a trip with Coco or take a trip with me… I park in the space in front of the bakery and dash up the steps. The little "Be right back" sign is turned and the door is locked. Checking my phone, I see it's noon, and I guess she must've walked to Betty's for a poboy.

"Emberly!" I exhale a little squeal of excitement and dash up the connected porches, past Wyatt's place and through the door. It rings loud, and I stop short. The place is full of people. Betty's standing at the counter with Roxanne talking to André about how he comes up with his recipes.

Roxanne's saying something about New Orleans when she sees me. "Hey, girl! That's my future travel partner, right? Ready to get crazy?"

André's eyebrows rise, and he gives me a look like *What?*

I just shake my head. "Hi, Roxanne, Hi, BP—is Emberly here?"

"She's in the back talking to Donna." Betty winks at me, and I freeze on the spot.

"What does that mean?" Seriously, I have no idea why BP is winking at me. It has never happened.

"Tabby!" Her voice is scolding. "Donna has a wedding coming up. Liam proposed… I told Emberly to tell her about the new offerings in cakes."

"Oh!" *Sweet mother Moses.* "I'd better get back there, then."

No telling what Emberly is saying to get out of this one—and poor Donna White. She's scared of her own shadow. I expect she'd pass out at the sight of a penis cake. Last time I'd checked, she'd never even seen the real thing.

"Mm, I love Emberly's cakes," André starts as I dash to the back. "The butterscotch sundae one she made for Thelma's birthday was like heaven in my mouth."

I'm cringing as I close the door. Poor André has no idea what those pervy old ladies are talking about, and he keeps going on about heaven in his mouth. I imagine Roxanne will need some alone time with her battery-operated boyfriend after this.

Pushing through the door, I see the two of them laughing and chatting. No signs of embarrassment or secrecy.

"Hey! What are you two doing?" I walk over to where Donna is sitting in the desk chair and Emberly's leaning on the edge of the table.

"Tabby!" Emberly hops up and runs over to give me a hug. "How'd Travel Time's big launch go?"

"Without a hitch, and I've got news—but first…" I lean forward. "I heard Betty's trying to get you some business."

Emberly turns so Donna can't see her face and mouths *No.* "Oh, I was just telling Donna about the different types of cakes people order for weddings or showers... stuff like that."

"Okay..." I glance at Donna, who's smiling innocently.

"It's amazing how creative people can get with cakes," she says.

"You can say that again." I'm doing my best not to laugh, but I'm already excited and now this.

Emberly grabs my hand and squeezes it hard. "I guess we'd better get on back to work. You come down and look at pictures with me when you get a chance."

"I will." Donna stands and follows us to the door leading into the store. Emberly and I are looking back at her as we open it. "I have time to plan, and... Oh, heavenly angel..." Donna's eyes are round, and her voice is a hushed whisper.

"What?" Emberly's head snaps to face forward. "Oh heavenly..." Her voice dies out.

I'm the last one to turn, and when I do, I have to grip my best friend's arm.

Chad is standing in the front of Betty's pack-n-save in his full dress uniform. It's white with gold buttons. Navy epaulets are on both shoulders with gold stripes on them. His hat is off, tucked under his arm, and his dark hair just touches the top of his collar. When he turns to face us, the breath leaves my body.

"Here you are." His deep voice makes my insides go liquid. He's possibly the handsomest thing I've ever seen.

I'm not the only one appreciating the view. Roxanne is frantically fanning herself with a paper plate, and Betty's hand is on her chest.

Emberly is the first one to finally speak. "Officer Tucker, you look so... dashing."

Chad does a little nod. "Thank you, Emberly."

"Give me a break, he officially looks like sex on a stick," Roxanne snarks from where she sits.

I still haven't moved. Chad's eyes are locked on mine, and a grin is curling those sexy lips. My favorite dimple ghosts his cheek. He isn't giving me the full-watt smile that melts my panties right off. He's waiting to see if I'll give him a sign. I don't make him wait.

Clearing my throat, I manage to speak. "I'm so glad you found me."

No truer words.

He takes the hat out from under his arm and puts it on his head, striding quickly up the aisle to where I'm standing in the middle of Donna and Emberly. With every step closer, my stomach gets tighter, my breath gets shallower.

I'm trapped in his gaze, unable to move and not wanting to get away. He doesn't stop until he's standing right in front of me looking down into my eyes. My eyes never leave his, although in my peripheral, I can see Emberly's hand go to her mouth and Donna clutch her heart.

"You are so beautiful." His voice is low, forceful, almost a command. "I've never wanted to kiss someone as much as I want to kiss you right now."

His clean, masculine Chad-scent surrounds me, and I can feel the heat from his body on my skin. I'm sure my nipples are visible through the thin red dress I'm wearing, but I couldn't care less.

"I've never wanted someone to kiss me so much in my life." My voice is breathless.

I'm surprised I can speak at all. I feel like my heart is beating out of my chest and the air all around us is electric.

It's a feeling I used to only have when I was being bad, breaking the rules, trying to get away or trying to feel like I belonged. Now I know, with this gorgeous soldier standing in front of me, exactly where I belong.

Chad's eyes darken, and he hesitates only a moment.

Emberly is beside me with both hands on her mouth, murmuring, "Do it… Do it…"

That full smile I love breaks across Chad's face, and he quickly bends down, lifting me in his arms, Cinderella style.

"An Officer and a Gentleman!" Emberly squeals.

André lets out a loud whoop from the front of the store. Donna sighs, and I put an arm around Chad's shoulder, pulling my face to his neck to hide the smile breaking my cheeks. He turns and heads to the door as Betty Pepper exclaims, "And in my store!"

Roxanne calls out, "That's my girl!"

Only one thing is on my mind, and as soon as we're out the door, Chad makes it happen. He stops and puts me on my feet, stepping closer to cup my face. His head lowers, and those whiskey eyes smile into mine. I'm breathing fast and my lips part before his even touch them.

Like the brush of a feather, he speaks against my skin. "I want you so much."

With that he kisses me, and my entire body ignites. Mouths open, tongues caress, and I grip his shoulders to stay on my feet amidst the onslaught of emotion sweeping through me like a tidal wave.

His lips move mine, and my lips chase after his. Our faces move, and his large hands are on my ass, gripping, sliding up to my waist, up my back and into my hair. A deep sense of home warms my stomach. It's unlike anything I've ever felt.

"Oh, man." He lifts his chin to kiss my cheek, my forehead. "It's just like I remember. We need a room."

My hands are on his neck, his cheeks. I run my fingernails through his beard. "My place is closer."

Looking down, he smiles again, placing his hand on my cheek, his thumb on my bottom lip. I want to pull it into my mouth and suck it. I want to hear him groan my name like he does when he comes so impossibly deep between my thighs.

Hot dark eyes burn me from within, and I know he's thinking the same thing as me. "Let's go."

Chapter 27

Chad

Tabby stands in the center of her living room, feet bare, silky dark curls all around her shoulders. Her fingers quickly unfasten the gold buttons of my jacket. I slide my fingers under the spaghetti straps of her dress, lowering them.

As soon as they pass her elbows, she straightens her arms and the entire garment slides to the floor. She sighs. "It's a little big on me."

She's not wearing a bra, and when I see her beautiful breasts, the semi I've been sporting since I saw her turns to a rod of iron. "I'm glad."

Sliding my hand up the soft skin of her waist, past her ribs, she does a little shiver. It's the sexiest thing I've seen today—since I found her standing at the back of Betty's store.

I cup her round breasts, squeezing them in my hands. Her nipples are tight, and I roll the hard tips between my fingers. She exhales a soft moan, and my jacket is open, revealing the white tank underneath.

She smooths her hands up my shoulders, and I temporarily release her to place my coat on the back of her office chair. Turning back, I have to take a moment to admire her standing in only a black lace thong before me.

"Damn, Tabby, you're sexier now than when I left."

Her cheeks flush a pretty pink and she shakes her head, crossing to me. "I look exactly the same. We haven't seen each other in a week."

"Longer."

She slides her hand up and down, cupping and stroking my dick through my pants, and a groan rumbles from my throat. "Don't make me come in my dress whites."

"That'd be an interesting story for the dry cleaners." Her green eyes glow and she gives me a naughty, sex-kitten grin.

I make quick work of removing the rest of my clothes, not missing the way her full bottom lip goes under her teeth at the sight of my cock.

"What did you call him?" I fist my shaft, sliding my hand up and down, running my finger over the drop of liquid on the tip.

"Andy the anaconda." Her eyes don't leave my hand, and I chuckle. "Andy misses your tight little pussy. I'll have to give her a name."

"I don't care what you call her. Just get over here."

Stepping forward, I grasp her neck with my other hand, tilting her head back and leaning down to pull her mouth with mine. I thrust my tongue inside and curl it with hers, then I release my dick and grab her by the ass, lifting her off the floor and pushing her back to the wall.

"Oh, shit yeah," she gasps, but I can't sink into her now. I'll come in two pumps or less. Instead, I take a knee, holding her open by her thighs, pulling those sexy panties away, and covering her pretty pussy with my mouth, sucking and licking, tracing my tongue all around the hard little button in the center.

"Chad… Oh… Oh!" Her fingers are in my hair, threading and pulling. I feel the muscles in her thighs jump with every pass of my tongue. "Chad... I'm going to come."

Moving my mouth to the crease of her leg, I kiss her, looking up at her heavy lidded eyes. "Say my name again."

"Chad," she moans, and I give her another lick.

Her hips jump and she breaks into trembling orgasm. A loud moan comes from her throat and I stand all the way, lifting her by the ass and wrapping those legs around my waist as I position my tip at her entrance and sink all the way, balls deep into her tight, wet heat.

"Yes..." I hold a second, her body pressed to mine, my mouth at her neck, feeling those little spasms all around me. "You feel so damn good."

On every breath, she makes a little noise. It's the fucking best thing I've heard in so long. She tightens her thighs, lifting herself and trying to move. I grip her ass and give her a firm thrust. It gets me another soft whimper. The sound is a match to gasoline. I'm thrusting fast and hard, and she's gripping, scratching my skin with her nails.

Our mouths chase each other's, kissing, tasting, sucking. "Chad... Chad..." She whispers my name between every kiss, and it's a shot of happiness, pure fucking joy filling my chest, blowing my mind. This is real.

Two more thrusts, and she breaks, coming again, and the sensation sparks my own orgasm. Pleasure snakes up my legs from the arches of my feet through my thighs, pulsing out into her, hot and hard, over and over.

My eyes close, my mind blanks as we're flying through the air, jumping off the highest cliffs into shimmering oceans below. I hold her tight against me

263

as the shudders move through us both, shaking us, changing us, bonding us together.

When at last we're able to open our eyes again, wonder is in our gaze.

Tabby places her hand against my jaw. "I don't ever want you to leave me again," she whispers.

I kiss her gently. "I won't ever leave you again."

She blinks, and I catch sight of something glistening in her eyes before she leans forward, wrapping her arms around my neck and holding me. My hands are on her smooth back, and I'm still buried deep in her sexy little body.

A sniff, and she tucks her head in my shoulder to kiss my neck.

"Hey," I give her a little shake. "Are you crying?'

She shakes her head and lifts it, but when I find her eyes, I see tears. She starts to laugh. "I'm so emotional lately. It's silly."

"As long as those are happy tears." I kiss them away. "I told you a while back you're mine, Tabitha Green."

Her hands are on my face again, and she runs her thumbs over my mouth. "I'm yours, Chad Tucker, and you're mine."

I kiss those fingers, kiss her lips. I never want to let her go, but I lower her, sliding out and going to the bathroom for something to clean us up. I return with a towel, and I see she's used tissues from her desk.

She's wearing her sundress again and sitting at her computer.

I clean myself up and toss the towel in the hamper in her closet. "How did the launch go?" I ask, walking back into the living room.

"Really well." Her eyes are focused on the screen, and I kiss her neck. "Hang on, I want to tell you something, but I need to see if it happened first."

"Here." I lift her out of the chair and sit down, positioning her in my lap like before.

She laughs. "Just hold that thought…" She types briefly, a few more clicks, then she lets out a little whoop and claps her hands. "It's there! Oh my goodness, check this out. Okay…" she wriggles around in my lap so cute, I can't help grinning in response. "So I know you told me to wait, but I went on and gave Rani and AJ my answer about their job offer."

My chest clenches and I sit up straighter, adjusting her so I can see her face. "What did you say?"

She places a hand on my cheek and leans forward to kiss me. Then she leans up and meets my eyes. "I told them no."

Happiness rises in my chest, but I tamp it down. I catch her arms and ask her seriously. "Why did you say no? Was it just because of me? Because —"

"It was because of you, yes, but it was also because of other things." Her pretty brow furrows, and she looks over my head. "I thought about being gone all the time, not seeing Emberly, missing Coco grow up… I guess I kind of love this town after all."

My hands are on her smooth thighs. I start to slide them higher, and she squeals. "Wait! There's more. Let me show you."

She rotates in the chair, and I lean forward exhaling a growl at her neck as I wrap my arms around her waist. "I haven't been with you in almost two weeks. Hurry up."

A shiver moves through her body, and her protests are less convincing. "You need to see this. It's important." She clicks over to a different screen. "When I first started working with Travel Time, the deal was my flat rate for web design, plus the hourly

265

rate, bonuses for making our deadlines... Well, they were so happy with how things turned out, they gave me bonus airfare and comps on several packages."

I sit up. She has my attention now. "They're letting you travel—"

"Whenever I want, as long as I want. Only, now you can come with me! Oceanside can be our home base, and we can still be together."

That makes me smile. I trace my finger across her cheek. "What changed?"

She looks down at her wrist. "I reminded myself to believe. I believe in us. I don't want to see the world with anyone but you. I love you."

Heat explodes in my chest, and I catch her face, kissing her roughly. "I love you, Tabitha Green." Tears are in her eyes again, and I kiss them away.

I lift her onto Andy, and for a little while, it's only us and love. Touching, feeling, our bodies becoming one. It's bliss, pure and simple, primal. It's the only thing I ever want.

When we're drifting down once more, from another incredible high, her soft body secure in my arms, I can't help teasing her. "Are you sure you want to be the girlfriend of a law man?"

"A sexy military man?" She arches an eyebrow and sighs. "I don't think I'll ever lose my love of being bad. Maybe you can help me find more creative ways to channel it."

"I found some fluffy purple handcuffs at a novelty store in Charleston. They're in my suitcase waiting to be tested."

"You're the only man I ever want to tie me down." Her nose wrinkles and she rubs it against mine.

"What are you saying, Tabitha Green?" I've also got a rock in my suitcase, and I can't wait to put it on her finger.

"I'm saying kiss me." Her voice is a purr.

And I do, because when we kiss…

Everything is exactly how it should be.

Epilogue

Tabby

Six weeks later…

Caribbean breezes swirl through the open doors of our cabana. We're lying in bed, sweating and breathing hard after another round of smoking hot sex.

"Best twenty-five dollars I've ever spent." Chad's hand is on my ass, and I chuckle.

One fluffy purple handcuff hangs from my wrist, and I lift it, unbuckling the straps. "Way less painful."

"I take it you're not into the pleasure through pain shit."

My nose wrinkles, and I toss the cuffs on a chair. "I don't really get that. Pain is just painful in my book. It's kind of a deal breaker."

"Got it. No metal cuffs." He rolls onto his side next to me, and I turn my face to kiss his chest. "How much longer do you think we'll be able to use them before it's too much?"

His eyes are on my flat stomach, where he slides his large palm down. I slide my hand to meet his, threading my fingers, and I can't believe it. A real bubble of happiness rises in my chest. No fear, no regrets, I'm going to be a mamma, and I absolutely can't wait.

"I'm sure it won't matter for at least a few more months. Should I ask Dr. Peters how long we can keep having kinky sex? My law enforcement boyfriend likes me in handcuffs?"

"Whatever you think is right, my love."

His arm tightens around me, and I exhale a lazy laugh. Since we found out two weeks ago I was pregnant, we decided to go ahead and get at least one trip in before we became a threesome.

We made the journey to Belize, and even though scuba diving is off the table for me while I'm pregnant, I still begged to take a boat out and at least look at The Great Blue Hole.

"Can you imagine what all is down there?" I'd looked longingly at the royal blue waters, leading to caverns and coral reefs far below.

"Giant squids and Anglerfish." Chad had sat behind me, strong arms around my waist, as we observed it from the boat. "No way in hell I'm letting you dive into that thing. It's creepy as fuck."

I'd only laughed and put my hand over his arm. "It's not so dangerous. We'll come back and check it out one day."

"In a submarine."

"Can you get one of those?"

That made him laugh. "No."

The rest of our visit is primarily lounging on the beach, snorkeling, and eating out. The pregnancy makes me so tired, and I've started taking naps. Chad is happy to join me, which leads to more than napping…

"Did you know Chad means protector in old English?" My cheek is against his chest, and my eyes are heavy.

"Did you know that Tabitha means beautiful in Hebrew?"

My head pops up. "Really? Does it matter if I'm not Jewish?"

"Apparently not. You are beautiful."

That makes me smile. "Did you know Andy means large dong in Greek?"

"Is that so?" He fights a laugh, but that dimple appears.

"Yes, and in Mesopotamian it means happy snake in pants." He loses the fight with laughter, and his fingers curl on my ribs, making me squeal in response. "No tickling! It's bad for the baby!"

He only tickles me more, and I struggle until I'm under him again, soft lips covering mine, scratchy beard roughing my skin. I thread my fingers in his hair as my stomach tightens and tingles move through my lower pelvis.

Chad's kisses are rich and delicious, and I could make out with him for hours.

"Since we're naming things, what's the name for hot little pussy?" His lips move to my jaw, down my neck.

"Mm, dirty talk. Jezebel?"

He continues down, pausing to kiss my right breast then my left before stopping all together at my navel. His eyes are on my skin, and he places his palm flat on my stomach.

"Do you think he can hear us yet?" He leans closer. "Hello in there?"

Propping up on my elbows, I look down at this great big man completely captivated by my midsection. It's not where I expected him to stop, but I love it just the same.

"So we're' having a boy?" Reaching down, I slide my fingernails through his beard.

"I don't care." He glances up at me, and I smile.

"I guess I should get one of those baby books. I was going to make Emberly tell me everything."

"Emberly might be a bit distracted."

"You're right. I'll get a baby book."

Shortly after Chad and I reunited, actually before we'd even gone public, Jackson came back to town. Completely out of the blue and with no warning. He just showed up one day answering Wyatt's ad for a painter.

Emberly was in the middle of making her first penis cake for Donna White's bachelorette party— ordered by Betty Pepper, of course—and it was like a major earthquake. It didn't just shake up my best friend, it shook up everything from her mother to my uncle to…

Well, that's a story for another time. For now, my sexy man is trying to make my heart burst with joy. He dips down and kisses my stomach. "Hey, baby. We can't wait to meet you."

I lean back and sigh, combing my fingers through his hair as he kisses my belly once more. "We love you."

So much love fills my chest. I never dreamed I could be this happy, and it really is like having it all. I'm closing my eyes, expecting him to travel further south when he's out of the bed so fast, my eyes pop open, and I sit up. "What's wrong?"

I watch his tight, sexy ass as he walks across our bedroom to where our empty suitcase is stashed in a closet. "I was going to wait until dinner for this, but I can't wait any longer. It's been six weeks of torture."

"What's wrong?" I have no idea what he's talking about. We already tested out the handcuffs. Several times. Pushing myself up in the bed, I wrap the sheet over my breasts.

He turns, one hand behind his back and pauses a moment looking at me with a strange smile on his face. It's happy but also a little hesitant. It's a smile I haven't seen since the first time he asked me to go out with him and I said no.

None of that matters. I'm too distracted by the sight of him standing in the light of the late afternoon sun. His shoulders are broad and his biceps are round and perfectly sculpted. The slanted rays make the lines of his torso deep and so lickable, and Andy standing at half-mast like a promise of all kinds of naughty pleasure has my thighs rubbing together.

His brow lowers, and that smile turns lusty. "If you don't stop looking at me that way, I'm going to have to fuck you before I can do this."

"I don't know what this is, but I have no objection to the fucking part."

A sexy laugh, low and rumbling comes from his chest. He walks back to where I wait in the bed, and I force my eyes off his swinging cock to his pretty, dimpled grin.

When he gets to the bedside, he stops, dropping to one knee. I sit a little higher, frowning as I try to understand. Reaching out, he takes my left hand, and my brow relaxes, my eyes get wider, and mist clouds my vision.

"Tabitha Green, I knew the first night I saw you standing in your transparent bra and panties beside the pool at the Plucky Duck I had to have you."

"Oh my God." I blink and a hot tear hits my cheek.

"I waited a year until I had my shit together to ask you out... Only, I guess I didn't completely have my shit together."

Shaking my head, I sniff. "You had it together. I was just too afraid to believe it."

"You're the greatest thing that's ever happened to me. You make me laugh. You bring out the best in me—and the beast."

"I love the beast."

"I would never change a thing about you. Except one thing."

My brow furrows. "What?" I'm ready to change anything about me to make him mine. Or to make me his. Or both.

"Your last name. Will you marry me?"

A little black box is in his hand, but I bypass it diving forward to put my arms around his neck. His body vibrates with laughter, but I only hold him, kissing his skin as tears flood my eyes. Strong arms hold me tight, and a deep sense of belonging warms my veins. It's something I lost when I was a very little girl, but now, with this sexy, hot, good man, it's given to me again.

My eyes are closed, and I'm holding him, letting happiness fill me when he gives me a little shake. "Hey, Tabby."

Lifting my head, I sniff, meeting his bright whiskey eyes. "Yeah?"

"Is that a yes?"

A laugh bursts from my lungs, and I nod. "Of course it's a yes. It's a yes yes yes yes yes!"

My favorite dimple appears, and he looks down. "Do you want to see the ring?"

"Oh, right." I relax my arms around his shoulders and lean back.

He opens the box, and it's a gorgeous, oval-cut diamond set in a white-gold, infinity-twist setting with little baguettes along the center swoop. It's just like my tattoo, only with a diamond where the word *Believe* would be.

"Oh my goodness." My hand covers my mouth as a fresh flood of tears heats my eyes. "How did you get this?"

"Had it custom made when I was in Charleston. I described it to the jeweler, and he found a setting in that style. Do you like it? It has a wedding band to match."

It's on the third finger of my left hand as he's still saying the words. "I'll never take it off." I'm still looking at it as I slide my arm around his neck again. "It's so beautiful."

His arms go around my waist, and he's smiling as he kisses the side of my neck, sliding us further into the bed.

Finally tearing my eyes off the delicate piece of jewelry changing my life, I find his mouth, kissing him gently at first.

His lips pull mine, and he lifts my chin, looking deep into my eyes. "I'll love you forever Tabitha Green Tucker."

I cup his face in my hand, stealing a glance at the sparkling ring lighting up my hand. My eyes return to his, and I'm smiling so big, my cheeks hurt.

"I'll love you forever, Chad Tucker."

With that his mouth is over mine again. He rolls me onto my back, and my thighs part instinctively for him. I'm caught up in the movement of our lips, the slide of his tongue against mine, the fast and slow, lips on cheeks and jaws and lips again...

I'm lost in his kisses.

The air is electric...

Because when we kiss, I'm not a bad girl. I'm his girl, and it's the only thing I ever want to be.

* * *

Thanks for reading **When We Kiss***!*

Want to know what happens when Jackson returns to Oceanside?

Get **When We Touch** *today, and fall in love with Emberly and Jackson's second-chance love story.*

Available in print and Free to borrow in Kindle Unlimited.

* * *

Never miss a new release!

Sign up for my New Release newsletter, and get a **FREE Subscriber-only story bundle!**
(http://smarturl.it/TLMnews)

Get Exclusive Text Alerts and never miss a SALE or NEW RELEASE by Tia Louise! Text "TiaLouise" to 64600 Now!*
(U.S. only.)

Your opinion counts!

If you enjoyed *When We Kiss*, please leave a short, sweet review wherever you purchased your copy.

Reviews help your favorite authors more than you know.

Thank you so much!

* * *

Books by Tia Louise

Save Me, 2018
The Right Stud*, 2018
Hit Girl, 2018
The Last Guy*, 2017
(*written with author Ilsa Madden-Mills)

THE BRIGHT LIGHTS SERIES
Under the Lights, 2018
Sundown, 2018
Under the Stars, 2018

THE ONE TO HOLD SERIES
One to Hold, 2013
One to Keep, 2014
One to Protect, 2014
One to Love, 2014
One to Leave, 2014
One to Save, 2015
One to Chase, 2015
One to Take, 2016

THE DIRTY PLAYERS SERIES
The Prince & The Player, 2016
A Player for A Princess, 2016
Dirty Dealers, 2017
Dirty Thief, 2017

PARANORMAL ROMANCES
One Immortal, 2015
One Insatiable, 2015

On all eBook retailers, in print, and audiobook formats.

Exclusive Sneak Peek

When We Touch
By Tia Louise
© TLM Productions LLC, 2017

Emberly Rose

Where we begin…

Jackson Cane tastes like red-hot cinnamon, salt water, and sin.

When he concentrates, his long fingers twist in the back of his dark hair, right at the base of his neck, and he tugs.

Tugs…

Tugs…

I like to weave my fingers between his and pull.

Then ocean-blue eyes blink up to mine, sending electricity humming in my veins. He smiles. I smile, and it isn't long before our lips touch. I straddle his lap as I open my mouth, and his delicious tongue finds mine, heating every part of my body.

Our kisses are languid and deep, chasing and tasting.

We sizzle like fireworks on a hot summer night.

Eventually, with a heavy sigh, I pull away, but hours later my mouth is still burning. I taste him everywhere I go.

Lying in my bed in the dark room, my heart aches, heavy and painful in my chest. Every breath is a burden. I blink slowly at the ceiling and slide my tongue against the backs of my teeth thinking about hot cinnamon, tangy salt, caramel and sugar, sunshine, and the best summer of my life.

The instant I hear it, I'm on my feet, tiptoeing to my open window. The low growl of an engine tells me he's there in the darkness, out on the street in the shadows just past the streetlight.

The late summer humidity hangs heavy in the air. Cicadas *scree* from the limbs of the mighty oak tree beside the house. Their damp wings make them too heavy to fly, and the sadness in my chest is replaced with breathless anticipation.

I'm panting. I've never felt this way for anyone, and I'm desperate to hold onto it. Somehow I know I'll never feel this way for anyone ever again.

Quiet as a mouse I scamper to my door and listen. The only sound is the hum of Momma's oscillating fan pushing the warm air around her room. I can't hear her breathing. I can't hear anything... except the noise of Jackson's engine on the street below, waiting.

Red-hot cinnamon.

Salt water.

Sin.

Pressure tingles around the edges of my skull, and a bead of sweat tickles down the side of my neck, dropping past my shoulder, slipping between my breasts.

I'm at the window slowly lifting the glass, and I don't care if she hears me. I dive through the space, out onto the cedar shake roof in my bare feet. I'll get a splinter if I'm not careful...

So many reasons to be careful...

I ignore them all.

I'm going to him like a siren's call in the ocean, like the mermaid story in reverse. I'm the hypnotized sailor. He's the promise of so many wicked pleasures.

Reaching for the tree limb, I swing my body across the narrow gap two stories high, gliding down the trunk as the skirt of my dress rises to my hips. My bike sits where I left it at the side of the house, and I carefully pull it away, holding it as I tiptoe down the gravel driveway to the street.

I can't take a chance on anyone seeing us together and telling my mother. Instead, I dash across the street between the thick beams of his headlights. He flickers them to let me know he sees me, and I plunge into the dark woods, pedaling fast.

Tires crunch on gravel, and I shoot down the pine needle path leading away from this place, through the tall, skinny trees, all the way out to the barren jetty of sand stretching under the moonlit sky filled with stars, surrounded by the clear blue waters of the ocean.

It's our place.

The place where we're the only two people on Earth.

In the summertime, the visitors to our sleepy little town use it to spend the day sunbathing and playing on the wide stretch of undeveloped sand. Now, on the edge of fall, with all the children back in school and Jackson leaving for college tomorrow, we have it to ourselves.

His engine roars on the road above, and I stand in the pedals to push harder, fueled by the burning desire twisting in my lower pelvis. I want to be with him now. I don't want to waste a moment.

I go even faster as the trail slopes downhill. A narrow wooden bridge *thump... thump... thumps* with the pressure of my tires distressing the aging slats.

The instant the trees part, I toss my bike aside and run out of the darkness onto the glowing white sand. The sizzle of waves crashing on the shore fills the night, and the black ripples are tipped with silver light.

Jackson stands in his canvas shorts, his hands in his pockets, and a thin white tee rippling across his back in the slight breeze.

I'm breathing hard when I finally reach him, and he turns. White teeth in a full-moon night, deep dimples in both cheeks, he smiles down at me, and I feel so small. A lock of too-long dark hair falls over his blue eyes, and my breath catches. He's so beautiful.

I swallow the knot in my throat as I gaze at him. What star crossed what planet in what solar system and said I could have him, even if it's only for a little while?

"You made good time tonight." His voice vibrates the warm air between us.

I force a laugh, moving to him until my hands are around his waist. My forehead rests on his chest, and I inhale deeply. He's leather and soap and a deeper, spicier scent that's pure Jackson Cane.

He feels so good in my arms.

His mouth presses against my head, and I lift my chin, reaching for his face. He leans down and claims my mouth, warm lips pushing mine open. I kiss him eagerly, curling my tongue with his, threading my fingers into the soft, dark hair falling around his cheeks, tugging.

An aching moan rises in my chest as he lifts me off my feet. Chasing his kisses, my mouth burns with cinnamon, my core tingles with need. He carries me to our place, a little shelter near the water's edge where an enormous log is slowly turning to driftwood. We lower to the sand, me on my back, him on his knees looking down at me.

My dark hair is all around us, my skirt is up around my waist. My panties are far away on my bedroom floor. A soft hiss comes from his lips, and he slides a finger down my center. My eyes flutter shut.

"Jackson..." I whisper. *I love you I love you I love you...*

He leans down to taste me, his tongue lightly tracing the line between my thighs, and my back arches off the soft sand. My body takes flight on the motion of his mouth, kissing me so deeply, tracing a pattern over my most sensitive parts.

The first time he did this to me, I didn't understand. I'd been embarrassed by how fast my body responded, the way I shook, how wet it was between my legs when the shudders subsided.

Then I was afraid of how I tasted. I was afraid it was dirty and wrong like my momma would say. *Sin...*

Then he kissed me, and my mouth filled with a delicate, clean ocean flavor, like the air after a storm. It was our first time, and when he pushed inside me, my mind came apart. My soul shifted, and I was forever changed.

I was forever his.

The flutters begin in the arches of my feet, and he kisses his way up my stomach.

"Jackson... Jackson..." I can't stop chanting his name as I thread my fingers in his soft hair.

At last his mouth covers mine. At last we're one.

"Ember..." His mouth breaks away with a groan, and I lean up to run my tongue along the ridges of his neck. *Salt water...*

I lick his Adam's apple up to his square jaw.

Rough stubble scratches my tongue.

My legs are around his waist and we're working together, chasing that glorious release. He stretches me and fills me, massages me so deeply, I feel it the moment I start to break apart.

"Oh!" My fingers tighten on his back as every muscle in my body clenches...

Tighter...

Tighter...

Then *Yes!*

Glitter gun showers of pleasure flooding my insides.

"Yes," he groans, and I feel him finish deep inside of me.

Our bodies unite, but at the same time we're flying apart as waves of ecstasy fill our veins. It's magical like the ocean, silvery water tipped in moonlight.

We kiss softly now, rich and gentle, over and over. His tongue touches my upper lip, and he pulls the bottom one between his teeth. *Red-hot cinnamon...*

We're breathing hard, and he slides a hand under my ass, turning us without ever losing contact, so I'm sitting in a straddle across his lap.

My dress is around my waist, and moonlight touches the tips of my breasts. We hold each other, skin against skin.

A hot tear spills down my cheek.

I'm not full-on crying. I'll save the ugly tears for tomorrow when he's gone. Instead, I find his blue eyes.

Dark brows quirk together, and he kisses my nose. "You're crying?"

My voice cracks with a whisper. "Aren't you sad?"

"I'm only going to college, Em. I'm not going to war."

"But we won't see each other for months."

I don't say what's truly scaring me. I don't voice the fear that I, a mere high schooler, couldn't possibly hold onto him.

He's traveling far away to where the girls are more mature, more experienced, more sophisticated.

"You're right," he nods. "It's going to suck. Especially when I want to kiss you."

He pulls me flush against his chest and groans deeply. Strong arms circle my shoulders, and I cling to him.

"But it's not something to cry about," he argues. "You're my girl, Em. That's never going to change."

My eyes squeeze shut, and I inhale his scent, doing my best to hold it in my memory, trying to absorb every part of him.

There's no way in hell I could even begin to argue. I am his, and he's... my everything. Jackson Cane is every first I've ever had. My first real kiss, my first real boyfriend, the first time I had sex... made love...

"Hey." He pulls back, blue eyes full of concern. "I'm right, aren't I?"

Blinking quickly, I try to find my bearings. "What?" I don't know why he looks so worried.

"You are my girl, right?"

My chin jerks forward, and I have to cover my mouth. "You have to ask?"

Warm hands cup my cheeks, and he trails his thumbs lightly along my cheekbones. "So beautiful," he murmurs. "My Ember Rose."

His eyes move around my face, along my hair, down the side of my jaw like a caress.

"I'll never forget this." I'm ashamed at how desperate my voice sounds. "I mean... I just..." I'm such a baby.

He blinks a few times, and a smile curls his lips.

With a nod, he pulls me against his chest, strong arms surrounding me. We stay that way a long time, listening to the crashing of the surf, the beat of our hearts. The seagulls cry, and the moon climbs higher. It's all so perfect, but it's all at an end.

Finally, with a sigh, he lifts me, helping me stand. We hold hands as he takes me into the gentle waves to clean up. I slowly restore my dress.

I feel so stupid. College girls don't need to be cared for like babies. They don't whine and cry about being left behind. They blow kisses and wink over their sunglasses. They sway their hips and turn the tables on saying goodbye.

My best friend Tabby is already one of those girls, and she's my age.

I'll never be one of those girls.

"Don't cry, Ember Rose," he says in a low whisper. "I never want to see you cry."

I hold him a while longer, listening to the steady rhythm of his heart. His hands slide up and down my back in a soothing motion.

After a while, they slide down my forearms to lace with my fingers. He steps back and leads me the way we came, stopping at the edge of the woods where I left my bike.

"Get on home before your momma wakes up."

That sexy smile curls his lips. He shoves his hair behind his ears, and I step forward again, clutching the front of his shirt before I press my lips one last time to his.

Red-hot cinnamon.
Sparkling blue sin.
Salt rocks breaking my heart.

* * *

287

Get *When We Touch* Today!

About the Author

Tia Louise is the *USA Today* best-selling, award-winning author of the "One to Hold" and "Dirty Players" series, and co-author of the #4 Amazon bestseller *The Last Guy*.

From Readers' Choice nominations, to *USA Today* "Happily Ever After" nods, to winning Favorite Erotica Author and the "Lady Boner Award" (LOL!), nothing makes her happier than communicating with fans and weaving new love stories that are smart, sassy, and very sexy.

A former journalist, Louise lives in the Midwest with her trophy husband, two teenage geniuses, and one grumpy cat.

Keep up with Tia online:
www.AuthorTiaLouise.com

50997653R00174

Made in the USA
Columbia, SC
17 February 2019